Master

By

Eve Vaughn

Master
Copyright © 2018 Eve Vaughn
Book publication July 2018

Dedication

To my readers. For as long as I could remember, the written word has given me joy. Somewhere along the line, I decided to write my own stories. To my surprise, people actually enjoyed them and because of that, it gave me the courage to live my dream. My books wouldn't be possible without all of you. Thank you for all of your support. It means the world to me.

Chapter One

Alasdair O'Shaughnessy had always been a man who dealt in absolutes. His world was black and white with very few patches of gray. Some called him ruthless, others would say he was a taker. Dare, however, saw himself as someone who wasn't afraid of going after what he wanted and taking it. It was why he was one of the wealthiest men in the country. He might have been born into a privileged life, but he'd more than doubled his father's net worth and quadrupled that of his grandfather's. Whenever he walked into a room, he was revered by all. He'd taken it as his due. He was, after all, one of the Elites; the very top of the social hierarchy. So, why shouldn't he have whatever he desired most?

And what his heart most desired was Aya Smith. From the moment he laid eyes on the feisty beauty, he'd recognized something special about her. It had only been a brief glance at first, a stolen moment when he'd witnessed her in the middle of a commotion that at the time merely peaked his interest. The fact that this woman had even caught his attention in the first place was an extraordinary feat, being that she was of no importance to him. Or so he'd thought.

A chance encounter had led him back to her in a part of town he normally wouldn't bother to be in were it not for business. There he'd seen her again as if fate itself had played a hand in the meeting. Seeing Aya up close felt like a punch in the gut, literally robbing him of his ability to breathe. Dare hadn't been able to tear his gaze away from the compact woman. Aya was unlike any of the elegant Elite women he'd taken as lovers in the past. She wasn't adorned in designer labels and expensive jewelry. Her face was free from the artifice of cosmetics, and she didn't need it.

Her dark skin, a shade so deep and rich, was smooth and blessed by the sun. It was rare, which would make her valuable to many who were wealthy enough to pay any price she named. Her hair was shaved close to her scalp and though Dare had preferred his women with long flowing tresses, this looked suited her. It made her already dark brown eyes looked larger, plush lips seem more kissable, and high cheekbones stark. Every single feature suited her from her slightly wide nose that still remained feminine to her thick, finely arched brows. There wasn't one detail he didn't notice about her. Considering the district she lived in, Dare deduced the reason for her oversized clothing was to hide her figure, but all it did was make him wonder what was beneath it. After a thorough inspection, he'd decided right then and there that he would have her.

What he didn't count on, however, was a resound rejection. From the time he was born, the power behind the name O'Shaughnessy had been drilled in his head. People revered them because they took what they wanted and no wasn't a word they accepted. Aya had taken him by surprise. She'd angered him, made him want to teach her a lesson. So, he'd set out to do just that.

He'd attacked her uncle's business knowing it was their only source of income and was instrumental in having her uncle sent to jail. He'd made sure Aya was in such desperate straits that she had no choice, but to participate in The Run, which was a game he used to own that catered to wealthy patrons looking for live entertainment. At least that's how he had once viewed it, a profitable venture. Aya, however, had opened his eyes to what it really was. A mill for down-on-their-luck, impoverished women in dire straits who were willing to prostitute themselves for enough credits to survive.

Dare shuddered when he thought about all he'd done to her. Though he didn't realize it at the time, he'd fallen for her at first sight. He never believed in love, thought it was a false emotion that only existed in fairy tales. He'd believed it was something that made people weak, turned them into fools. Dare had fought against his feelings for her which made him do disgraceful things. He'd hated himself for making her pay because he didn't know how to handle his emotions.

But now he wasn't afraid to shout it to the world that he loved this woman to distraction. It wasn't simply her beauty that drew him to her, but her spirit. He liked that she stood up for herself and others who couldn't do it for themselves despite her below average height. She was a pint-sized ball of energy who was protective of her friends and family. Aya was the type of person who actually cared for other people. It was uncommon to find people in this society who were as genuine as she was. Dare liked that she didn't pretend to be something she wasn't, and you always knew where you stood with her.

Aya had changed him, made him a better person. It was almost scary how much she'd come to mean to him in such a short time. She was the light in his darkness, his everything. She was the very oxygen he breathed, and he realized that he'd merely been existing before he met her. Now he knew what living was. But his biggest fear was on the verge of coming true.

He was going to lose her.

For the past few weeks, things were different between them. Aya had grown more distant. The smiles she used to gift him with were becoming fewer and further between. Her light had seemed to dim. And it was all his fault. He knew what he was doing to her, but he couldn't help himself. Every time he found himself acting out, it was like he was having an out-of-body experience. His jealousy, possessiveness, and need to know where she was every second of the day drove him to the edge of insanity. Dare would snap at any other man she even looked at. Aya would get angry with him, and each time he'd apologize.

At first, his need to know her whereabouts stemmed from the fact that women had randomly started disappearing. Illegal sex trafficking operations were a lucrative operation for those who chose to make their wealth through underhanded means. Women were valuable commodities, particularly the young and attractive ones. But then his quest to protect her had warped into something more, something dark and scary. He'd been reminded of the time he'd unselfishly let her go once he realized his true feelings for her. Those months without Aya in his arms were absolute torture. Looking back on those days, he wasn't sure how he'd managed to survive them. By some miracle, she came back to him.

However, knowing what life was like without her made Dare not want to live that way ever again, which was why he couldn't let her go again. He would die without her, maybe not physically, but on the inside, he'd be absolutely empty. And no matter how he tried to back off and stop being so crazy when it came to his woman, he just couldn't. Something within him simply couldn't let things be.

Dare rolled to his side and rested his head in his palm as he stared at a sleeping Aya. She turned away, presenting her bare back to him. Her hands rested beneath her head. Unable to keep himself from touching her, Dare ran a finger down her spine. Her skin was like smooth dark brown satin. He loved the contrast of his hands against her body.

A soft moan escaped plush lips as she rolled over to her back to reveal a perfect set of breasts capped with nipples the color of black diamonds. She was probably tired, but he couldn't resist dipping his head and capturing one tempting tip between his lips. Dare sucked gently at first and then with more fervor. Whenever he touched her, something came over him. He couldn't get enough of her. He raised his head and gave her other nipple the same loving attention.

As he licked and laved the now taut peak, he slid his hand down her flat belly and cupped her hot sex.

"Mmm, Dare," Aya moaned. Her voice was heavy with sleep. "So tired."

He lifted his head to meet her hooded gaze. "Should I stop?"

"Don't you dare." She threaded her fingers through his hand and pulled his head back to her breast.

He alternated between each mound, sucking, laving and tasting her as he eased two fingers inside her slick channel.

"Feels so good. What are you doing to me?"

He chuckled, loving how responsive she was to his touch. "Making you nice and ready for me."

"When am I not ready for you?"

The question didn't require an answer because they both already knew. Despite the tumultuous nature of their relationship, sex had never been a problem between the two of them. Sometimes Dare wished that he could keep her in his bed all the time and there wouldn't be any problems between them. This was where he best communicated with Aya. Here he was free to express his feelings for her and show her how much he loved her. Dare could use his mouth, hands, and cock to worship her like the goddess she was. Words were never his strong point, but at least here, in bed, he made sure Aya had no doubt how he felt about her.

Dare pressed kisses in the valley of her breasts before moving lower, placing his lips against her stomach, and stopping long enough to circle her belly button with his tongue. Finally, he settled himself between her thighs. His treasure. She smelled amazing. She was already slick and hot for him.

Aya inhaled sharply as he gently slipped his fingers out of her, brought them to his mouth and licked them clean. "I'll never get tired of this. You taste so good," he groaned before parting her labia which was still swollen from their earlier lovemaking session.

She was an addiction he couldn't shake, one he didn't want to.

Burying his face between her thighs, he licked and nibbled her pussy, making Aya moan and cry out in pleasure.

"Dare, you're killing me." She tightened her grip on his hair to the point where it felt like she might actually pull some out by its root, but he was too focused on his task to care. He captured her clit between his teeth and bit down just enough to give her the right amount of pleasure. He knew her spots and knew exactly what she liked. He'd mastered her body and knew all of her erogenous zones. And he especially knew how she liked to be licked and loved.

Aya smashed her pussy against his face, coating his face in her juices and he loved every second of it.

"I'm going to cum."

"Don't hold back, doll. Give me everything you've got."

"Dare!"

He lapped up her sweet cream, making sure not to miss a single drop. Dare ate her delectable pussy until he could no longer ignore the hardness of his dick. He had to be inside of her or else he'd go insane with need.

Bracing his arms on either side of her body, he aligned his cock against her weeping entrance. "Take me inside of you," he commanded.

He gasped as she circled his cock with her small hand and guided him inside of her. Dare closed his eyes and bit his bottom lip to savor the sensation of being inside her tight velvety walls. It felt like home. No matter how many times they had sex, it was always like the first time. He couldn't get enough and didn't want to. He thrust forward, sinking balls deep inside of her.

Aya clasped his shoulders and wrapped her legs around his waist. They moved together, slowly at first, finding their rhythm. But as they made sweet love, something came over him. Something animalistic. With a growl, he grasped her hands and pinned them above his head. The next thing he knew, he was pounding in and out of her. It was almost as if it wasn't him even though it was.

Aya whimpered beneath him and he honestly couldn't tell if she was into it anymore, but he couldn't stop even if he wanted to. This need to place his mark on her, to claim her permanently, drove him to plow in and out of her with reckless abandon.

"Dare!" She thrashed her head from side to side, but he kept going.

He wasn't sure how long he went on, but when he finally spilled his seed and collapsed on top of her, he was covered in sweat. His lungs felt tight from exertion as he fought to catch his breath.

Once he got his bearings, it had finally dawned on him what he'd just done.

"Shit." He rolled off her and cupped the side of her face. "I'm so sorry. I was too rough."

Aya didn't answer at first. Instead of looking him in the eyes, she stared at the ceiling, that distant look that she'd gotten of late was there and it scared the fuck out of him.

"Aya? Please say something."

She sighed. "I'm not sure what you want me to say, Dare."

"Call me an asshole. Tell me that I went too far or was too rough. Say anything."

"I…I didn't hate it. I actually liked it."

He raised a brow, surprised at her response.

"You did?"

"Yes." His relief was short-lived when she added, "And that's part of the problem."

Dare felt his heart plummet. He should have known there was a but in there somewhere. "I'm sorry.'

"Don't apologize. Look, I'm not upset, just…I mean, what started out as something beautiful just became another exercise of possession for you. I don't know what it was, but it felt like you were an animal and I was a juicy piece of meat you were laying claim to. But the crazy thing was, I didn't dislike it. I was still aroused.

Maybe the blame falls on me because you keep doing things that make me question my sanity for being with you. I'm not sure what scares me more sometimes…the way you act or the fact that I sometimes like it. I'm just so confused."

It felt like his worst nightmares were coming true. "Are you saying you no longer love me, because I will do whatever it takes to—"

She placed her finger over his lips. "I didn't say that. Of course, I still love you, Dare, or else I wouldn't be here with you right now. It's just…sometimes you go overboard and it's getting harder to justify why we're still together. Tonight, for instance, we were at a formal function you dragged me to. You know I hate those stuffy events, but I go because I want to support you. I was only making polite conversation with a man who was probably only being nice to me because we're dating. I understand that most of these snobs only see me as some Dreg you rescued from the gutter. But then to almost start a fight with him because you thought he was coming on to me was a bit much. This kind of behavior has got to stop, Dare."

It was painful to hear the sadness in her voice. Her anger he might have been able to handle, but this, he wasn't sure how to fix it because no matter how hard he tried, he couldn't shake this feeling that he was somehow going to lose her. It drove him crazy because he lived in a world of paranoia, but to realize he was the one pushing her away made him feel helpless. This wasn't something he was used to. He, by nature, was a fixer, but he didn't know what to do about this. Not being jealous where Aya was concerned was easier said than done. "I know. It's just…" He couldn't bring himself to finish. Every time he wanted to explain what was going on in his head, the words just wouldn't come. Something was holding him back and even he couldn't figure it out.

She touched his cheek, her dark eyes, filled with concern. "What is it? Tell me?"

"I...I just love you."

"You keep telling me that, but there's something you're holding back. Whatever it is that's going on with you, we can't work through this unless you open up."

Dare opened his mouth, but the words remained stuck in his throat. He wanted to tell her how he felt, but he'd never been good at expressing himself. It was difficult to share when the vast majority of his life he'd been taught to suppress his emotions. Those were for the weak. The specter of his father still haunted him. Memories of those times when he'd lived in fear until that very same fear had hardened him, had made it damn near impossible for him to care about anyone other than himself. But somehow Aya had found her way into his heart and he was screwing it up.

When he remained silent, Aya sighed. "Dare, I'm tired. It's obvious that you're not up to talking and I have to get up early to open the bar." She yanked the covers over her body and turned her back to him.

"Didn't your uncle hire more people to help around that place?"

"He did, but it's my turn to open up in the morning."

"You know you don't have to work there. You're my woman and I'm more than capable of taking care of you."

"I'm not having this conversation with you right now. I'm going back to sleep. Goodnight."

"Aya—"

"I said goodnight." There was a finality in her tone that left no room for argument.

Dare cursed under his breath. He'd fucked up again. It killed him to know that his relationship was falling apart and he didn't know how to fix it.

Chapter Two

"So, are you going to tell me what's been bothering you for the past several weeks or do you plan to continue to mope around this place like you've lost your best friend?" Uncle Arthur walked behind Aya as she was taking inventory of the afternoon delivery.

Aya kept her eyes firmly glued on the holopad as she scanned each item. "I don't know what you're talking about and frankly I don't have time. We've been inundated lately since the expansion and it doesn't seem like there are enough hands to go around. I'm thinking we should probably look into hiring a couple more locals to help around this place. There are always eager people looking for work."

The older man released a heavy sigh. "Aya, put that damn thing down and look at me when I'm talking to you."

The sharp edge in her uncle's tone was one he rarely took with her, but when he did, she could not ignore it. Aya put the holopad on the closest box and turned to face her uncle with crossed arms. She raised a brow, waiting for him to continue.

"Don't give me that look, girl. You come to work with those big bags under your eyes like you haven't slept for days. You don't smile like you used to and you've been short-tempered. The regulars are even taking note of it. You're not your cheerful self and if that's not enough, every now and then I catch you on the verge of tears when you think no one is looking. What's going on, Aya? Does it have something to do with O'Shaughnessy? If that boy is doing something to you, I swear I'll put my foot so far up his ass, he's going to be spitting out my insole."

And that was exactly why she'd kept it to herself. Uncle Arthur had made no secret of the fact that he wasn't a Dare fan. In fact, he only seemed to tolerate Aya's lover for her sake. It was understandable considering all Dare had done. But he didn't know about Dare's past and how it had shaped him. He didn't see what Aya saw in him and the last thing she wanted was to give Uncle Arthur a reason to dislike Dare even more than he already did. But she had to tell him something or else he wouldn't let it go. "It's nothing Dare did. I've just had a lot on my mind lately, with the expansion of the bar and helping Tori and Macy with their shelter, and Dare has had a handful of business arrangements lately. I'm just stretched a little thin right now." It wasn't exactly a lie. Aya really did have a lot going on in her life at the moment, but it wasn't anything she couldn't handle. Besides, she didn't want to make a bad situation worse by getting her uncle in the middle of it.

Uncle Arthur gently grasped her by the chin, forcing her to meet his gaze. "You're not lying to me are you?"

She shook her head. "Of course not."

He stared at her with narrowed eyes before releasing her. "Well, if something was the matter, you'd tell me wouldn't you?"

"Of course."

"Fine, but if that man gives you problems, you let me know. You can't fault me for thinking he was the source of your problems considering the rocky start the two of you had."

Aya snorted. "That's putting it lightly, but you don't need to worry about Dare. I can handle him if he gets out of line."

"Hmph. If you say so. But maybe you should take it easy with all the things you've been doing lately. It's okay if you take a few days off from here. The bar won't fall apart if you're not around and I'm sure your friends would understand if you can't volunteer for a bit. You need rest."

She pasted a smile on her face, hoping it was convincing. "Honestly, I enjoy what I do. I'm sure things will settle down shortly. So, if you don't mind, I really need to get back to cataloging this inventory before the afternoon rush."

Uncle Arthur leaned over and pressed a kiss to her forehead. "You take it easy, okay?"

She nodded. "Of course."

Once he was out of sight, she released a deep sigh of relief, but along with that, a tear escaped from the corner of her eye and then another until they ran freely down her face. Once she started to cry, Aya couldn't stop. She hurried to the office so that no one would witness her emotional breakdown.

Aya hated that she'd lied to her uncle, but she didn't think she could handle being caught in the middle of a battle between the two men she loved the most in the world. She hoped her talk with Dare had sunk in to some degree because if it hadn't she didn't know how much longer she'd be able to deal with his outbursts. Sometimes it felt as if she was dealing with two different men. One moment he'd be tender and loving, making her heart and body soar to heights beyond her wildest imaginings, and the next he was a jealous and possessive monster who made her afraid to even look at another person of the opposite sex out of fear of causing an argument.

Most of her life, Aya had never backed down from anything. She stood up for others who couldn't defend themselves and she'd never taken shit from anyone. Yet here she was hiding in the bar's office so no one would see her crying. She loved Dare so much, and she'd tried so hard to make allowances for his past, but she wasn't sure if her feelings were enough to hold them together any longer. Aya shuddered as the events from the night before bombarded her mind.

Aya glanced at herself in the full-length mirror to make sure her appearance was in order. She patted her curls which now hung past her ears. It had been a while since she'd allowed her hair to grow to this length. For safety purposes, she'd kept her head shaven close to her scalp as not to draw attention to herself. Many unattached women incorporated tricks to make them go unnoticed when they were out in the open due to the high rate of rape and kidnappings that occurred simply for the fact that women were vastly outnumbered. This was mainly due to the Deregulation Act that had gotten rid of all the oversights of corporations that protected the people. Because of that, pharmaceutical companies were able to introduce drugs to the public that had not been properly tested. A lot of people fell ill because of these dangerous practices, but the most detrimental product introduced to the public was a vaccine called Prozoxodril, which was marketed specifically for women and used to eradicate breast cancer.

Because the pharmaceutical company who'd produced it had several government officials in its pocket it wasn't hard to have a law passed that all women and girls over the age of ten were to be vaccinated in order for them to even obtain basic life necessities like government IDs or a job.

It had ended up wiping out half the female population. It had a disastrous worldwide effect because several countries had followed suit with the vaccinations. With so fewer women, laws were passed under the guise of protecting the women who were left, but in essence, it left them at the mercy of men's laws. The only women who seemed to come out on top were among the Elite. Women without the protection of a husband or without monetary means were often at the mercy of those who simply saw them as chattel.

Aya had kept her hair short and had worn baggy clothes at her uncle's insistence at first until it had become natural for her. It still took some getting used to, seeing herself dressed in an outfit that cost more than what the bar made in profits in a week. Her make-up was expertly done by a stylist as was her hair. Again, she touched her artfully styled curls. A diamond pushed her hair up at the temples. Her white gown was floor length and gave the appearance of modesty with its long sleeves and scoop-necked cut. But the back of the dress dipped dangerously low to the top of her ass, exposing the expanse of her back.

It was the most modest dress the store had. Some of the dresses that she'd been shown, Aya figured she might as well have been naked. Aya wasn't a prude, but the habit of dressing conservatively was deeply ingrained within her. Besides, Dare always seemed to act even more possessive whenever she showed any skin.

As if her thoughts had conjured him, he stepped into their bedroom. "You look amazing." He was behind her in an instant. Grasping her shoulders, he lowered his head and pressed his lips against her bare neck. A shiver of pure pleasure raced up her spine and her nipples hardened. The familiar tingling in her pussy made Aya squirm. Dare only had to touch Aya for her to be putty in his hands.

She melted against him, accepting the caress of his mouth against her flesh. "Mmm, do we have to go to this dinner tonight? We just went to one a few days ago?"

"Unfortunately, we do. I must put in an appearance as head of the board of O Corp. It's part of the job to have occasional engagements with my business associates, besides, there'll be someone in attendance there whom I'm interested in meeting."

She raised a brow in question. "Oh? Who is it?"

"Just a company head from an international conglomerate who has a business under his umbrella that I'm interested in purchasing."

"I see." Most of this talk went over her head, but Aya was interested because it was important to Dare.

As he pulled away from her with obvious reluctance, she noticed his expression change through the mirror. The slight smile he'd sported just seconds ago had now morphed into a ferocious frown.

Aya stiffened. "What's wrong?"

"I trust you'll be wearing some kind of jacket to cover all this skin you're showing."

She rolled her eyes. "Don't start. We've been to plenty of these functions before and I'm always the most covered up out of all the women in attendance. I'd rather you didn't start on this tonight." Aya moved away from him and headed to the closet to get her shoes.

Dare followed closely behind. "Start what? Do you realize what's going to happen when you walk into that place looking like that?"

"I appreciate you have that much confidence in my sex appeal, but trust me, Dare, every man I come in contact with does not lust after me. That's all in your head." She grabbed her shoes and pushed past him. Aya refused to continue this conversation with him. For once she wanted to get through one night where he wasn't acting like a jealous idiot.

Maybe it was a mistake moving in with Dare despite her misgivings. Part of the reason she'd decided to take the final leap and officially move in with him was to give her uncle some privacy since he'd moved his girlfriend Mera in with them. Aya liked the other woman and was happy for Uncle Arthur, but she felt they deserved their space. Another reason she'd taken the leap was that she'd hoped that Dare would calm down. Ever since they'd become a real couple he'd insisted that she move in with him, but Aya had wanted to maintain some of her independence and have her own refuge. But she had spent most nights with him anyway and after some thought on her end and a lot of convincing on Dare's part, he finally convinced her to take the final step. Things were great at first. While Dare was at work, she still continued with her daily tasks at the bar while helping her friends out with their projects in her spare time. And the nights were spent making love until the wee hours of the morning, which kept a smile on her face.

But then something happened Aya couldn't explain. Dare would show up at the bar unexpectedly and make a fuss when one of the customers looked at her too long. He'd treat her like a possession whenever they were out in public barely allowing her to stray from his eyesight. It was exhausting, more than a little embarrassing and frankly, she was becoming more certain as time passed that she couldn't deal with this much longer.

On the ride to the function, Aya stared out the window as Dare tried to engage her in conversation.

"Do you plan to give me the silent treatment for the rest of the night?"

"I don't know what you want me to say."

He sighed. "I'm sorry, okay. You look so beautiful tonight and sometimes I lose my head a little." He took her by the hand and kissed her knuckles. "I'm an idiot. Forgive me?"

Though she wanted to stay mad at Dare, it was hard when she heard the genuine contrition in his voice. Finally, she turned in her seat to face him. "Dare, just promise me that you won't do anything crazy tonight? Let's just get through this dinner without incident."

Dare kissed the inside of her wrist. "I'll do my best."

It wasn't exactly the promise she was looking for, but knowing Dare, it was probably the best she was going to get for now.

At the actual dinner, Dare seemed to be on his best behavior. Even some of the usual Elite snobs she had to deal with at these types of functions weren't as insufferable as usual. The meal was uneventful and afterward, the guests mingled for after dinner drinks. Aya had somehow found herself in a circle of wives who were discussing topics she was vaguely paying attention to. She remained focused on the champagne in her hand, trying not to be bored out of her skull while Dare was talking to some man in the corner. She assumed he was a potential business associate.

Unable to take any more of the conversation about absolutely nothing, Aya politely backed away from the group and found a spot in the back of the room where she could people watch.

"These little get-togethers can be tedious, can't they?"

Aya turned to see the source of the voice that had intruded into her thoughts. She had to crane her neck to meet his gaze, which wasn't unusual for her since she was shorter than most people she encountered. She nearly gasped at how good-looking he was. If it weren't for Dare, he would have easily been the most handsome man in the room with his dark red hair that fell past his neck in careless waves, eyes so deep a blue, they were nearly purple, and strong-boned features on a deeply tanned face that almost seemed unreal. And when he smiled with perfect, blindingly white teeth she couldn't help but smile back. "Absolutely, but I guess they're a necessary evil if you're trying to get what you want."

"Exactly." He grinned at her again before holding out his hand to her. "Thor."

She shook his hand and returned his smile. "I'm Aya. Nice to meet you. I don't remember seeing you at dinner."

"Oh, I just flew into town today, so our host was aware that I'd be missing the dinner portion of the evening."

"Where did you fly in from?"

"From Nuldanria."

Aya frowned. "I'm not sure I've heard of that country."

"It's a fairly new country, about ten years old. It used to be part of Spain and Portugal before the war."

She nodded. World War IV had split several European, and Asian countries, making it hard to keep up with the ever-changing geography around the globe. "Oh, well, I hope you had a productive trip."

"I did actually. Everything is coming along quite nicely and soon, I'll have everything I want."

"Well, good luck with that, Thor. Interesting name. Greek mythology?"

"Norse actually. God of Thunder."

"I'll have to read up on that."

"Norse mythology is quite fascinating actually."

"The next time I have a chance to read, I'll definitely look through the archives for that."

"You enjoy reading?"

"I do. But like I said, I don't have much time for it lately."

"Beautiful and smart. The gentleman you're here with is a very lucky man." Thor raised his glass to her in a silent salute.

Before Aya could respond, Dare appeared next to her and hooked his arm around her waist. He pulled her roughly to his side. "Is there a problem?"

"We were just talking, Dare." Aya didn't appreciate the proprietary way he was holding on to her. And when she tried to pull away, he held her closer.

Thor smiled as he held out his hand. "O'Shaughnessy. Didn't expect to see you here tonight."

Dare looked pointedly at the hand, making it clear that he had no intention of shaking it. Instead of answering the other man, he looked down at Aya who at this point was embarrassed at his rudeness. "I asked if there's a problem."

"There wasn't until you came over," she answered through gritted teeth.

Dare flexed the muscles in his jaw.

Thor dropped his hand, but his affable smile remained. "I was just having a conversation with this lovely young lady. I'm assuming you came together."

"Now that we've established who she belongs to, perhaps you can stop undressing her with your eyes," Dare practically growled the words.

Thor raised his brows in apparent surprise and held up his hand. "Whoa. I meant no offense. I was just paying her a compliment."

Without a reply, Dare turned away from Thor, dragging Aya away.

If she wasn't so furious in that moment she would have given him a piece of her mind, but she was far too overwhelmed to get the words out. She yanked herself out of Dare's hold. "I can't believe you did that. I'm leaving and I'm going to spend the night at my Uncle's. You just can't seem to help yourself, can you?" She stormed out the room, uncaring of the eyes that followed them. She didn't care about the gossiping bunch. They didn't matter to her. What did was, yet again, Dare had treated her like she didn't have her own autonomy.

He caught up with her by the time she made it outside. "Aya, wait!"

"Leave me alone!"

He grabbed her wrist. "Please. I don't know what came over me. But you should have seen the way that guy was looking at you."

"Who cares how he was looking at me. I didn't do anything for you to warrant treating me like I'm some

scatterbrained tramp who intends to spread her legs for the first guy who shows interest in me. And Thor was just being polite. He was talking to me while you were busy making business deals. I should have known better than to come out with you tonight. It's always the same thing with you, Dare. You can't keep doing this."

He pulled her against his chest and wrapped his arms around her. "I know. It's just…I love you so much Aya. You know how things are around here. Men in these circles are unscrupulous. They take what they want. You don't understand men the way I do. I just want to keep you safe."

Aya didn't doubt that was one of his motives, but it was more than that. She had this feeling that he wasn't telling her something. Since she'd known him, Dare had never been strong on sharing his feelings, often bottling things up until they spilled over in an unhealthy way. He was holding something back from her and she couldn't help him if he didn't tell her what the matter was about. She certainly had no intention of allowing things to continue the way they were if he kept acting this way.

She shook her head. "I've lived twenty-three years without your protection and I've done just fine."

"Did you really?"

She twisted out of his hold to glare at him. "That's right until you decided you wanted me so you set out to destroy everything I cared about just so I'd be forced to compete in that disgusting game of yours. Maybe you're the one I should be wary of." The second the words left her mouth she regretted it. One of the things she'd told herself when she decided to give their relationship a chance, she would truly forgive him for what he did to her. But in forgiving him that would mean she wouldn't get to throw the past in his face every time he made her mad. Instead of focusing on his current transgression she'd brought up the one thing that should have been off limits.

She could see the pain in Dare's eyes, but she remained silent. "I'm sorry. I shouldn't have said that."

He shook his head. "Don't apologize. It's no more than what I deserved."

"No, not that. Look, I know that topic is off limits and that was a low blow, but like I said before, you can't keep doing this."

He nodded. "I'll try harder, just please...stay with me tonight. I need you."

"Okay."

By the end of the night, she regretted the decision. The second they got home, he wasted no time tearing off her clothes and taking her in every which way he could. Normally Aya didn't mind and was, in fact, an active participant, but she couldn't help thinking that instead of making love to her, he was staking his claim somehow as he chanted mine, over and over again.

She'd barely gotten a wink of sleep. Aya realized she couldn't go on like this. Something had to change soon because she was tired of giving him chances. If things didn't get better and fast, it was over.

Chapter Three

Aya had the strangest feeling she was being watched. The feeling was so strong that she couldn't shake it. She looked over her shoulder, but there was no one there, at least no one who was looking in her direction. The streets of the shopping district weren't as crowded as the busy section she lived in, which was usually littered with loiterers and homeless people lying in the alleys.

In this area, the sidewalks were free of litter and enforcers patrolled the streets to protect the Elite who frequented the area shops. It still made her a bit uncomfortable visiting this part of town considering the fact that before she'd become the lover of Alasdair O'Shaughnessy, she was just another Dreg. In fact, shop owners had looked down on her because they thought she'd steal something while the patrons made no secret that she didn't belong there.

It wasn't very long ago, before some of the more exclusive shops knew of her association with Dare, that she'd been arrested by the enforcers simply because an Elite customer decided to antagonize Aya with no provocation. That humiliating experience was still fresh in her mind. It wasn't lost on her how the same store managers who once looked down on her now seemed to trip over their feet to help her. She hated the hypocrisy of it all. Sometimes she felt like a fraud in these ridiculously expensive clothes and that her life should have belonged to someone else.

The second she walked into the restaurant, a maître'd was at her side in an instant. "Miss Smith, your table is ready. Miss Preston is already here."

"Thank you." She followed the man to the preferred section of the restaurant where only the VIP customers were usually seated. In this section, instead of one dedicated server, the entire staff waited on the table so that there would never be any unnecessary gaps in service or at least that's how it was explained to her. It was slightly embarrassing to be catered to this way and to see all the other VIP patrons who seemed to take it as their due made the stark differences of her home district even more obvious.

A smile curved her lips as she spotted her friend looking through the holographic menu items.

"Sorry I'm late. I was making sure the bar was sufficiently covered before I left."

Tori smiled and stood to greet her friend as Aya approached the table. Once the two women exchanged hugs and took a seat, Tori pressed the button on the side of the table to make the menu items disappear. "I'm glad you could make it. I thought it would be nice to see you in a more relaxed setting."

"I wouldn't have minded meeting you at the boarding house."

Tori Preston and she had become fast friends shortly after meeting. Tori was one of the women who had also participated in the Run. Unfortunately for her, she had been tagged by an unscrupulous owner who sold her to an auction house where women were sold to the highest bidders, most never to be heard from again. Foster Graham, who happened to be best friends with Dare, had been a hunter in the Run where he and Tori had first met. From Aya's understanding, Foster had been the one to tag her and thus ensued a relationship where the two of them had fallen in love. Foster, however, had been too scared to share how he really felt for the tawny-skinned beauty and had let Tori go. Tori had had no choice, but to enter the Run again for the large fee she'd receive so that her family would be taken care of. The second hunter who had taken possession of Tori was abusive. When he was finished torturing her, he'd sold her to the auction house.

Around the time Tori had been sold off, Macy, a girl who Aya had met at the Run, had gone missing. Aya and Macy had become close friends after Aya had enlisted Foster and Dare's aid to get Macy away from the man who'd tagged her in the Run. But shortly after Macy had been saved, she had disappeared. Foster once again had set out to rescue Macy by participating as a buyer in the auction in hopes of finding Macy. Who Foster had found, however, was Tori.

Foster had made sure to outbid everyone for a chance to make things right with Tori. The two had been going strong ever since. Macy was eventually found as well and it had turned out that Macy and Tori were sisters. Since then, Aya had become as close to Tori as she had with Macy if not even more so because they were closer in age.

Besides going back to school to further her education, Tori used a house that Foster had purchased for her as a shelter for women who had escaped abusive situations. There were also spaces for women were kicked out of brothels because of their age or whatever reason made them a no hire. Tori's work had expanded, enabling her to make three more safe havens. Aya often helped her out as that was a cause she was also passionate about. If she didn't have the bar to occupy most of her time, Aya would help them out full time.

"I'm sure you wouldn't have minded and that's exactly why I asked for us to meet here. You already do so much at the bar."

Aya waved her hand dismissively. "It's nothing. I've been working with Uncle Arthur for years. I can run that place with my eyes closed."

"But you do way more than run the bar. You make sure that all the left-over food gets distributed to people in need. You give meals to the ones who can't afford it. You give people odd jobs around the bar which instills a sense of pride that they're earning their keep. I'd say you're doing way more than you have to do. And on top of that, you come by the shelter to help me. Aya, when do you even get the chance to sleep?

Aya squirmed in her seat, feeling slightly uncomfortable at Tori's words. It wasn't like she was a saint, she was doing what she could to help out the people in her district who were suffering from an unjust system that took advantage of the poor. "You make it seem like I'm doing something out of the ordinary. I'm sure anyone in my position would do the same thing."

"If that were the case, the world would be a lot better place and you know it. Most people are only out for themselves and I've seen the way you care for the people in your town. They respect you and look out for you. Why do you think your bar has never been robbed or you assaulted in a district riddled with crime? It's because people know to leave you alone."

Aya shrugged. "I think you're making a big deal out of nothing. Besides, I think the boarding houses you've opened up are a pretty extraordinary thing."

"An idea I got from you. You inspired me to do what I'm doing right now. Without you, I don't know what I would have done with myself. I'm not cut out for living a life of leisure and being Foster's arm candy for the rest of my life."

"May I interest you in an appetizer today? We have fresh beluga caviar on water crest." He filled their wine glasses with some expensive drink brand that Aya had no intention of touching. She was grateful however for his presence because it had stopped Tori in the middle of her speech.

"None, thanks. But I'll have a house salad."

He nodded punching her order into the holoscreen that was projected from his wristband. "And you Miss Preston?"

"I'll take the veggie platter with a side of lemon chicken."

"Very good. Your orders will be out shortly."

Aya shook her head. "Isn't it still strange being able to order real meat?"

Tori nodded. "It's a guilty pleasure of mine. Even protein bars made from insects was a little too expensive for my family to afford, but I've gotten a bit spoiled."

"I have to admit that I have enjoyed the occasional steak. I sometimes feel guilty eating the way I do knowing there are people out there who sometimes don't know where their next meal is coming from, let alone some of these items. At the last Sapphire Ball, there were foods I couldn't even name."

"I know what you mean, but don't beat yourself up for being able to treat yourself every now and then. Dare would want you to have whatever you wanted."

At the mention of his name, Aya picked up her wine glass and took a healthy gulp. She didn't plan on drinking a thing, but she needed something to calm her nerves. Even hearing Dare's name these days put her on edge.

Tori narrowed her hazel gaze and gave Aya a discerning look. "There it goes again."

"There what goes again?"

"That look. Whenever I bring Dare's name up. It's not the first time you tensed up when I've brought him up. It's kind of the reason I wanted to meet at the restaurant, away from anyone who would pry into our conversation."

Aya took another swig from her glass, draining its contents. "I don't know what you're talking about. You're imagining things."

"Oh? It's true, I may not have known you very long, but I've never seen you drink alcohol that way. As a matter of fact, while at the last formal dinner we attended, you mentioned that you rarely drink unless you're nervous. So, what are you nervous about?"

Aya held up her hand, and a waiter appeared with the bottle of wine. He refilled her glass before discretely slipping away. "Well, maybe I just want to cut loose today. I didn't think when you invited me to lunch I was going to get the third degree."

Tori raised a brow. "I didn't realize I was giving you the third degree. I'm just concerned is all, but if you don't want to talk about what it is that's bothering you, I will mind my business. I apologize for actually caring."

Aya saw the flash of sadness that entered Tori's eyes and she felt like an asshole. She was certain Tori meant well, but if she said what was wrong out loud, she'd be forced to do the thing that scared her the most; end things with Dare.

"I'm sorry. I just..." She sighed, looking down at the table, unable to meet her friend's gaze.

Tori reached across the table and grabbed Aya's hand. "Aya, we're friends. You can tell me anything."

Tears blurred her vision as she raised her head. "If I told you, you must promise to keep this between the two of us. Don't tell anyone. Not Macy and not Foster. Especially not Foster."

"It's about Dare isn't it?"

"How did you know?"

"It wasn't hard to figure out. You wouldn't ask me not to say anything to Foster considering he and Dare are best friends. It stands to reason that it may concern Dare. Has he hurt you? I mean...I know he's intense, but I never thought..."

Aya shook her head vehemently. "No. He hasn't laid a hand on me, at least not in a violent way, but..."

"But what?"

"Sometimes when we make love, I feel like he's trying to mark me or something. It's hard to explain. He's rough, and I don't mind that sometimes, but it's like he's trying to stake some kind of claim over me. And when we're out in public together, he thinks every man wants me, which is absolutely ridiculous. I can't even talk to someone of the opposite sex without him going nuts. He's so possessive and jealous, and he smothers me. He shows up at the bar randomly to make sure I'm not flirting with the customers. He has to know when I'm coming and going, and I just can't take it anymore. But every time I think about breaking up with him, I start to cry because I do love him. What's wrong with me? Most sane women would leave and never look back, but I feel like there's something going on that he's not telling me, something deeper. Maybe it has something to do with his past, but I can't keep making excuses for him. I've been trying to hold it together, but people are starting to notice. My uncle brought it up the other day and now you are as well. It's tearing me apart." Aya bit back a sob, not wanting to embarrass herself in the middle of the restaurant.

Tori squeezed her hand. "I'm sorry you're going through this. I must be honest when I say, I'm not exactly surprised. I don't think Dare is a bad guy or else I don't think he and Foster would be friends. He has his demons I'm sure, just like Foster, but the first time I met Dare, my first impression of him was that he is real intense. I noticed how possessive he was of you from the beginning and I could tell that it seemed to bother you a little then. But as I got to know him and I had a chance to observe him, it became clear that he's head over heels in love with you. When you're in a room together, his expression softens when he's looking at you, and his gaze follows you around the room. That he cares for and loves you is an absolute certainty, but is this love for you healthy? I don't know."

"Do you think I'm a fool for sticking around? I feel like an idiot for putting up with him. You probably think I'm one of those weak women who will stick with a man only for a sense of security."

Tori shook her head. "I don't think that at all. In fact, you're one of the strongest people I know. You stand up for people who can't stand up for themselves. You do so much for others that I can't even begin to tell you how many lives you've probably touched. So don't be so down on yourself. The thing is, you have a good heart and you don't want to hurt Dare. Like you said before there is something you think he's not telling you. That could be the reason he's acting this way. You two have to have a serious conversation to work out your issues, otherwise, you'll worry yourself sick. Ultimately, only you can decide what the best course of action for you is."

"I'm going to talk to him."

"Good. Like I said before, I don't think he's a bad guy and it's obvious he loves you. Things will work themselves out, I'm sure."

Aya wished she shared her friend's confidence where her relationship with Dare was concerned. No matter what the outcome, Aya had a feeling that things weren't going to go well.

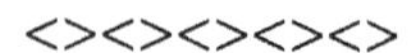

Where was she? Aya had promised to come straight home after the bar closed and she still hadn't arrived. He'd called her holophone several times, but there was no answer. He stopped himself from tracking her through her VC, reminding himself that she probably wouldn't forgive that invasion of her privacy. She was probably on the verge of hating him already, but he couldn't help himself. He loved her so much he didn't know how to deal with these feelings.

Growing up, he'd been encouraged to swallow his feelings or else face the wrath of his father. By the time he was ten, his father had tortured all real emotion from him until he was completely screwed up. He didn't know how to express himself in a healthy way. Dare realized this but didn't know how to fix it. He had to find a way to make things right before it was too late.

He pushed himself from away from his desk, admitting defeat. There was absolutely no way he would get any more work done. He'd come home early to work in his home office so that he could meet Aya, but apparently, she had no intention of coming home anytime soon.

"Ms. Smith is home." The home alarm alerted him on his holowatch. Dare was on his feet in an instant.

By the time he made it to the foyer, Aya was heading up the stairs.

"Aya."

She stiffened before turning to face him. There were shadows under her eyes and the wariness in her expression was his fault. Guilt assailed him. He'd done that to her. If only she knew why he was acting like an overprotective jerk, maybe things would be different. Maybe he would be different.

"I'd like to take a shower and relax for a few minutes before you start bombarding me with questions. I've had a long day and before you ask, I was with Tori this afternoon. We met for lunch and then after I closed the bar for the night, I went over to her house and we talked. I didn't answer your calls because I wanted to have an enjoyable afternoon without arguing."

Dare flinched at her matter of fact attitude. Was he that big of a monster that Aya was constantly on the defensive? "I was…actually going to ask how your day was."

She raised a brow. "Were you really?"

He couldn't hold her gaze because the lie refused to come. Dare had intended to ask where she'd been, but seeing how wary she was of him, had changed his course.

Aya gave him a narrowed-eye stare before snorting. "Yeah, that's what I thought." And with that, she turned around and headed up the stairs.

Chapter Four

Dare shrugged out of his clothing and headed into the bathroom. The bathroom was so steamy he could barely see, but he could make out the outline of Aya's body through the glass shower door. Though she was petite and fine-boned, her curves were generous from the swell of her breasts capped with nipples the color of black diamonds to a round firm ass which molded beautifully into his palms.

His cock stiffened and body throbbed in anticipation. Dare found it hard to believe that he once believed that he could actually sate himself with her. He now knew that wasn't possible. Every time he made love to her, it only made him crave more. Though he didn't have the words to tell her how much she meant to him, he always knew how to tell her with his actions. Deep down, Dare was aware that sex wouldn't always fix things, but for now, it was something that sustained them.

Aya's back was turned to him and she rested her forehead against the tile as the water beat down on her dark skin. He opened the shower door and stepped inside the stall with her. Aya must have been deep in thought because she didn't seem to notice that he'd entered. He flinched when he felt the water. It was hotter than he liked but now wasn't about him. Dare was focused on Aya. He gently grasped her by the shoulders and peppered light kisses against her neck.

She stiffened as if finally sensing his presence. "Dare..."

He continued to place kisses, running his lips down her spine. Dare went to his knees and kissed each one of her luscious ass cheeks. He went lower still, placing his lips along legs and didn't stop until he connected with her feet. Then, he made his way back up as he remained on his knees.

A soft moan escaped her lips as he went about the task of worshipping her with his mouth. Remaining on his knees, he gently grasped her waist and guided Aya's body until his face was flush with the front of her body, giving him access to her breasts and pussy.

He circled her navel with his tongue before kissing her along the flat expanse of her belly.

Aya moaned, gripping his shoulders. "Dare...you know this can't always be the solution to our problems."

"I know, doll," he murmured as he continued caressing her skin with his lips. "Just, let me have this. I need you so much." He squeezed her breasts in his palms, tweaking and pulling on her nipples. The taut tips puckered beneath his touch and Aya released a soft sigh. He loved how responsive she was to him. But Aya was right, sex wouldn't solve the underlying issues between them, but for this brief moment in time, he could love her in the purest way possible and pretend that he wasn't on the verge of losing the love of his life. While she was in his arms, he could make believe that everything was just fine. And Dare intended to prolong this as long as possible.

Aya tightened her grip on his shoulders but didn't pull away. Dare took it as an encouraging sign.

He continued to pluck the hardened nubs between his thumb and forefinger, never taking his gaze from her face. Just seeing her head thrash back and forth while gasps of pleasure escaped her lips, made his dick so hard, he didn't know if he'd be able to hold out for long before plunging into her cunt. Damn, she was beautiful.

And for now, she was his.

Dare ran his tongue across her belly before burying his nose against the juncture of her thighs. Nudging her legs apart to gain access to her treasure, he slid his middle finger along the length of her slit. She was soaking wet, and despite the shower spray beating against their bodies, Dare knew that most of the wetness dripping from her juicy pussy had come from Aya herself. He wanted to take his time exploring every inch of her, but he felt like he would die if he didn't get a taste.

"Hold on tight, doll." Dare gripped her leg and lifted it over his shoulder so that he could feast on her hot sex. He eased a finger inside her tight sheath. It was so warm and welcoming. Her walls clenched his finger and when he slid his cock inside of her it would take a considerable amount of control to not shoot his seed inside of her right away.

Dare pushed his finger as deep as it would go before pulling it out. He repeated the motion several times as her cream slid down his hand.

"Dare!" she cried out. "I can't take it."

A smile twisted his lips. He'd found her spot. He added another finger and relentlessly fucked her pussy with his digit before capturing her swollen clit between his lips. Aya's moans grew louder and she dug her fingernails into his skin as he continued to suck on her the sensitive little nubbin. As always, she tasted of pure heaven. Dare couldn't get enough of her.

"I'm going to cum!"

Her words only encouraged him to pump faster and suck harder. Aya clawed into his flesh, releasing a primal scream as she reached her peak. He was certain she'd broken skin, but when it was all over, Dare would gladly wear these scratches as a badge of honor, knowing he'd pleased his woman. Slowly, he removed his fingers and lapped at the juices flowing from her pussy.

Gripping her firm ass cheeks, he spread them apart and licked Aya from her clit to her rosette. He circled the tight ring with his tongue, savoring the taste of her on his tongue. He continued to lick her with long, broad strokes. Dare couldn't get enough.

"Dare, please…" she groaned.

Finally, he raised his head to look at her face. Aya's lids were at half-mast and her eyes, which were already dark seemed to have turned obsidian and filled with lust. Her bottom lip was between her teeth, inviting his kiss and the way she looked at him, there was no doubt in his mind what she wanted, but he wanted the gratification of hearing her say it.

"Tell me, baby. What do you want?"

"I need you. Inside of me. Now."

Dare licked his lips in anticipation. "You don't have to ask twice." Gently, he placed her leg down and stood up. He pressed her against the wall and captured her mouth in a heated kiss. Cupping the side of her face, he pushed his tongue past her lips, sweeping it along the cavern within. She twined her tongue with his as she threaded her fingers through his hair. Aya pressed her breasts against him, giving back as much as she got.

He gripped Aya by the ass and lifted her off the shower floor. She automatically wrapped her legs around his waist.

Dare pulled her away just enough to align his cock with her moist entrance. "Are you ready for me, doll?"

She bit her bottom lip again and nodded.

With one strong surge, he slammed into her pussy. Dare sighed with relief. Being inside of Aya was like home. She was so warm and welcoming, fitting around his cock like a tight, velvet glove. He held on to her for several seconds just savoring the feel of her walls surrounding him.

Aya circled her arms around him and buried her face against his neck. "Please." She squirmed against him signaling her need for him.

Dare chuckled at her eagerness. "Anything you want. I'm here to please you." He jerked his hips back until only the tip of his cock remained before thrusting forward. Dare moved slowly at first, finding his rhythm before picking up the pace. Aya ground her hips, meeting each one of his thrusts with an enthusiasm that matched his.

She ran her nails down his back and nibbled on the side of his neck. Aya's erotic ministrations drove him insane with lust. He'd intended to take her gently, but all niceties flew out the window as she licked the shell of his ear.

"What are you trying to do to me woman?"

"Tasting you."

Her matter-of-fact words were enough to snap the little control he'd been hanging on to. He pounded in and out of her as she moved her body in time with his. Dare grit his teeth and tried his best to hold out, but when she clenched her muscles around his dick, he lost it.

"Aya!" He shouted her name as he released inside of her.

Slowly, as he came down from his sexual high, he placed his hands between their bodies and found her clit. He caught it between his thumb and forefinger and twisted it until she moaned out loud. Dare wanted to make sure she reached another climax. He didn't have a long wait before she stiffened against him. Dare captured her scream in his mouth, kissing her in earnest.

His semi-erect cock still rested inside of her, but he could feel himself getting hard again. He wasn't finished. Dare broke the tight seal of their mouths.

"Shower off," he commanded.

The water stopped flowing.

With Aya still in his arms, he opened the shower stall and carried her out to their bedroom. It didn't matter that they were soaking wet, he would take Aya anyway he could get her.

"Dare, the sheets are going to get wet," Aya pointed out as he placed her in the center of the bed.

He smirked. "We've gotten the bed wet before, at least you have."

She raised a brow as she returned his smile with one of her own. "You're so bad."

Dare slid on top of her. "And that's why you love me." He covered her mouth with his again. With his first orgasm out of the way, this time, Dare was able to explore Aya at his leisure. He placed a kiss on her forehead and more all over her face. He didn't leave a single inch of her unexplored from the spot behind her ears that made Aya whimper in pleasure, to the soles of her dainty feet.

Dare took care to suck and lick each one of her toes because there wasn't a single part of her he didn't love. He rolled her over and licked and caressed the dark expanse of Aya's back, running his finger along her spine.

"You're going to be the death of me," she murmured the words that came out more like a moan.

He massaged her legs and buttocks and gently pushed her legs apart. Dare lowered himself to suck on her pussy some more. She was an addiction he couldn't fight and he had no intention of denying himself while he still had her.

"It's my turn," Aya said in between moans.

While the thought of Aya's luscious lips wrapped around his dick was a temptation that was nearly impossible to resist, this was her night. He wanted to make sure she was thoroughly pleasured.

"Not tonight. I need this so badly."

"What do you mean?"

Dare rolled to his side pulling her with him, her back was flush with his chest. He then positioned their bodies until her ass rested against his hardness. Dare lifted her leg and slid into Aya's pussy from behind. "I mean that I want you to feel very satisfied by the end of the night.

She leaned her head against his chest. "You do satisfy me, Dare."

He circled her throat with his hand and kissed her cheek. Instead of answering her, he began to move inside of her. She was just as wet and ready for him as she had been in the shower.

This time, he was able to go slow. From this position, he could place his free hand between her legs and play with her clit as he moved in and out of her. "You're so beautiful. Love you so much," Dare whispered against her skin.

He noticed that Aya didn't say it back as she usually did and his heart broke a little bit, but he continued moving inside of her, holding on to this as long as he could. The one consolation he had was that she was definitely into this from the way she wiggled her hips and met his cock whenever he moved inside of her.

Dare held back just long enough for Aya to climax again before he finished inside of her. Reluctantly, he pulled out of her and then wrapped his arms around her, with her back still against him.

He kissed her shoulder. "Aya. I love you."

Dare waited but was greeted with silence.

It was like a punch to the chest, but he forced himself to continue talking. "I know I get out of control sometimes, but it's only because I'm so scared of losing you. I can't forget what I did to get you. And my biggest fear is that one day you'll realize that you can't forgive me after all and walk out on me. And it drives me crazy because I know I don't deserve you. As you already know, I wasn't raised in a home where I was able to express my emotion so instead of telling you how I feel, I act like a huge idiot sometimes."

Aya sighed. "Dare, I do love you. That's why it's been so hard for me to reconcile how you treat me versus how I feel. There are times when you're attentive and thoughtful and sometimes even very sweet. Like the time you sent me a message while I was working that you love me and you're thinking about me. You can afford to give me anything I ask for, but that note meant the world to me. I still pull it up on my holowatch to look at it to remind myself why I love you. But I shouldn't have to constantly remind myself why I love you. And as for me not forgiving you, I already did. Will I ever forget, probably not, but I was able to open my heart up to you anyway. The fact you can't accept that shouldn't be placed at my feet. I can't go on like this, Dare."

"Please don't say it."

Aya didn't reply at first and as the silence lengthened Dare's anxiety grew. Aya had a big heart and she was probably looking for a way to let him down gently. But there had to be something he could say—to do to make things right. He could tell her the other reason he was so worried about losing her, but he didn't want to frighten her. Besides, he wasn't sure he wanted to speak that scenario into reality.

"Dare I think we should—"

"Wait before you say anything, can you please give me another chance. I'll do better."

"The second a man looks at me for longer than a few seconds, you'll want to start a fight. I don't want to be placed in the middle of your testosterone-fueled aggression. It puts my nerves on edge so that I have to constantly be on guard."

He placed kisses on her shoulder. "And I'm so sorry for making you feel this way. If you want, I'll do whatever it takes to put you at ease with me again. I want you to love me again."

Aya turned around within the circle of his arms so that they were facing each other. She cupped the side of his face with her small hand. "But I do love you, Dare. And therein lies the problem. If I didn't love you, don't you think I would have walked away a long time ago? The only reason I'm still here is because I love you. All I was going to say, was maybe we're taking things a little too fast. It was a mistake for me to move in with you so soon without resolving some of our underlying issues. I think I should move back to my old apartment. Uncle Arthur and Mera are in the process of moving to a condo closer to the city. And it would be more convenient for one of us to live in the unit over the bar."

"Aya, that neighborhood isn't safe."

She narrowed her eyes. "I lived there long before you came along without any incident."

"It's still a dangerous area, full of Dr—" He stopped himself before he could finish. That word was derogatory and it was ironic that a word he once used freely was now something he cringed at whenever he heard it.

"Go ahead and say it. Full of Dregs. Right? If you haven't forgotten. I'm one of those Dregs you're speaking of."

Dreg was a term used by the Elite to describe people they saw as lower than them in society, usually ne're do wells and those who were too lazy to find jobs so they resorted to crime or begging on the streets. Having met Aya and actually getting to know a few of the people in her life prior to him, Dare had learned just how offensive that word was and he hated himself for using it in the heat of the moment. He understood most of the people in Aya's former district were victims of their own circumstances and most of them wanted to work and make an honest living. But it didn't change the fact that there was still an element that worried him. Just because some people didn't want to voluntarily commit acts of violence to get what they wanted, didn't mean that it wasn't there. Besides, rape was still one of the leading violent crimes in the country, and doubly so in the area Aya hailed from.

"No. I don't look at you that way. And that was a poor choice of words on my part. I'm sorry for even forming the word, but the fact of the matter is that I can keep you safe over here. It's one thing that you work there in the daytime, but I'm terrified of something happening to you. You're so trusting of everyone."

Aya pulled away from him. "Now you're making me sound like an idiot. Gosh, however did I make it before the great Alasdair O'Shaughnessy came into my life?"

Dare could tell that no matter what he said he was only making things worse. And maybe Aya was looking for a fight so that she could use it as an excuse to get out of the relationship. He wouldn't fall for the bait, though. Dare refused to stop fighting for them. "You're right. You were doing just fine. I just don't want to lose you. Please, stay with me." He pulled Aya against him and held her tightly. "I can't breathe without you. Please give me another chance. I won't let you down."

The pregnant pause stretched throughout the room, but Dare refused to release his grip on her until he had an answer.

"One more chance," she finally whispered.

Dare released the breath he didn't realize he'd been holding. "Thank you." She was still his.

For now.

Chapter Five

"You seem to be in better spirits lately," Tori noted as they sat in the salon.

Being pampered was still a luxury that had taken Aya some getting used to, but she found that full body massages and pedicures had quickly become her guilty pleasure. There were robots that could give you each service quickly and at a fraction of the cost, but nothing beat the human touch.

She and Tori were in the middle of getting pedicures, each with two diligent workers taking care of their feet. Aya sighed in pleasure. Whatever they were doing to her, she wished she could bottle that feeling up and take it out whenever she was feeling stressed. "Wouldn't you be in great spirits if someone as skilled as Evita and Calise was working on your feet? They have magic hands." She smiled at the ladies who seemed to appreciate that she actually took the time to learn their names. Most of the clients received services from the workers as their due, most of the time not even making eye contact. Having worked in the service industry herself, Aya knew what it was like to work on the other end, which was why she always tried to be polite.

Tori shook her head. "That's not what I meant. I'm talking about in general. The past few times we've gotten together, you have actually been smiling. You even look like you've been sleeping better. Can I take this to mean that things are going better with you and Dare? According to Foster, Dare hasn't been his usual gruff self. Foster says that he seems a bit mellower."

"Did he? I guess you can say things are getting better. Dare and I had a long talk and it's almost as if a light switch went off in his head. He's actually been…great. I'm not sure what the exact word for it, though, the past few weeks, he hasn't been on my case. He doesn't demand to know where I am every single second of the day. We've even gone out a couple times and he's been normal. Things are good. He's the Dare I fell in love with."

"I'm so glad to hear that. It's nice to see you smile."

"It's just nice to be treated like I have my own autonomy. Dare came by the bar the other day and at first, I was worried that he'd do something crazy like pick a fight with one of the patrons like he's done before, but he was on his best behavior, in fact, he'd come by to give me a gift."

"What did he give you?"

"A handwritten note. On real paper."

Tori raised a brow. "What? That's something special. Actual paper is hard to find. I've only seen it in Dare's library."

"I know, but I guess when you have unlimited credits, nothing is too difficult to acquire."

Tori smiled. "That's really sweet. What did the note say?"

Aya grinned to herself as she thought of his handwritten words. *You own my heart, always and forever. Without you, there is no me. I love you. Dare.*

"Basically, it was just a message telling me that he loved me." Aya didn't want to share the exact wording because it was something special she wanted to hold close to her heart. She touched the antique gold locket that Dare had gifted her with. She had folded the piece of paper up and placed it inside the locket so she could have it always.

"That's pretty romantic. I think I should ask Foster why I've never gotten something so nice."

Aya waved her hand dismissively. "Oh, come on, Foster spoils you rotten. He bought you and your family a house and three more for the shelters you run. That sounds like love to me."

"It is incredibly kind of him and I appreciate all he's done for me and my family, but when you have that amount of wealth, that's like buying a bar of protein. It's nothing to him. But taking the time out to do something creative like that...well, that's pretty special."

Aya absently touched the locket again. "It is, but don't be so hard on Foster. He adores you."

"Oh, I'm not. I love Foster to pieces and I wouldn't trade him for the world. I'm just in awe of your gift."

"I'm so glad you two are doing well."

"We've been talking about getting married."

Aya raised a brow. "Really? That's exciting."

"I know. I never thought I'd get married since marriage is such an Elite thing to do."

"That's true," Aya agreed. Marriages were expensive affairs. Even regular town hall weddings presided over by judges were costly because of the amount of credits it took to purchase a marriage license. Most people in her town couldn't afford the two thousand credits it took to get one. Most people barely made enough to feed their families so marriage was a luxury. And normally when the wealthy wed, they put on grand celebrations that were televised and lasted days at a time to show off their riches. Some of the more generous couples donated their excess food to charities and soup kitchens, but the others just threw it out, which was a complete waste. She even heard of some of the Elite using the food as bait to get free labor out of hungry people.

Aya generally saw those big extravagant parties as just another way for the Elite to live in excess and flaunt the differences of their lifestyles with those who came from humbler backgrounds like hers. But then there were those rare weddings where people actually scrapped the little credits they had because they wanted to make a lasting commitment to each other that would be recorded for all time. Aya thought those were more heartfelt and earnest.

"I see the wheels working in your head and no, if we do get married, I don't see myself getting holovision sponsorship and it wouldn't be over the top. I'd just want a simple ceremony with friends and family and maybe some of our old neighbors."

"That sounds really lovely."

"I'd, of course, want you to be one of my attendants."

"Aww, I would be honored."

"So, what about you and Dare? Do you think the two of you will take that final step together?"

Aya shrugged. "I never thought about it really? I do love Dare, but marriage is so final. We're just getting to a good point in our relationship. Although he has mentioned it, I want to take things slow."

"Well, I'm glad that the two of you are at least in a good place because I was worried about how you'd handle the bodyguard situation."

Aya furrowed her brows together. Maybe she'd misheard her friend. "Bodyguard situation?"

Tori opened her mouth in a big oh, and gasped. "Nothing." She shook her curly locks vigorously.

"No, don't do that. If you know something I don't regarding me and Dare, tell me."

"It's nothing really. Something Foster said in passing. I might have misheard him."

Aya folded her arms across her chest and narrowed her gaze as she focused on the other woman. "Tell me."

Tori squirmed in her seat and looked like she wanted to bolt. "Well, it's just that I thought I heard Foster say something about Dare having bodyguards following you around so they can report on your comings and goings."

"Well, if there are bodyguards, I'm unaware of them. I haven't seen anyone near me."

"Exactly. That's why I must have misheard it. Forget I even mentioned it. The last thing I want to do is cause any dissension between you and Dare."

"If anyone is the cause of any problems between me and Dare it would be either me or him and in this case, it would definitely be him."

Aya didn't know what to think. It was obvious that Dare hadn't gone through with his plan to have her flanked by bodyguards because she was certain to have noticed them, but the fact that he'd discussed it with Foster without bringing it up to her bothered Aya. Maybe she was overreacting because after all, she had Tori and sometimes Macy as her sounding boards. It was just unsettling to know that he'd even considered this. She wasn't sure how long ago this conversation had taken place and maybe it was better if she didn't know.

"You've gone silent, Aya. I hope you won't be angry with Dare. I'm sure if he even brought it up it was because he wants to keep you protected."

"No, that's not it. He'd do it to keep tabs on me so he could have another reason to act like a possessive jerk.

But I'm not going to get angry about it. As long as he didn't go through with it, all is good."

But as the day went on she couldn't get that conversation out of her head. Were things as good as she thought?

Aya's driver, Ben was waiting outside for her. Aya didn't have plans to go back to the bar because her uncle was closing that day, but Mera had slipped on a spill on the floor and had hurt her back. Uncle Arthur had taken her to a medical facility to get treatment so he'd contacted Aya. She didn't mind since Dare had planned on working late that night because he said he had some big deal in the works. Going to that huge mansion without him would be lonely enough. Sure, he had the finest home entertainment money could buy, but there was only so much holovision she could watch and hologames to play.

She could catch up on some reading, but as Ben drove her home while they exchanged light conversation, a little building caught her attention. "What's that?"

Ben looked out the window briefly before turning his attention back to the road. "Oh, that's a new restaurant. It's a twenty-first-century style dinner. They serve breakfast food all day long which seems to be a big draw for a lot of people. I've heard that the prices aren't that bad so most people can afford the occasional meal there."

"Have you tried it?"

"Not yet, but Macy and I were talking about going there. She gets an allowance from her sister and she wants to pay for everything, but I have my pride, you know?"

Aya smiled at the mention of her friend Macy. When Macy had come for a visit, Ben had been the one to pick her up. Apparently, the two had hit it off because they'd been seeing each other for a few months much to their mutual friend Mac's dismay. Poor Mac had had a crush on Macy since he'd met the adorable brunette. And while Macy had tried to have a romantic relationship with Mac, it had felt more like a brother and sister relationship even though Mac had felt otherwise. Aya felt bad for Mac, but he'd taken it in stride and she was glad that Macy was happy. Ben was a good guy and the two of them were cute together. "That's understandable. It's good that you want to maintain your independence. Sometimes wealth corrupts people."

"You make it sound like having money is a bad thing."

Aya shrugged. "Not really. I think it can do a lot of good for those in need, but people with too much of it can buy and sell anything they want."

"And that's a problem because?"

"The issue lies in what happens when you have a lot of credits at your disposal. When you've already bought everything you could possibly think of so you get bored and start creating entertainment for yourself. That's how programs like the Run come to be. Yes, brothels are legal and I wouldn't knock women for doing what they have to do to support themselves, but think of all the depraved acts that happen in some of the less scrupulous ones. And then there are things like the Auction." She shuddered when she thought of how Tori and Macy had to deal with that revolting organization."

"I guess I know what you mean. But I suppose that it isn't the money that changes people. It only enhances who they were in the first place."

She sunk into her seat. "I never thought about that. That's a pretty profound statement."

"I didn't come up with that myself. I heard it from somewhere else, but in my observation of being around the Elite, I've noticed that statement to be true."

"I suppose you're right." Aya wondered what Dare would have been like if he hadn't been born into wealth. Would he be the hard man that he'd once been who disregarded others so casually? And what would she eventually become? Would she end up like the horrible wives of Dare's business associates? There were only one or two that she could actually stomach being around without wanting to commit an act of violence and that wasn't saying a lot considering they were all terrible people. Or maybe she was just being too judgmental.

The closer they got to home, the more Aya didn't want to be there without Dare. And eating alone at the huge marble dining room table was never fun. "You know what, Ben, would you mind terribly if we turned around and went to the diner? I think I might want to catch a bite to eat there."

"By yourself?"

"Well, it wouldn't be that much different from going home and eating alone. At least at the diner I would be surrounded by people."

"If that's what you want."

"Thanks, Ben. You wouldn't want to join me, would you?"

He laughed. "I see you are in good spirits tonight to even suggest such a thing. But that's a pretty funny joke. Thank you for the offer, but I'd like to keep my job."

"Dare wouldn't fire you. I'd make sure of it. It could be our little secret."

"He would find out."

"Because you'd tell him?"

"I wouldn't have to. He'd know because of..."

She frowned when he trailed off. "Because of what?"

Ben didn't answer.

"Ben, what aren't you telling me?"

"Nothing. Here we are." He brought the car to a halt in front of the diner.

"Ben. Tell me."

"Miss Smith, I—"

"Oh, so it's Miss Smith all of a sudden? It's Aya. You know I don't like formalities."

"We're here," he repeated.

Aya realized he wasn't going to budge, but there was definitely something he was keeping from her. "I thought we were friends, Ben. But if that's the way you want to play it, I understand."

"I do consider you my friend, Aya, but I'd also like to keep my job. There aren't that many that pay as generously as this one. I have enough to take care of myself and I'm able to help my family with the excess. Please try to see things from my perspective."

"I do. I'm sorry for pushing."

"Don't apologize. I shouldn't have made you think there was anything more to my statement."

But there was, although Aya decided not to say it out loud. Feeling slightly frustrated, she got out of the vehicle. "I'll buzz you when I'm ready to go home."

Ben nodded. "I'll be ready when you are."

When Aya walked inside the diner it was like stepping into the past. She didn't recognize the décor but it had a retro feel to it. There were red vinyl booths lining stark walls with framed black and white pictures that looked as if they should have been in a museum. Lively music she didn't recognize played in the background and the servers, all males were dressed in white uniforms with red bow ties and triangular white caps. It reminded Aya of an old movie she'd once seen.

The place seemed packed and she wondered if she'd be able to get a table. "May I help you?" The host gave her the once over, taking in her appearance.

Since Aya had come straight from the bar, she was casually dressed in a pair of slacks and plain black top. There was nothing about her that screamed money, but she didn't feel too out of place.

"I'd like a table, please."

Again the host looked her over. "I'm afraid there are no tables available."

"I don't mind sitting at the bar if there's a seat open there."

He shook his head. "No, there isn't. Sorry." This host didn't particularly seem to sound the least bit regretful.

"That's no problem. The lady can dine with me. Any friend of O'Shaughnessy is a friend of mine."

Aya looked up to see the man she'd met at the dinner she'd attended with Dare a couple months back. His name escaped her at the moment, but she definitely remembered his face.

"Oh, Mr. Reichardt, my apologies. I didn't realize she was your guest. And did you say this was a friend of Mr. O'Shaughnessy's? Mr. Alasdair O'Shaughnessy?"

The redhead grinned. "That's correct. This is his very close friend. You might have seen her on his arm at the last Sapphire Ball."

The host's eyes widened as realization dawned on his face. "I'm so sorry, Ma'am. I swear I meant no offense. We do in fact have a table for you but it was reserved otherwise it would have been yours. It's in the best spot in the house."

Aya might have actually been amused at his change of tune if she wasn't annoyed by the fact that he'd completely dismissed her out of hand before he found out who she was. She would have walked out, but by now she was starving and just wanted to get a quick bite.

"It's okay."

"No, it's not," Mr. Reichardt spoke up. "You should be careful how you treat your customers. You never know who you're dealing with. Perhaps I should have a word with the owner."

The host turned bright red.

Aya shook her head. "That won't be necessary. Could you just show me to a table please?"

"Of course." He nodded before turning to her rescuer. "Mr. Reichardt, would you like to remain at your table or would you like to sit with Miss…"

"Smith."

"With Miss Smith."

"Best table in the house you say? If the lovely lady is in agreement, I'll join her."

Aya shrugged. She didn't mind the company and he seemed nice enough.

Once they were seated, the host mumbled something about letting him know if there was anything else they needed before scurrying away. Aya turned to the redhead and smiled. "Thank you for stepping in for me. But I'm going to sound like a huge jerk when I say I don't remember your name."

He raised his brows in apparent surprise before smiling. "Well, I don't hear that often since my name is what most people would call eccentric. It's Thor. Nice to meet you again." He held his hand across the table.

With a giggle, she took it and gave it a shake. "It's nice to meet you again as well. I'm surprised you remembered me."

"You're not that easy to forget."

She felt her cheeks heat up. The way he looked at her made her think he might have meant more by his words, but Thor was fully aware that she was with Dare. Instead of responding to his question, she switched topics. "I didn't realize you and Dare were friends, considering how rude he was to you at the dinner. I apologize for that by the way."

"I don't take it personally. I've known him for a long time and I understand him. So, what brings you here tonight?"

"I suppose, the same as you. I wanted to get something to eat. I've never noticed this place before. Have you ever eaten here before?"

"Yes. I suggest you try the sirloin burgers. They grind their own meat here. It tastes better than some of the more upscale spots."

"Well, I'll give that a shot."

A server stopped by their table to take their orders and once that task was accomplished, he left Aya and Thor alone again.

"So why aren't you with O'Shaughnessy tonight?"

"He's working late, but it's not like our bodies are connected. I come and go as I please."

"Hmm." Thor took a drink from his water glass.

"What's that supposed to mean?"

"I don't mean to make you feel uncomfortable by bringing up the topic, but I couldn't help but notice that he's...very intense when it comes to you. I was actually a little worried about you."

"You don't mean to make me feel uncomfortable, but you're doing a pretty good job of it."

"I'm sorry if I'm overstepping my boundaries. We hardly know each other after all, but I do know Dare. I've known him for a long time and I've just seen what he's like if something doesn't go his way. His temper is legendary, and I don't want you to get hurt."

Sure, Dare had a short fuse, but hearing this practical stranger tell her about it made Aya defensive. Thor seemed like a nice enough guy, but she didn't need his relationship advice, especially since things were back on track with her and Dare.

"You know what, I'm not that hungry anymore. I'm sorry, but I have to go." She pressed the call service button on the table that brought up a holographic screen and then hit the pay bar. And infrared scanner appeared and moved along her arm until it came to where her VC would be and debited credits for the meal she'd ordered.

Thor stood with her. "I'm sorry that I said something to offend you. You don't have to go."

"But I do. Thank you, Thor, for speaking up for me. I know you meant well, but there are certain things that are better left unsaid. Enjoy your dinner." She walked away without waiting for his reply.

Chapter Six

Dare's tongue bled from how hard he'd been biting it. It took a lot of his will power to remain silent even though he knew Aya was keeping secrets from him. He didn't understand why she didn't tell him about that dinner with Reichardt even though he'd found out about it. The only reason he didn't bring it up was because apparently the meeting hadn't been planned and from what he could tell it had ended abruptly.

If Aya knew he was having her watched, it would be the end of them without a doubt, but he had to do it, for her own protection. He was a wondered how she hadn't been snatched off the streets before he'd met her, despite her saying that her neighbors had always looked out for her. That might have been true enough, but Dare lived in a world where when someone saw what they wanted, they didn't take no for an answer, himself included.

He still cringed when he thought about the lengths he'd gone to make her his. But even still, there were far worse people out there, like the people who had taken her friend Macy off the streets. Or people who used wealth and influence to capture and abuse people, mainly women, for their own sick pleasure. Depravity was a well-known secret among the Elites. Most of them didn't bother to hide their sick inclinations because most of the enforcers and government officials were in their pockets. It didn't excuse what he'd done, but he knew there were far worse people than him.

It was quite possible that it was his fault that Aya was on someone's radar. He was after all a visible figure in society and his name carried weight wherever he went which in turn would give Aya attention. Maybe she would have been safer being left to her life running her bar and living in peace. The guilt ate at Dare that he was the reason Aya was in possible danger.

It didn't help matters that Aya seemed to be so naïve to how valuable she would be to men or Elite women who preferred women over men because of her looks. Yes, she was a beautiful woman, but she stood out for her skin color, a throwback to a few decades ago. As far as history had taught him, racial ethnicity mattered a lot more in past centuries before a huge portion of the female population was wiped out. Many ethnicities intermarried to the point where not many people were either ethnically Caucasian like himself or not much darker than Foster's lover, Tori who appeared to be multi-racial in appearance. Aya, however, was a dark shade of brown, which wasn't common in this country. Wealthy people loved having something others didn't and Dare could only imagine those who would want Aya for that very reason. Perhaps it was her appearance that had garnered his attention in the first place, but it was his heart that had kept him interested. And he intended to keep her safe even if she didn't appreciate it.

Besides, until he could figure out who was sending him coded messages, he would continue to keep tabs on her.

She touched his arm. "You've been very quiet tonight."

They were on their way to another party, this one was a lot like the Sapphire Ball, but on a smaller scale and all the proceeds went to charity. Dare hated going because he would have to mingle with people who acted like they gave a damn about the cause the party was supporting. Most of the people in attendance were there to be seen and to show off how much money they had. The only reason he attended any such events was because his corporation was one of the sponsors so for appearance sake, he had to show up. Since Aya had come into his life, she made these functions bearable. He could get through the night as long as she was by his side.

Dare took her hand and brought it to his lips. "I just have a lot on my mind. Did I tell you how beautiful you look tonight?"

Aya's smile lit up her face. "Several times."

"That's because it's true." And she did. Aya wore her favorite color green, which suited her, but then again, she looked good in any color in his opinion. Her beaded gown was strapless and figure hugging with a slit that went up to her thigh. Her hair was slicked back and her makeup was subtle. Her naked shoulders seemed to be inviting him to place kisses all over them and her exposed leg was making his dick so hard, he had to shift in his seat several times to get comfortable. He had every intention of fucking her senseless when they got home.

"What are you thinking about?"

"You," he answered truthfully.

"Oh? What about?"

"Just how much I love you and I'm also wondering how I'm going to get through the night watching other people lust after you."

Aya rolled her eyes. "Don't start that again. You think everyone wants me and I can assure you that they don't. Maybe I look nice when I'm in these fancy clothes, but I'm just me."

He kissed her hand again. "And that's why I love you." Dare decided not to push the issue because he didn't want to cause an argument. He'd been on edge since her meeting in the diner that she didn't tell him about. It was hard to drill her like he wanted to but he'd promised her that he'd try harder not to question her every movement. It would indeed be a long night. In his mind, he was already planning his escape from the party, the people he would have to say hello to and how long he would have to be before leaving without appearing rude.

"How long before we get there?"

"Roughly fifteen minutes give or take a minute or two."

"Great, just enough time."

For what?"

Instead of answering the question, she focused on the driver. "Jim, would you mind putting up the partition, please?"

"Yes, ma'am."

Dare raised a brow.

"You seem tense and I think I know how to relax you" She placed her hand on his thigh and immediately encountered his cock that was already rock hard. Aya grinned. "Oh, you are tense. But I'm going to make it all better."

He inhaled sharply. "Aya, you don't have to do this."

She fumbled with his zipper and reached into his pants. "But I want to."

Dare lifted his hips and groaned when she circled his member with her fingers and freed him. Aya slid off her seat and positioned herself between his thighs. He held his breath as she lowered her head and ran her tongue around his sensitive tip. She licked his entire length before teasing the top again. Dare, balled his fists at his sides to keep himself from grabbing her head and forcing her to swallow his dick.

While her tongue felt amazing, he needed more. Aya continued to tease him alternating between stroking him with her tongue and placing kisses on the head. Dare didn't think he could take any more of this erotic torture. "Fuck, Aya. Feels so damn, good. More. Please."

She raised her head to meet his gaze. He focused on her full lips coated with a cherry-colored gloss and he raised his hips, silently begging her to take him fully into her mouth.

"Tell me what you want. Do you want me to suck your cock?"

"Fuck yeah," he groaned.

"Anything you want." She circled him with her lips and began to take him into her mouth one excruciating inch at a time. She stopped only when she nearly had his entire dick within the warm cavern of her mouth. She slowly bobbed her head up, down, sucking on him with a precision that made him moan. Dare cupped the back of her head and raised his hips, careful not to thrust too hard.

Aya pushed her free hand inside his pants and found his balls, caressing them, never missing a beat as she continued to suck him with even more vigor with each stroke.

"Feels so fucking good, doll." Dare raised his hips to thrust each time her head moved down. When Aya began to hum around him, he nearly lost it. The vibration of her mouth as it moved along his shaft was too much for him to handle.

"Shit! I'm going to cum!" Dare tried to pull away from her, but Aya gripped his sac more firmly as she tightened her lips around him. He shot his seed down her throat while she greedily continued to suck.

She licked, kissed and fondled him with reckless abandon. With one last swipe of her tongue along his length, Aya raised her head and casually wiped away the string of cum that had slid from the corner of her lips. That sight alone was enough to make him hard all over again. He pulled her against him and slammed his lips against hers in a hungry kiss. Dare could taste himself on her lips, but it wasn't unpleasant. It only made him hornier. He turned his head to break the kiss before panting, "Lift your dress."

Aya nibbled on her bottom lips. "Do we have time?"

"We do now."

As he commanded, she gingerly raised her dress to reveal a barely there thong. Dare pushed the crotch aside as she straddled his dick.

"Mmm," Aya moaned as she sunk on his cock. "I love it when you're inside of me." She wrapped her arms around his neck and buried her face against his neck. Dare gripped her tiny waist and he proceeded to move her up and down his shaft.

"That's it doll, bounce that ass on my cock."

He fucked hard and fast, thrusting so deep inside her warmth, they were like one sexual entity. It felt so good and there was nothing he wanted more than to have her in his arms like this forever.

Aya was the first to scream her release. "Dare!!"

"That's it. Cream on my cock. Let it all go."

The feel of her muscles squeezing the life out of his dick triggered another climax.

By the time they untangled themselves from each other, their clothing was disheveled and Aya's face had a glow. She wore a smile as if she were hiding a secret that only she knew.

"I must look a mess." Aya frantically fixed her hair and dress."

"You look beautiful." Dare liked that Aya had the look of one who was freshly fucked and that he had been the one to do the fucking.

"'I'm sticky between my legs. It's going to be slightly uncomfortable walking around like this the rest of the night."

Dare leaned over and gave her a quick kiss on the corner of her lips. "Good. It's a reminder of what just happened and what's to come."

"You are insatiable."

"Only when it comes to you, my love."

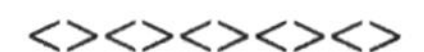

Aya was happy to see a familiar face when they finally walked into the ballroom. She immediately spotted Foster and Tori talking to the Deacons, a couple she'd seen at another one of Dare's business dinners. If there were two people who loved talking about themselves as much as them, Aya had never met them. Tori looked as if she was about to fall asleep on her feet so Aya thought it was her duty to rescue her friend.

"There's Foster and Tori," she pointed out to Dare. "Let's go over and talk to them."

"As you wish."

Tori spotted them when they approached and she didn't bother to hide the relief on her face. "Aya! Dare."

Aya and Tori exchanged hugs. "You look amazing." Aya took in her friend's shimmering gold gown with spaghetti straps. Her curls were piled on top of her head.

"You look fantastic as well, you didn't look like you were having much fun."

Tori rolled her eyes. "Uh, we've been here for at least a half an hour and those two over there corned us and have been talking our ears off ever since. I've never met anyone who said so much but so little at the same time."

Aya nodded in agreement. "The best way to handle it when people go on and on is nod and smile, then after a couple minutes excuse yourself by saying you see someone you want to talk to on the other side of the room. That's a trick that's worked for me so far."

"I'll keep that one in mind because my eyes were starting to water."

"Aya, you look beautiful tonight, as always," Foster greeted as he approached them. He dropped a kiss on her cheek.

Though Dare and Foster were best friends, Aya had come to value his friendship as well. She was happy that he and Tori had found each other again. It was clear that the two of them were deeply in love. Considering what Foster and Tori had been through, they deserved the happiness they'd finally found in each other.

"Hi, Foster. Good to see you again."

"Did you two just arrive?" he asked.

"Yes, we only made it here a few minutes ago and not soon enough I imagine." Aya pointed in the direction of the Deacons who appeared to be in the middle of another drawn out conversation with another poor couple.

"Oh, them." Foster shook his head. "If you two hadn't arrived, I think I would have committed murder."

"They weren't that bad," Tori chided. "Boring yes, but worth killing? Not so much."

"You're much nicer than me, Foster because I wouldn't have entertained them. They know better than to waste my time with their stories about nothing. Besides, from my understanding, Deacon is looking to resurrect the Run." Dare dropped that bit of information so casually that Aya thought she might have misheard him.

"What? Can't he be stopped?" Aya demanded.

Dare shrugged. "Yes and no. Even though I shut the Run down and own the rights to the name, I can't stop him from opening up something similar. Jackson Deacon used to be one of the frequent clients of the Run and one of the most vocal dissenters when I shut it down."

Aya frowned. "But you own the land it had taken place on."

"And he could easily purchase land elsewhere for it to take place."

Aya wasn't happy to hear this. "You don't sound like you care. You know what happens to those women. To be humiliated and hunted like animals, it just isn't right."

"I know, doll. If it will help things, I can talk to my lawyers to see if there's some legal action that could be taken. At the very least, I can have it tied up in the court for so long that he'll eventually lose interest."

"Or until someone else comes up with the idea." Aya felt dejected at that thought. She should have known with the closing of the Run, someone would come up with something else even more depraved. And since Foster and Dare had been behind the shutting down of the Auction there was no telling what people were planning next.

Dare must have sensed her sadness because he wrapped his arm around her waist and dropped a kiss on her forehead. "It will be all right. I'll take care of this."

"Dare, there's something I've been meaning to talk to you about. Do you have a minute? I'm sure the ladies will be fine without us for a bit."

Dare looked at Aya. "Go ahead. I have Tori to keep me company."

When the men were out of earshot, Tori gave her a quick hug. "It's going to be okay. I'm sure Foster and Dare will make sure the Run or anything similar isn't reopened."

"That isn't the problem. It just makes me think that something far worse is coming along. I don't know what it is, but I can't seem to shake the feeling that something bad is going to happen. At first, I thought it was because of the problems me and Dare were having, but now that things have gotten better, that sensation is still there. I don't know why I still feel this way."

Tori gave her a sympathetic smile and patted her shoulder in comfort. "Maybe it's because you're feeling guilty. I know what you're going through because I felt the same way."

"I don't understand what you mean."

"Of course you do. Sometimes it's just hard to reconcile. You and I came from practically nothing. We were labeled Dregs and lived hand to mouth. Sure, you and your uncle had the bar to run, but it wasn't as if it was one of those fancy establishments in the shopping district. Poverty was all around us but look at us now; at a fancy ball, wearing gowns worth more money than both of us could have even imagined and rubbing elbows with people who have never had to lift a hand to do hard labor. We live in grand houses with lots of servants and our men give us everything we could possibly want. And the kicker is, we like it. You can't tell me you don't enjoy being pampered every now and then. It's okay that you enjoy your new life. No one holds it against you that you're with Dare."

Aya didn't realize she was carrying around this weight until now. She'd been in denial, afraid of letting this life change her. Maybe she had contributed to the problems in her relationship with Dare as much as he had with his stubbornness. "I guess I never thought about it. I mean deep down I knew this, but I didn't want to acknowledge it. It just feels strange going to restaurants and people are falling over themselves to serve me because of who I'm attached to. And then I go back to the bar and our customers are working class people."

"But I'm sure those same people who frequently patron Arthur's place are happy for you. And the ones who aren't, well, that's their problem. You do so much for other people. It's okay."

Aya gave Tori a quick hug. "Thank you."

Tori laughed. "For what?"

"For making me see things clearly. I need to go find Dare."

"And leave me at the mercy of the Deacons? If they see me alone, they may tell me another one of their boring stories."

"Oh, I'll wait."

Tori waved her hand in dismissal. "I'm kidding. Go find him. I'll just use your tip if I encounter those two. In the meantime, I'm off to the bar to order one of those pretty purple drinks I see some of the people drinking."

"Thanks."

Aya searched the ballroom but didn't catch sight of either Dare or Foster. It then occurred to her that they may have taken their conversation outside. Once she was outside of the ballroom, it didn't take long for her to spot them and they appeared to be having a heated argument even though they kept their voices low. They were so deep into what was being said to each other that neither man noticed her approach.

"You're going to have to tell her." Foster seemed to be lecturing Dare about something and Aya was almost certain that she was the *her* in question.

"I'll tell her in time, but for now, it's better that she doesn't know."

"Tori told me that she nearly let it slip when they were in the salon together. She doesn't want to keep secrets from her friend."

"Maybe you shouldn't have told Tori what I told you in confidence."

"She was worried about Aya and I assured her that things would be okay once things settled down. I honestly never meant to tell her, but when she asked what I meant, I refused to lie to her."

"Look, if I tell Aya, it's over with us. How do you think she's going to react when she finds out that I've had her VC hacked so that I'm aware of her comings and goings and that I'm having her discretely followed?"

Chapter Seven

Aya had heard enough. Storming over to the two men, she cleared her throat to gain their attention.

The second Dare noticed her, he lost all color. "Aya. What are you doing out here?"

She shook her head torn between screaming at him or slapping his face. The rage she felt, that he would go behind her back and do the very thing he promised he wouldn't do, angered her beyond words.

"Judging from the look on your face, you probably overheard our conversation. But I can explain." Dare reached out to her, but Aya swatted his hand away.

"Don't fucking touch me! How could you?"

"Maybe I should leave the two of you alone." Foster backed away.

Aya turned her narrowed gaze in the blond's direction. "Yeah, you do that. And you can tell that *friend* of mine, thanks a lot for keeping me in the dark about something that pertains to my life."

"Please don't blame Victoria. I swore her to secrecy. She wanted to tell you, she really did," Foster defended his lover.

"Of course she did. Just like you, right? I thought we were friends too, Foster. Does Macy know?"

"No. Victoria didn't tell her and neither did I."

Aya snorted, not the least bit mollified. "But I'm sure she would have found out before me. Some friends you turned out to be. Go ahead and run away."

"Aya…I'm really sorry. It wasn't my place to tell you. Just give Dare a chance to explain and you'll see that it wasn't out of completely selfish reasons."

"Just go away okay?" She turned her back to him.

Foster sighed before walking off.

"Aya," Dare began. "I couldn't tell you because I didn't want to worry you. I—"

She held up her hand. "Save it. You didn't tell me because this was your way of controlling me. You have absolutely no trust in me."

"It's not you I don't trust. It's—"

"Stop lying! I'm tired of you telling me that you'll do better and then you pull some shit like this. And here I was coming out here to tell you how much I love you and that I'm looking forward to our future together and you've been monitoring me? You don't get to dictate my comings and goings. You treat me like I'm your little lapdog and you're my master. You might as well just put a collar on me that says property of Dare. Well, I'm done being your pet. Fuck you Dare, and fuck this relationship. It's over." By the time she was finished with her rant, tears flowed down her cheeks unheeded because despite being angry, her heart was breaking. She'd given this man so much; heart, body, and soul and he just saw her as another one of is acquisitions.

"Don't do this Aya. Just hear me out. Please. I did it to protect you. If anything were to happen to you, I don't know what I would do with myself. I love you."

"You have a funny way of showing it. Goodbye, Dare."

When she attempted to leave, he grabbed her by the wrist and swung her around to face him making her collide with the hard wall of his chest. "Please. I don't want to be without you. I can't be without you. You're everything to me."

She tried to break out of his grip, but he was too strong for her. "Then maybe you should have thought about that before you had me stalked. Let me go, Dare. You disgust me." Aya realized her words were harsh, but she wanted him to feel as much pain as he had caused her. Besides, the longer he held her in his arms, she was scared that he'd change her mind. She didn't want to be weak. If she kept taking him back every time he fucked up, then she'd have to continue to take whatever he decided to dole out to her.

"No! I won't let you go. You're mine. From the moment I laid eyes on you, you belonged to me."

Hearing his possessive words made her struggle even harder. "I'm not a thing. I'm a person! This is exactly why we can't be together because you keep treating me like I'm something to own. I can't do this anymore. I should have known that things were going way too well for us."

"Aya if you'd just let me explain it to you, then you'll understand why I had to do it. I suggested you have bodyguards. I'm an important man and because of that, there are unscrupulous people who will try to hurt you to get to me. Why is it so wrong for me to want to protect you? Yes, you belong to me, but I belong to you as well. We belong together. Don't do this to me. Don't do this to us."

"Dare, if you really loved me like you claim you do, you would have been honest with me. But you knew I didn't want anyone following me so you went behind my back. And what's worse, you told your best friend who in turn told my friend, leaving me in the dark completely. I've had it. You can overpower me and keep holding on, but the second you release me, I'm walking away and not looking back."

Dare tightened his grip on her and buried his face against her neck. "I'm begging you."

Aya remained limp in his arms, not bothering to respond. There was no point. No matter what she said, Dare wouldn't listen. When had he ever? She'd been the fool who had always looked deep to find the good in him, but maybe it was her imagination. Perhaps she'd convinced herself that there was another side to Dare to justify her being with him.

She didn't know how long they stood there, but it felt like Dare was squeezing the life out of her. Aya forced herself not to feel anything because the emotional pain was unbearable.

"Dare, I think you need to let her go." It was Foster. Apparently, he'd returned with Tori in tow.

Aya didn't want to look at either one of them. She felt so betrayed.

"No." Dare held her even tighter, causing Aya to gasp for air.

"You're hurting me," she managed to say between breaths.

"Dare, people are starting to stare," Tori spoke up.

"Fuck those people."

"Dare, you can't hold on to me forever and even if you could, it doesn't change the fact that I hate you."

The second those words left her mouth, it seemed to do the trick. Dare released her so abruptly she nearly stumbled to the floor, but Foster steadied her.

Aya didn't miss the hurt in his eyes and she almost wished she could take those words back, but she was too angry and not in the mood to be reasonable. She pulled away from Foster.

"I'm leaving." This time when she turned away, he didn't stop her.

Aya stormed out of the building uncaring about the curious onlookers who had gathered to watch their confrontation.

By the time she made it outside, however, Aya realized too late that she had no way of getting home without counting on Dare for a ride. It was too far to walk all the way to her former apartment. And even if it wasn't, it was too dangerous to be out on the streets at this time of night. It didn't matter that she knew most of her neighbors, Aya wasn't that unaware despite what Dare thought.

"Let me take you home." Foster walked into her line of vision.

She frankly didn't want to have anything to do with him at the moment either, but she had little choice. "You should have told me."

He released an exasperated sigh. "Like I said before, it wasn't my place to tell you. I know now isn't the time to bring this up, but maybe you should talk to Dare. I know he can be very intense at times, but I think his heart was in the right place. When he set this up. Maybe he didn't go about it the right way but—"

Aya shook her head not wanting to hear anymore. "You know what? If you're going to spend the ride home discussing Dare's virtues, I'm not in the mood. I don't need you to defend him."

"I understand but—"

"I said I don't want to hear it."

"Fine, but please don't be mad at Victoria. She feels absolutely horrible for keeping that information from you. She wanted to tell you. She's the reason why I pulled Dare aside in the first place, so I could make him tell you."

Aya folded her arms across her chest. "Just as you are Dare's friend, Tori is mine. One of you should have told me. It doesn't matter. But at this point, I think I can figure out another way to get home. I don't want to talk to you either."

"Then how are you going to get home?"

Before she could answer, Tori appeared. "Aya, I'm so sorry."

She couldn't even look at her friend. Aya had confided in her about the problems she'd been having with Dare and all along Tori had known this was going on. It was hard to stomach right now.

"Victoria, I told you to stay inside. It's probably best to leave Aya alone right now," Foster said gently."

Tori placed her hand on Aya's shoulder but she shrugged it off still refusing to meet the other woman's gaze.

"Look, Aya, I can have my driver come get you and take you where you want to go. Victoria and I won't be in the vehicle with you so that way you can be alone."

This offer made the most sense.

"Or I can take you home if you'd like." A familiar voice joined the conversation.

Aya turned to see Thor Reichardt. She wasn't sure if she should have been relieved or annoyed at his appearance, but at the moment she wanted to get out of there.

"Reichardt. This matter doesn't concern you." Foster glared at him.

"Relax, Graham. I saw a lady in distress and I was offering my assistance. And don't you think the decision should be up to her? What do you say Aya?"

Seeing how vehemently Foster didn't want her to go off with Thor was enough to make up Aya's mind. "Okay, Thor. Thank you for the offer. Let's go."

Thor smiled. "Right this way, I was on my way out so my car is ready." He placed his hand on the small of her back to guide her away.

Foster caught her by the arm as she started to walk away. "Aya, don't do it."

"Fuck off." She yanked her arm away and walked away with Thor.

<><><><><>

"Oh my, goodness, Dare, I saw the entire thing. I'm so sorry about that. But what did you expect from a Dreg? An eligible bachelor shouldn't have had to lower himself for the likes of her. Angelica just completed finishing school and we're having a huge to do for her. You should consider coming. She'll be so happy for your attendance."

Dare was in the same spot he'd been in since Aya had stormed out of his life. He stared at the door waiting for her to come back to tell him that she forgave him and that everything would be all right. He wanted her to wrap her arms around him and say that she loved him. Only then things would be right.

Subconsciously, Dare realized that they had drawn an audience and in the morning the gossips would be working overtime to spread the salacious tale of the prominent head of O Corp's downfall at the hands of a petite woman who had left him completely broken. None of those people, however, had had the gall to come over and talk to him. Even Foster and Tori had the good sense to give him space. But not Maxine Walters. She and her husband Geren were leeches of society. They were barely hanging on to the little bit of wealth Geren's failing company provided. They were empty people who lived for the downfall of others and took delight in being assholes. Dare saw them for the roaches they were. According to the rumors, they'd sold off their youngest daughter to maintain a lifestyle that was quickly slipping through their fingers, although they claimed she'd gone missing.

He knew they were bottom feeders with Maxine being the worst of the two, but he didn't think even Maxine would stoop so low."

He didn't answer her immediately because he was very close to committing physical harm to her and hitting a woman in a non-sexual way was a line that even he didn't want to cross. Dare mentally counted to ten to calm himself down. But when she placed her bony hand on his arm he lost it.

He gripped her by the wrist and squeezed until she gasped in obvious discomfort. "What kind of psychotic bitch are you? Do you think because you married a rich man that you're any better than Aya? She's worth more than ten of you. Everyone knows he found you in a high-end brothel and how you were there is still a mystery but you're nothing but a two credit whore. Now if you don't get out of my face, I will forget that you're a woman and do physical harm to you. And then I will crush whatever's left of Geren's pathetic little software company so you and your precious family can be where you belong, on the streets. Now leave me the fuck alone!" he roared as he released her wrist.

Maxine had gone bright red and her eyes glistened with tears. "I'm sorry. I spoke out of turn." She couldn't get away from him fast enough. The other people who had gathered scattered as well, apparently not wanting to incur his wrath.

After several agonizing moments staring at the door, waiting for Aya's return, he realized that she wasn't coming back. He figured since she had no way to get home without him than she'd have to come back. Was she foolish enough to walk back home? When that idea occurred to him, he rushed outside to see that Aya was nowhere in sight.

He pressed the side of his holowatch and the screen popped up in front of him. He pressed in a few coordinates to locate her. The tracker read that she was already a few miles away. She couldn't have gotten that far by foot. She must have gotten a ride.

Foster. If his friend had intervened then he'd let him have it. But to his surprise, Foster appeared at his side.

"She's gone, Dare."

"How, I didn't call the car? Was this your doing? You let her get away before we could work things out?"

"I offered to have my driver take her home, but she didn't take my offer either. She went off with Reichardt."

An explosion went off in his head. "What the fuck? And you fucking let her?"

"Lower your damn voice," Foster glared at him. "I couldn't stop her if I wanted to and secondly, she's an adult. She can come and go as she pleases. Maybe if you would have figured that out, you wouldn't be in this predicament."

"I was trying to protect her!"

"Please guys," Tori got in the middle of them. "Don't argue. It's not going to bring Aya back.

Dare turned his attention to her and his anger flared even hotter. "This is your fucking fault. Why couldn't you keep your damn mouth shut?"

Tori's lips quivered and her eyes glistened with the suspicious sheen of tears. But Dare was beyond caring. Aya had told him it was over and he was on a warpath.

Foster nudged Tori aside and moved in front of Dare, so close that their noses nearly touched. "I understand that you're upset, but if you ever disrespect Victoria again like that, friend or not, I will fuck you up. And the only reason why I didn't just now, is because you're clearly upset. This is your one time. If you're looking for someone to blame, how about taking a look in the mirror. If you had been honest with her in the first place, maybe this wouldn't have happened. But then again, your psychotic ass would have figured out a way to screw things up in the end anyway."

Shooting him one final narrow-eyed stare, Foster stepped away, took Tori by the hand, and went back inside.

Chapter Eight

Aya felt numb. She couldn't believe she'd finally ended things with Dare, but it needed to be done. She stared out the window, not looking at anything in particular. The stars usually fascinated her, but all she could think about was how she could have allowed herself to be with someone who clearly didn't respect her personhood. Sure, Dare said he loved her, but would someone who loved her do things behind her back or act so jealous all the time. It was obvious he had no trust in her. What annoyed her most was that he said, he'd done it for her own protection as if she hadn't been taking care of herself long before he came into the picture.

"A penny for them."

Aya was so caught up in her own problems that she'd barely registered that Thor was in the car with her. Instead of having a chauffeured vehicle, Thor drove his own compact luxury car. Aya sat beside him in the front passenger seat. "I'm sorry, what did you say?"

Thor smiled, seeming unbothered by the fact that she'd said very little since agreeing to let him give her a ride. "I said a penny for them, as in a penny for your thoughts."

"I don't know what that means. What's a penny?"

He chuckled as he casually threaded his fingers through his auburn waves. "It's an old saying meaning, I'll pay you for whatever it is you're thinking. A penny was a form of currency that became obsolete at the turn of the twenty-second century. Apparently, it's worth back then would only be a fraction of what one credit would be now, but they're very valuable for collectors now."

"You sound like you know a lot about them."

"When I take an interest in something I do my research. Anyway, it's a bit of a quirk of mine to use colloquialisms, no one uses anymore."

"Then how will people know what you're talking about?"

"I find that they're an interesting conversation starter. Speaking of which, back to my original question, what's on your mind?"

She shrugged. "Nothing I want to talk about."

"But you're here with me and not with O'Shaughnessy, so I'm assuming all isn't well between you two?"

"If it's just the same to you, I'd rather not talk about it."

"Fair enough. I'm kind of glad we ran into each other tonight."

"Oh?"

"Yes. When we were in the diner, I was out of line and I apologize for that. It was none of my business and I had no right to bring up anything regarding your relationship. I don't know the situation well enough to voice an opinion."

Aya slumped deeper into the plush seat. "It's okay. Truthfully, you were right. Dare was a little too intense for me. I was just seeing things that weren't there."

Thor thankfully didn't respond. The remainder of the ride was in silence until they neared her old district. "Umm, I really appreciate you bringing me home."

"I thought you lived in the Garden District."

"You mean with Dare? That's not my home anymore. This is."

When he pulled his vehicle in front of the bar and frowned. "It looks really dark up there. Are you going to be okay?"

"I've lived in this area most of my life. You don't have to worry about me."

"Arthur's. I've seen this place before. You live with your uncle, right?"

"Actually, he moved into one of Dare's rental buildings but the apartment is still livable. When I'm working at the bar, I take my breaks up there and have some meals. And I still have clothes here so I'll be fine."

"That's good to hear. Aya, I know we don't know each other well, but I'd like to be your friend."

She turned to eye him warily. Aya really hoped that he wasn't coming on to her so shortly after she'd broken up from a relationship with someone she still had feelings for. "Uh…"

He smiled, showing off perfect white teeth. "I'm not trying to make a move on you. I'm just offering my friendship. You look like someone who could use one. Whenever you're ready, contact me, that's if you need someone to talk to."

Maybe it was the enormity of what had happened earlier, or it could have been the compassionate sound of Thor's voice but without warning, she broke down. Her body began to shake from her sobs. It hurt so damn much. When it was over, the feelings were supposed to go too.

So wrapped up in her own emotions, she didn't fight Thor when he reached across his seat and pulled her into his arms for a hug. Under normal circumstances, Aya would have been embarrassed to cry on a virtual stranger's shoulder, but all the pent-up angst from earlier came pouring out.

Thor held her close and rocked her in his arms while stroking her back in a comforting gesture. By the time she was all cried out, Aya felt incredibly awkward. She pulled away from him abruptly. "I'm sorry. I probably messed up your suit with my snot and tears."

"It's perfectly fine. I can buy more suits. I'm just glad you were able to get that out. It's not healthy to hold in your emotions. I'm not unfamiliar with loss myself."

Aya sniff. "Loss? It's not like anyone died."

"But when you end a relationship, sometimes it feels like it. So I understand. Allow yourself to mourn so you're able to fully move on with your life. Use that grief to find purpose."

"Who did you lose?"

"My parents. They were good people and they were murdered by a really bad person."

"Oh, no. I hope your parents found justice."

A humorless smile briefly curved his lips. "Not right away they didn't, but he eventually got what was coming to him."

"Well, there's that at least. My parents died when I was younger as well. My father was killed by enforcers during a protest for fair wages and my mother, she was killed by someone who was very bad. I never found out who did it, but not long ago, my uncle told me he'd died of natural causes so I assume he was very old. I think my uncle kept the identity of my mother's killer from me because he feared I'd find him and do something to him."

"And would you have?"

"I don't know. Maybe. I guess before I met Dare, I didn't have a high opinion of any member of the Elite. No offense."

"None taken. So what was it about Dare that made you change your mind?"

Aya folded her hands in her lap and looked away from Thor's intense blue-violet gaze. "It's hard to say. I thought I saw a softer side to him. I saw a man who seemed to carry this heavy burden on his shoulders and maybe it was the fixer in me that attracted me to it. When we were together, he was attentive. He was affectionate and surprisingly had a sense of humor, but a lot of people never see it because he's so reserved." By the time she was finished speaking, she realized she was talking about a subject she really didn't want to.

There was just something about Thor that made it so easy to share her feelings, but she'd said too much. "You're pretty easy to talk to."

"So I've been told. Can I offer you some advice?"

"Ugh, depends on what advice that is."

"Just take your time to grieve. And then be happy."

His words were touching. "Thank you. That's really sweet. I should be going in. I see some guys hanging out on the other side of the street eyeing this car. You should probably get going."

"No worries. I can take care of myself. It's not like I haven't been in this area before."

"That's surprising considering most Elites wouldn't be caught dead in this area."

"I'm not like everyone else. Go ahead. I'll watch to make sure you get in safely. Do me a favor and turn on a light to signal that everything is all right."

"Okay." Impulsively, she leaned over and gave him a quick peck on the cheek. "Thanks for everything."

"I'll be seeing you."

She smiled before sliding out of the car.

Thank goodness she and Uncle Arthur had decided to leave the apartment furnished and ready for use in case either one of them suddenly needed a place to stay. Maybe in the back of her head, she always knew that things wouldn't work out with her and Dare. She even had spare clothing here. When she made it inside, she pressed the button to turn on the light so they would be seen from the outside.

It was very nice of Thor to drive her home and be a shoulder to cry on. She really hoped he wasn't looking for anything more serious than friendship and even then she needed more time before she could forge any type of relationship. It was bad enough that Dare had done what he did, but the fact that her friends knew and she didn't hurt doubly.

Aya undressed and tossed the expensive dress to the side. As she lay in her bed, she placed her hand against her heart feeling the pain from earlier creep up on her. She noticed that she was still wearing the locket that Dare had given her. With one angry tug, she yanked the chain from around her neck, breaking the clasp.

She tossed it on the floor, unable to stand the sight of it. It was something that had symbolized her love for Dare, but it was all a lie. When her head hit the pillow, Aya tried to fall asleep, but she couldn't. As she thought about Dare, her heart began to ache again. She could barely breathe. Tonight, she should have been lying in bed with Dare and held tightly in his arms. Instead, she was alone in bed. Again, the tears came and didn't stop until the wee hours of the morning.

Dare ripped the paintings off his wall and then slammed his fist into a mirror, shattering it into several pieces, all while holding onto a nearly empty bottle of absinthe. He picked up a vase that was probably priceless, but he didn't care as he violently threw it to the ground. He knocked tables over and tore through his house causing damage. For each item he damaged, he took a swig of alcohol. It didn't matter that it would take him thousands of credits to get the mansion back into a livable condition but he couldn't fight the anger raging through him. He'd begged her and had done everything short of getting on his knees. He would have if he thought that would have made a difference. He wanted to be angry at her big mouth friend for telling Aya something she had no business doing. Dare wanted to be angry with Foster for telling Tori. But he especially wanted to be mad at Aya for giving up on him so easily. But he couldn't. The only person he had to blame was himself. If he could have done things differently, he might have taken a different approach, but he felt justified in wanting to protect her.

"Mr. O'Shaughnessy. What's wrong? Is there anything I can help you with?" His estate manager appeared in the room. The man had seemed to pop up out of nowhere. His usual stoic expression seemed slightly fearful and he seemed hesitant to be in the same room with Dare.

"Go away!" Dare roared.

The older man scurried away without being told twice. He didn't know how to fix this. He was able to tell by her tracker that she'd gone back to her apartment over the bar. Without her, his house was no longer a home. It was just a cold dwelling with nothing but possessions that didn't mean a thing.

Aya was wrong about one thing, she thought he saw her as a possession, but instead he saw her as his savior. She was his heartbeat, the air that he breathed, his reason for being. Aya was his everything. She'd taught him love when he didn't think it existed. She made him believe in a happily ever after even when he knew he didn't deserve it. He didn't know how to win her back short of going to her apartment, kidnapping her and chaining her to his bed. Though that thought did cross his mind, that was the old him speaking. Because he felt so helpless, he continued to tear shit up. It was the only constructive thing he could do.

Dare punched and kicked holes in the walls, hurting himself in the process. His fists ached and his body was sore from exertion, but he kept going until he couldn't move anymore. Finally, he collapsed into a heap on top of the destruction he'd caused. His house was now like his life. In ruins.

Dare didn't know how long he was on the floor, but the next thing he realized, he was being shaken awake. He didn't realize he'd dozed off. "Get up."

Foster's voice sounded like a sonic boom, making his head throb so badly that Dare didn't want to open his eyes. "Go away," he groaned, rolling over to his side. He winced as he felt one of the broken shards of glass scattered on the floor cut into his side but he relished in the pain. The physical pain was at least a brief reprieve from the emotional hurt.

Before he knew what was happening, he was being partially lifted off the ground and dragged across the floor. He didn't have the will to fight even when he was being pulled up the stairs. Nothing really registered until he was thrown in the shower stall.

"Cold water on," Foster commanded.

The water cascaded over his head and soaked through his clothing. "What the fuck!" he screamed, getting to his feet and getting out of the shower. He turned his angry gaze on the blond now leaned against the wall with his arms crossed over his chest.

"Are you finished with the histrionics?"

"Fuck you! How the fuck did you get in here? I didn't invite you. In fact, I want you out." The more Dare yelled the more his head ached. He stormed past Foster and grabbed a towel to wipe the water out of his eyes. "Medicine table," he spoke to the automated home system. A portion of the wall opened and a drawer appeared from it with an array of medications laid out. Dare selected a pain tablet and placed it on his tongue. Once the medicine dissolved on his tongue its effects began to work. Within seconds the throbbing pain in his head was just a dull ache.

With that taken care of, he turned to Foster. "Well? Are you going to answer my question?"

Foster shrugged. "Shouldn't it be obvious? Garrison let me in. He contacted me because he was concerned for your welfare and judging from the looks of the disaster zone I walked into, I couldn't have come soon enough."

"I'm going to fire his ass. He had no business contacting you."

"You're lucky someone still gives a damn about your disgruntled ass. Give that man a raise because the amount of shit he has had to put up with dealing with you would have driven most people insane."

"Well, now that you've seen that I'm all right, you can fucking leave. I didn't ask to care, let alone come over. You just couldn't keep your mouth shut could you?"

Foster huffed, his exasperation evident. "Do you need me to apologize for something you're essentially at fault for? Fine, I'm sorry. Maybe I shouldn't have told Tori, but unlike you, I'm not going to lie to my woman if she asks me what's happening."

"I didn't lie to her. I just didn't tell her because I knew she'd make a big deal about it so I did what I thought was best."

"So you basically lied by omission. There's not much difference. Don't you think Aya has the right to know that she's being threatened?"

"If she would have known, she would have been frightened. I didn't want to worry her."

"But in this need to play the protector, you became an overbearing jerk who had a hand in driving her away. I'm not the only one who noticed Aya looking sad when the two of you were together. It wasn't this mysterious person sending you messages that he was going to take her, who did that to her. It was you!"

As much as Dare wanted to deny it, he couldn't, but Foster didn't know the entirety of the story. "There's something I need to show you. Go wait downstairs for me while I get out of these wet clothes."

Foster raised a brow but didn't argue as he left Dare alone in the bathroom.

Dare was relieved to finally be alone to clear his head. He quickly got undressed, happy to peel away the damp clothes that clung to his body like a second skin.

He released a satisfied sigh as the hot water cleansed him. Images of Aya filled his head and the ache returned. He'd never allowed himself to cry, but he felt a few tears slip from the corners of his eyes blending into the shower's spray. He touched the scar on his chest where he'd been shot. It was a souvenir from an explosive fight he'd had with Aya. From the beginning, their relationship had been rocky and most of it had been his fault.

Dare cursed the day he discovered Arthur's Place. Maybe then he wouldn't hurt so much. But then again, he wouldn't have met Aya. Despite knowing he didn't deserve her, he wasn't sure how he would be able to live without her. He couldn't actually believe she had wanted to be with him after all the bad things he'd done to her so he had made it his mission to give her anything and everything she wanted. But it turned out that Aya didn't require much. The expensive gifts didn't seem to impress her and he had no clue what to do, so he floundered a lot and took several missteps.

And then he'd see the disappointment in her eyes and he'd get scared that she wanted to leave him. It made him paranoid and jealous whenever she so much as looked at another man because, in his mind, he believed she would find something in someone else that clearly wasn't in him.

Maybe he was more like his father than he realized. Aeden O'Shaughnessy had been a hard man who didn't give a damn for anyone but himself and everything in his world had been disposable, even his wife. Dare didn't have too many memories of his mother except that she was extremely beautiful and she was very skittish. Whenever his parents were together, he noticed the fear she seemed to wear like a shroud and it wasn't hard to figure out why as Dare had personally witnessed his father choke and slap his mother for saying or doing something he felt was out of line.

And then one day his mother was gone and his father was responsible for it. Aeden had killed her and the only time Dare had brought it up, had earned him a punch in the face that had broken his nose.

Was Aya as fearful of him as his mother had been of his father? Dare shuddered at the thought.

Chapter Nine

By the time Dare made it downstairs, freshly showered and dressed there was a flurry of activity. A handful of servants were busy cleaning up the mess he made while Garrison directed the inventory of what was destroyed, more than likely for the purposes of replacing them.

"Good afternoon, Mr. O'Shaughnessy. Mr. Graham is waiting for you in the library."

Dare halted to look at the other man. "The next time you want to invite someone over on my behalf, think twice. Your job depends on it."

The older man turned red. "I apologize, sir. It won't happen again."

"See that it doesn't."

Just as Garrison had said, Foster was in the library thumbing through some of the books on the shelves. "Took you long enough," he spoke without turning around to face Dare.

Dare shrugged, not caring in the least that he'd made his friend wait. "Well, seeing as I didn't invite you over, I took my time."

Foster turned to look at him then with a half smirk curving his lips. "So, this petty passive aggressiveness is how it's going to be?"

"Maybe if you lost Tori, you'd be able to snap back from it right away, but I just lost the love of my life and the man who's supposed to be my best friend is here to gloat. So pardon the fuck out of me if my attitude isn't to your liking at the moment."

Foster clenched his fists at his side and blew out his deep breath. "You're right. I'd probably act like a huge jackass if Tori and I were to break up. It really doesn't matter who's at fault when the result is the same, so I'm sorry if you think I'm not being supportive. If I didn't give a shit about you, I wouldn't even be here. But I'm not going to coddle you and I'm certainly not going to pretend that this couldn't have been avoided.

"Fine, I get it. I was wrong. And I lost Aya because of it. Anything else you want to get on my case about?"

"I'm not going to argue with you, Dare. What was it you wanted to show me?"

Dare felt like being recalcitrant and telling Foster to fuck off, but he needed to shut the other man up to show that he hadn't been too hasty in hiring protection for Aya. Dare realized that he was more than a little possessive where Aya was concerned and he'd really tried to work on it. But then the messages started coming around the time that her friend Macy had been kidnapped.

Someone had hacked into his cyber network and every time he'd open one of his holo devices he'd see them. He'd never forget that first message.

I'm going to take your most prized possession.

At first, he didn't think too much about it because there were always cyber terrorists who made it their mission to try to take down members of the Elite for some social justice cause. He'd asked his cyber security team to take care of it so that it wouldn't happen again, but they were unable to trace where it had originated from.

And then came the second message.

She's going to be mine.

And without a doubt, he knew whoever was sending these messages was talking about Aya. He panicked. Dare had to know about all of her comings and goings out of fear that she would be snatched. It wasn't until one night Aya had stayed out late when his fear had escalated to the point where he would do anything and everything to ensure he didn't have to go through that again. Although it had turned out that she'd just stayed late at the bar, he still couldn't stave off the fear that something was going to happen to her.

He'd show up at the bar unannounced and even though he could see there were times when Aya was annoyed with him for brooding around her place of business he couldn't stop himself. But with his a very large corporation to run, it wasn't feasible for him to constantly show up, so Dare got the idea to get her bodyguards. He'd even brought the idea up to Aya which didn't go over well because she believed that he was only doing it so that he could keep track of her and make sure no one else was hitting on her.

While he did want to keep track of her, it wasn't for the reason she was thinking so he let her go along with the idea because he didn't want her to be concerned. Because Aya had been so upset about the bodyguard idea, he'd backed off, hoping that the messages were just some random troublemaker who wanted to needle him.

And then the pictures came. There were images of Aya's coming and goings that could have only been taken if someone was actually following her. But those weren't the scariest ones. It was enough for Dare to make the unilateral decision of having her protected no matter the price he had to pay to do it.

He'd hired an expert to hack into Aya's VC to track her every move. Dare's person was also able to connect her to a monitored system where he could pull it up on any of his holo devices at will. There were also guards who were connected to this system to keep an eye out on her. These were people Aya wouldn't notice and would blend in where she went, like a patron at her bar or someone sitting in the salon she frequented, Aya was completely unaware and things seemed to be working out. But then he'd mentioned what he'd done to Foster. That apparently was a mistake.

He pressed a button on the side of the wall and a huge holographic screen appeared in the center of the room. "Pull up the hack folder and open images," he ordered.

The screen shuffled producing a holographic image of the folder before opening up. A splash of photos spread across the room."

"What the fuck is this, Dare?" Foster demanded.

"This is the reason I've been on high alert. I didn't take these. Whoever is stalking Aya did."

As Foster took in each image, his mouth fell open. "Fuck. Why didn't you tell me?"

"So you could tell me that I was being paranoid or that Aya had the right to know? How do you think she would feel knowing that some sick fuck has pictures of her like this? It's apparent someone was able to use some kind of mobile camera to get these."

"But the ones inside the house....fuck!" Foster shouted angrily raking his fingers through his hair.

A chill ran down Dare's spine as he stared at images of Aya at the bar, and out with Tori at a restaurant. There were even pictures of Aya inside of one Tori's shelters. Most of them were of her alone. But the scariest ones were of Aya sleeping. There were even a few of her in the shower. In his shower and one at her apartment. There was even one of them making love. He was aware that there were micro drones that the government owned to spy on people. He even had a company that invested in them, but they were typically used by government officials to spy on their enemies. These tiny cameras could follow people unawares and it appeared that whoever was controlling this had their sights set on Aya.

Dare had had an entire team to do a test on every square inch of his house to make sure none of those drones were lurking in his home. They'd found three. It was why he'd had an electromagnetic field set around his house so one of those little things could no longer get past his property line. He, however, couldn't do anything about the bar without Aya's knowledge so he'd placed the pressure on her to move in with him. He wanted her with him anyway, but in his mind, this justified him putting on the pressure.

"Close folder," Dare commanded when he was certain Foster had seen all of the images.

"I didn't know."

"You knew about the messages."

"I just thought it was one of those typical hacker assholes. I've gotten similar messages before."

"But not about someone you love, have you? You were too busy on your pedestal of self-righteousness that you didn't stop to think that maybe I had my reasons. Yes, I have a history of doing things that only suit my best interests, but you're supposed to be *my* friend and have my back." Dare patted his chest to emphasize his words as the anger resurfaced. "When I saw how judgmental you were about me having Aya watched, I kept the rest to myself. So tell me, do you still think I should have told Aya and have her looking over her shoulder every minute? Like I said before, I didn't want her to be afraid."

Foster remained silent seeming to take in everything Dare was telling him.

"And now that she's back in her old apartment, there's no telling what that person is doing. They could be watching her now for all we know and there's not a damn thing I can do about it short of going over there and dragging her back here where I know I can keep her safe. Hell, I might as well. She already fucking hates me thanks to your big mouth, right?"

"Dare..."

"You don't know everything Foster, so don't pretend like you do because if you were in the same predicament I was in you'd probably do the exact same thing."

Foster collapsed into the nearest chair. "Maybe you're right. I didn't try looking through things from your perspective. My only excuse is that Victoria was worried about her and I found myself opening up about what I knew. I swore her to secrecy, but sometimes things slip. It wasn't done maliciously. And if it's any consolation, Victoria, feels awful."

Dare shrugged. "Join the club. Now that that's out of the way, you can leave now."

"Please Dare, don't be like this. I fucked up okay. I should have tried to understand. Maybe if I talked to Aya—"

Dare shot Foster a narrow-eyed stare. "Don't you think you've done enough?"

"No. I haven't, at least not to make it right that is. Maybe if Aya knew—"

"No! I don't want her to find out about this. I'll figure out who's behind these threats and then I'm going to work like hell to win her back."

Foster stood up. "You know what? I get it. You're upset with me right now and I'll allow it. You deserve to be angry for a little while, but it doesn't change the fact that we're friends. When you need me, I'll do whatever I can to help. We've been friends for too long and been there for each other for too long for us to stop speaking. I'll be in touch."

Foster walked out of the room, leaving Dare in the same spot, fists clenched at his side. He would probably hold on to his anger for a bit longer, but Dare already knew he'd eventually forgive Foster. Like the blond had pointed out, they had been through a lot together, had their share of arguments and even fist fights but whatever conflict they had was always squashed. They'd even taken down The Auction together. Though he had a considerable amount of resources at his disposal, Foster had his own sources as well, some of them underground. He would probably need them. But for now, he'd mourn for a day or maybe two. But then he'd set forth on his mission of keeping Aya safe and finally winning her back.

"I know you probably don't want to talk about it, but I can't help notice that your eyes are red and you look like you've been crying," Mac pointed out as they were closing the bar down for the night. There were only a few stragglers left and Aya didn't anticipate many more people coming in at this time of night. Uncle Arthur had volunteered to close, but now that Aya had moved back into the apartment, she sent him home since she was so close by. Besides, she wanted to keep busy to stop herself from thinking about Dare. Every time she was idle, the image of him holding her and begging her to stay with him tore at her heart. It almost made her want to contact him, but she had to remain strong.

If he didn't respect their relationship enough to not have her stalked then she was better off by herself. She was almost certain he could still track her through her VC and she would have to go to the registry center to get her chip fixed. But for now, she simply didn't have the will to do anything other than work and go to sleep. Even sleep was a luxury she couldn't quite afford because she dreamed of Dare.

She'd already had this conversation with her uncle earlier and didn't particularly feel like having it again with Mac, but she could see the genuine concern in his eyes. "Dare and I are no longer together."

He raised his brows in his obvious surprise. "Whoa! When did that happen?"

"Last night."

"Damn, take a day off and all the drama happens."

"Gee, thanks, Mac. I'm glad you've found amusement in my life."

"I didn't mean it like that, little bit. I'm just shocked. I imagine that you were the one to break up with him."

"Why do you think that?"

"Because that man was absolutely obsessed with you. I could feel the temperature drop several degrees whenever he walked into the bar and he'd sneer at anyone who so much as looked at you."

"Obsessed seems like such a strong word, don't you think?" Aya hated that even when she wanted nothing else to do with Dare, she was defending him.

"Okay, maybe that wasn't the right word, but it's pretty clear the guy was smitten with you. He looks at you like I look at food."

Aya giggled a little at Mac's silly attempt at a joke. It was the first time she'd smiled since yesterday. "Thanks for that, but I honestly don't want to talk about it since it's so fresh."

"I understand. I felt like crap when Macy and I broke up, but I guess romance isn't in the cards for me."

"Don't say that. Just because it didn't work out with her doesn't mean that there won't be someone else."

"Well, it's not like there's an overabundance of women in this neighborhood and most of them are attached. Maybe when I save up enough credits I can move to another region where the ratio between men and women aren't nearly as unbalanced. I here there are pockets in the world where the gender ratio is almost equal."

"Well, I hope you don't plan on leaving anytime soon because I'd certainly miss you."

"I still have a significant amount to save let alone to afford a passport. The government practically wants a body part to get one of those so maybe when I'm old and gray I can see some of the world. It helps that I'm able to work here full time. Maybe you should consider letting me take on more responsibility around here. After all, you do so much already and I've been doing stuff at this place for years."

"If that's what you want, you can close up some nights. I'll talk to Uncle Arthur about changing your pay rate to reflect the extra duties."

"Thank you, Aya. I could really use the extra credits."

Aya frowned. She knew that Mac didn't have a lot of money like most of the people who lived in this area, but he'd never brought up needing credits for as long as she knew him. "Are you trying to save up so you can be able to move?"

"Yes."

He said that a little too quickly for her liking, but it wasn't that big a deal. What he did with his credits was none of her business. "Could you do me a favor and take care of that inventory in the back. I'll handle the rest of these customers so we can close up shop.

"Aya?"

"Yes?"

"Uh, never mind, I completely lost my train of thought."

"Oh, that happens to me sometimes."

"I'm going to the back now."

"Okay." Aya had the sudden feeling that Mac was hiding something from her and she couldn't figure out what but it didn't matter right now. She had way too much on her mind like trying to figure out how to get over Dare.

She would have to find a way or else she would drive herself crazy.

Chapter Ten

Aya walked aimlessly down the sidewalk of the shopping district looking at items, but nothing really caught her attention. She should have been at the bar, but her Uncle Arthur had put his foot down and told her in no uncertain terms that she had to take a few days off. Staying holed up in her apartment only lasted a day because she was bored out of her mind, and while she had all that time alone, her thoughts were centered on Dare.

But coming to the shopping district wasn't exactly a good idea either because everywhere she looked she saw places that she and Dare used to frequent together. Her eyes began to tear up a little as she caught sight of the antique shop across the street. That was where Dare had purchased the gold locket for her.

She absently touched the spot where her locket would usually be hanging and found nothing but skin. Then she remembered that she'd ripped it off in a pique of rage. It was probably still on the floor where she'd discarded it. Aya remembered how happy she'd been that day.

Dare had been working so hard lately that she barely saw him except late nights. A couple nights this week, she was asleep by the time he made it home so today she had planned to surprise him with a lunch that was packed by his staff. When she made it to her building, the receptionist alerted Ronald

Briggs, Dare's executive assistant of her presence. Ronald had come down and had personally escorted her to Dare's office. He pressed the intercom. "Mr. O'Shaughnessy. There's someone here to see you."

"I told you no interruptions. Send them away."

"I think you'd like to see this person."

There was a pause on the other side of the door before it slid open. As Aya stepped into Dare's spacious office with a lunchbox in hand Dare's stern expression had turned to one of surprise and then of delight. An actual smile split his handsome face.

"Will you be needing me for anything else, sir?" Ronald asked with more than a hint of smugness in his voice.

Dare waved him off as he stood up. "Aya, what are you doing here?"

"I've barely seen you this past week. I know you're working on a very important deal, but I thought you needed a break."

"While this is quite unexpected this is a very welcome surprise. You look beautiful today."

She was just wearing a pair of jeans and a plain white top. She still dressed casually since she was with Dare, but the items she chose were more form fitting. "Thank you. I brought some lunch."

He licked his lips. "Oh, yeah? Looks like you brought my favorite."

Aya raised a brow. "Unless you have x-ray vision or someone tipped you off that I was coming and therefore you know what I have packed for you, then how do you know?"

Dare stalked toward her with purposeful strides. "I wasn't talking about what was in the box baby. You know my favorite thing to eat is your pussy, so I suggest you hop that cute little ass up on my desk and spread those legs." He wrapped his arms around her and give her a long deep kiss.

She melted against him, pressing her tongue forward to meet his. He tasted of rich hot java, mint and a flavor that was uniquely him. Finally, she pulled away from him, panting. "Dare, you have a one-track mind. How about we eat first and then we'll have dessert." She wiggled her brows suggestively.

"Not interested in food. Want pussy now." Dare didn't seem to be in the mood to take no for an answer. He grasped Aya by the waist, lifted her off her feet and carried her the short length to his desk. Dare placed her on the edge in a sitting position and went to work unbuckling her pants. Aya barely had a chance to protest, not that she wanted to, before she was completely naked from the waist down.

Dare pushed her legs apart and knelt in front of her. "I've been thinking about this all day," he groaned, running a finger along her already damp slit."

"Mmm," Aya moaned. "Looked to me like you were pretty focused on your work when I stepped into the office.

"Multitasking," he murmured before replacing his finger with his tongue. He pressed a deep kiss against her pussy and then sucked the plump lips in his mouth.

Aya gripped his shoulders as heat spread throughout her entire body. Her pussy ached with need and only Dare could provide the cure. He took his time licking and sucking on her sensitive flesh. He slid two digits into her wet channel, easing them in and out as he slurped greedily at her cunt. Aya gripped his shoulders and grinded her pelvis against his face. "Dare, this feels so good, but I need your cock."

He played with her pussy for several more moments before pulling away with obvious reluctance. Pulling her off his desk, he turned her around until her back was flush with his chest. "Bend over, doll, because I'm going to give it to you, just like you like it."

Without hesitation, Aya placed her hands on the desk and poked her ass out to give him the access he required. After undoing his pants, he guided his cock against her entrance.

"Now. I need it, now, Dare," she moaned.

"As you wish." He slammed into her with one powerful thrust.

Aya gripped the edge of the desk to hold herself steady. As Dare began to move in and out of her, he wrapped one hand around her throat, applying just the slightest bit of pressure. Somehow, when he did this, it made the high of their lovemaking even more intense. She threw her hips back, meeting him thrust for thrust.

"That's it, just like that," she moaned so close to her climax as he found her g-spot.

"You're so damn tight. Trying to hold on," he moaned.

"Don't hold back," she cried. "I want you to cum with me."

As she felt him spill his seed deep inside her channel, it triggered her own orgasm. "Dare! Yes! Yes! Yes!" She collapsed over the desk and he bent to rest his upper body against her. They lay like this for several breathless moments. Dare was the first to move. He headed to a room at the side of his office, which she assumed was his private bathing area. Dare returned with a damp sponge and proceeded to gently clean her between her legs. He was so tender and careful as if he was handling the most delicate of possessions.

She practically purred in satisfaction by the time he was finished. Aya turned his head to meet his lips in a hungry kiss.

"Mmm, if you keep that up, we'll have round two before either one of us has the chance to properly recover. I'm glad you came by today?"

"Oh? Because I gave you some pussy?" she teased him.

He grinned. "Well, there's always that. But no, it's because I'm always happy to see you. And plus, I have a surprise of my own for you. I was going to wait to give it to you tonight, but now that you're here I don't see any point in waiting until then. Why don't you get dressed and I'll go wash up real quick?"

"Should I set up the food?"

"Sure."

Aya dressed and pulled out the box of foodstuff that she'd had prepared. There were all of Dare's favorites. She carefully laid everything out on his desk. By the time she was finished setting everything up, Dare had returned.

"This all looks good. You didn't have to do all this, doll."

"I wanted to."

"Sometimes, I ask myself what I did to deserve you because I really don't think I do. But a word of warning, now that I do, I'm not letting you go."

"I don't want you to. So what was it that you said you had for me?"

Dare opened a drawer in his desk and pulled out a small rectangular box that looked to be made of crystal before handing I to her.

"What is it?"

"Open it and find out."

And she did just that. A gasp escaped her lips when the contents of the box was revealed. "It's…it's beautiful. I saw this before…how? How did you know?" It was an antique, solid gold locket on a chain of like metal that looked like it had been designed in a past century. She'd seen it when she, Tori and Macy had gone shopping. Tori had wanted to look in the antique store. Aya was fascinated by all the old jewelry which was a lot less ostentatious than the stuff that Elites usually sported in this era. What had really caught her eye was this locket. She'd even pointed it out to Tori.

"I asked your friend what gift she thought you might like and she suggested this. If you open the locket up, you'll see that I've had it engraved."

Inside was a message that simply read: To Aya with love always, Dare.

"I love it, so much." It was one of the best presents he'd ever given her because it was something from the heart.

"May I?"

She nodded, handing him the necklace.

Dare moved behind her and fastened it around her neck.

Aya touched the locket resting against the center of her chest. "I'll never take it off."

She wiped away an angry tear.

"Do you need this?" Someone handed her a handkerchief.

Aya looked over to see Thor. Up until a couple of months ago, she'd never seen him, but now he was everywhere. "Where did you come from?"

"I was actually coming out of a restaurant with my companion here and I saw. You looked rather upset so I thought I'd come over to see if you were all right."

For the first time, Aya noticed a tall redhead resting her hand possessively on his arm. She took the offered handkerchief and dabbed at her face before handing it back to him. "Thank you, Thor. I'm so embarrassed that every time we see each other it isn't the best of situations."

"These things happen." He looked to the redhead. "Freya, would you please excuse us for a moment please."

She smiled and kissed him on the cheek. "Sure." Without acknowledging Aya, she walked a few feet away.

"You didn't have to send her away. I don't want to interrupt your date."

"Freya doesn't mind. She understands that I saw a friend in distress and wanted to see if she was okay. Are you?"

"You caught me at a bad moment. I'd usually be at the bar, but my uncle forced me to take these past few days off and I'm actually kind of bored. There's only so much holovision I can watch and reading is almost impossible because I can't really concentrate on the words with so much on my mind. I'm not a huge shopper, even though I do like window shopping and walking through this district to people watch."

"Ah, so you're a people watcher too. Do you by any chance sit back and make up stories in your mind about complete strangers?"

Aya found herself smiling despite her melancholy. "Actually, I do, how did you know?"

He smiled. "Because I like doing the exact same thing. Take that couple for instance," Thor pointed to a couple across the street. They were clearly Elite but the man was much older than the woman he was with, and the intimate way he had his hand on her rear made it quite obvious those two weren't related by blood. "When I see them, I'm guessing he's a lonely old man who recently lost his wife. He didn't love his wife, he was just with her because it was expected of him. But now that she's gone, he can finally declare his love for the mistress he's been seeing for the past few years. A mistress he probably met in one of the brothels. She, on the other hand, plans on getting him to sign over a significant amount of his credits and then kill him. She'll make it look like an accident because he's so old there will be little to no investigation."

Aya raised her brow at the detail in the scenario. "Wow, you're good. I don't think I've ever come up with a scenario that elaborate."

"I've been called a thinking man. I meant to be in touch with you, but I figured you needed your space."

"And the fact that I never gave you my coordinates."

He chuckled softly. "No you didn't, but since I took you home, I do know where you work. I could have easily stopped by."

"But you didn't and that's fine. You're not responsible for me. I have to be honest with you, Thor. I'm not sure why you're even interested in me."

"Maybe because I sense a kindred spirit. And maybe I think you deserve to smile."

She raised a brow. "And you think you could be the man to do it?"

"Possibly."

"And yet you have your friend standing over there." Aya looked at the redhead and frowned. Freya, she believed he'd called her, was standing in the exact same spot Aya had seen her in only a few minutes ago. Her head was bowed and she looked stiff.

"Is your friend all right?"

Thor gave a quick glance in his friend's direction. "Oh, she's fine. Her mind wanders quite a bit. She'll snap out of it soon enough."

Aya shrugged. "Well, I guess you know best. Look, I appreciate your kindness, but as I've stated before, I just got out of a long-term relationship and I'm not looking to jump back into one. It may take me a while to get over Dare. And even when I am over him, I'm just not sure if I'm cut out for romantic love. It's so messy and complicated."

"You're very young to be so jaded. It's unfortunate to hear you talk like that, but I'm not asking you to run away and elope with me. I'd like to take you to dinner and talk, as friends. As I said when we first met, I've been out of the country for a long time and now that I'm back, I don't have that many friends and I could use one. Besides, you seem to have an interest in history. I have an extensive collection of turn of the century artifacts at one of my residences. I'm having a little get-together tonight, nothing formal, but I'd like it if you could come. And before you say no, there will be other people there."

"I don't know..." It would probably be another sleepless night and if she did eventually doze off her dreams would be filled with Dare. But then again, she hated Elite parties and even though Thor seemed nice enough, she didn't know him well enough to put up with a bunch of insufferable snobs. "I don't think that would be a good idea. I don't mean to come off as rude, but I'm not really into those types of parties."

He raised a questioning brow. "What kind of parties are you referring to?"

"Look, you seem very nice. In fact, you've been very sweet to me, but I don't feel like being around a bunch of people who stand around bragging about how much money they have and the latest gadget they purchased. And then the self-congratulatory air in the room. It's a little overbearing."

"I can assure you that I will have none of those types of people at my party. Believe it or not, I haven't always been what most people consider an Elite."

She gave him the once-over, taking in his very expensive suit. And even though his auburn locks fell in careless waves, Aya was certain it had been expertly styled. "You could have fooled me."

"It's true."

"But you said you grew up with Dare."

"I said I've known him for a long time. I never said in what capacity. At this point, you're looking for excuses. Do you want to stay home tonight and mope or do you want to come out for a few hours to take your mind off things?"

When put like that she didn't feel like being alone tonight and she didn't really have anyone to talk to. She could stay with her uncle and Mera for a few nights because they had a spare bedroom at their place, but she didn't want to intrude on the two lovebirds.

What did she have to lose? "Okay. Why not? I'll stop by for a few hours."

"Do you have a vehicle?"

"No. But I'll contact a car service, it's how I've been getting around."

"Don't worry about that and save your credits. I'll have a driver come pick you up around eight?"

"That should be fine. I guess I'll see you tonight. Thanks for the invitation."

"Trust me, it's my pleasure."

Aya jerked her thumb toward his friend who was still in the same spot. "Think you better go check on her."

"Yes, I'll do that. See you tonight."

She wasn't one hundred percent sold on the idea of going to a party, but at least she'd have a few hours reprieved from crying.

When she made it back to her apartment, she was surprised to find that she had a visitor standing outside her door.

"Dare!"

Chapter Eleven

Dare knew he was taking a big risk coming here, but he had to see Aya and convince her to come away with him. He didn't think she was safe all by herself in this apartment when someone was probably watching them at this very moment. Maybe if he explained to her the danger she was in without giving too much away, he could at least get her to move to another location even if it wasn't with him.

He had tirelessly been working with a cyber team trying to figure out where those messages were coming from and all they had come up with were dead ends. One thing in particular that kept coming on was some code, 110503. He didn't know what that meant, but he had his crew on it. Until they could crack this code there wasn't much he could do. When he'd walked into the bar, he was surprised to see that Aya wasn't working that day. That kid Mac who also worked there had said she'd taken the last few days off.

So, he'd waited. In the meantime, he'd discreetly placed a disk that generated the same electromagnetic pulses that he'd had placed at his house. At least that way he would disable any micro drones that were lurking around the building. It sickened him to think some creep was spying on Aya. He'd received more pictures of her. None as intimate as the ones from before, but it was at least enough to let him know that her stalker was still out there.

Seeing Aya again after nearly a week of not being able to hold her in his arms was like a man who'd been underwater for a very long time getting his first breath of fresh air. He couldn't stop staring at her. Judging from the bags under her eyes, she'd gotten as much sleep as he had, which wasn't much.

"I had to see you."

She rolled her eyes. "Of course. You just had to come despite me telling you I wanted nothing further to do with you."

"Can we please talk? I know I screwed up, but there was a reason I did what I did."

She shook her head. "There's nothing you can tell me right now that could possibly explain what you did. So I don't want to hear whatever story you have brewing. I don't want to hear about your fucked up past as the reason either because you have officially tapped out all of my sympathy."

Dare flinched at the harshness of her words. It wasn't like his sweet Aya to be so callous, but he'd done that to her. For as long as he lived, he'd never forget the pain he'd seen in her beautiful brown eyes when she'd learned what he'd done. But it was no more than he deserved. "Okay. You have the right to be angry, but you have to listen to me."

She shook her head. "Do you hear yourself? I don't have to do anything and that includes listening to you. Now if you would leave, I'd really appreciate it."

Aya made her way to her apartment door, but he grabbed her by the wrist. "Wait. Aya, I think you're in danger." There. It was out. If telling her the truth was the only way she'd listen to him then so be it.

She glared at him. "Really? From you, I suppose? What are you going to do to me this time? Make sure the bar closes again? Make it impossible for me to find work somewhere else?"

"You think that little of me?"

"Have you given me any reason not to?"

Dare knew he deserved some of the criticism, but she was very close to crossing the line. "I think I have. Can you tell me that all the time we were together that you didn't enjoy any of it?"

She hesitated for a moment and for a nanosecond he thought she would waver, but instead, she raised that stubborn little chin of hers in defiance. "I don't have time for this. I have things to do."

"Someone is stalking you," he blurted out.

"I know. You're the stalker and I want you to leave me alone."

Dare shook his head vehemently. "No, that's not what I meant. Someone has been monitoring you. They've been sending me threatening messages telling me that they're going to take you away from me. I have proof, I can show you."

The incredulous look she shot his way spoke volumes. "I don't believe you."

"I wouldn't make something like this up. You're not safe here. Someone could be watching you right now. Look, you don't have to move in with me right now, but I have other properties you can stay at where you'll be safe. You could live in one of the units in the building your uncle resides in. Please, you have to believe me." Dare gripped her arms, pleading with her in earnest.

For a moment, Aya appeared as if she might relent, but instead, she pulled herself out of his hold. "No! I can't keep doing this with you. Please leave."

"Aya—"

"Leave!"

Dare realized then that no matter what he said, Aya wasn't going to listen, so he had to resort to other tactics. "Well, if you won't listen to me, then I'll just keep coming back until you hear me out."

"Don't bother."

Winning Aya back was going to be difficult enough as it was but if he just tossed her over his shoulder and took her with him against her will, then he'd be damning himself forever but at this point, he had no option.

"You know what? Fuck it." He grabbed her arm and propelled Aya against his body, catching her by surprise. Dare then lifted her and tossed her over his shoulder.

"Let me go!" she screamed as she rained blows on his back with her small fists. For such a petite woman, she packed a punch, but Dare refused to be deterred as she screamed and wiggled as he carried her downstairs.

By the time he made it outside, Aya was cursing his name. "Put me down, you bastard! Why can't you take no for an answer? It's over between us!"

Her words were like the proverbial dagger to the heart, but Dare ignored them. If keeping her safe meant that she would hate him, then so be it. He carried her out to the waiting vehicle, opened the door and tossed her inside. He immediately slid in next to Aya to prevent her from getting out.

"And this is exactly why we aren't together. You just do whatever the hell you want. I'm never going to be through with you am I?" She slumped in her seat as if finally realizing that it was futile to fight him.

"Aya, this isn't how I wanted things to be."

She shrugged. "I don't care. Did you come over because you could no longer track me? I went to the registry earlier today to get my VC reset and updated so that it's hacker proof."

Dare didn't point out that nothing was exactly hacker proof. And with his cyber team, he could figure out a way to get into it again, but he wouldn't need to if he knew she was in the area. This bit of information he decided to keep to himself. There was no point in further agitating her.

"I don't want to go back to your place."

"Fine, I'll take you to the building your uncle is in. There are furnished units ready for use."

"How convenient. I'm sure there are hidden cameras all around to monitor me. Thanks, but no thanks. Dare….whatever it is you think you feel, it's not love."

Dare had allowed Aya a lot of latitude considering the situation, but he refused to let her disparage the love he felt for her. "You can say whatever you want about me, but you don't get to tell me how I feel."

"What else am I supposed to think? I'm just an obsession to you. If you had it your way, I'd be sitting at your feet all day or chained to your side."

He gripped her chin between his thumb and forefinger, forcing her to meet his gaze. "Aya, I may be new to this emotion, but I know what love is. It keeps me up at night and makes me think of you when I wake in the morning. These last several days without you have been torture. I miss your smile, I miss the way you kiss me, and the way you'd wrap your arms around me and make me feel like no matter what was going on in my life, everything would be okay. If it were possible to give you the sun and the moon, I'd figure out a way to make it happen. I'd die for you Aya. There isn't a thing I wouldn't do for you. If that isn't love, then you tell me what it is.

"If you love me, then you'll let me go."

"Aya, maybe you're fighting so hard because you still love me too." It hadn't been his intention to beg for her to come back to him, that was something he'd planned on for later, but being this close to her, he couldn't help himself.

She twisted her head away, breaking his grip. "It doesn't matter. Just let me go, so I can get over you." Tears slid down her cheeks and the sight of her crying broke his heart all over again. He'd done that to her.

Dare could take the anger and even the hate Aya threw his way. But he couldn't take that broken expression. His Aya was a fighter and it was one of the things he loved about her. Foster had been right. He should have told her the truth from the beginning because now they were in a situation he wasn't sure he could fix. Sure, he could have her locked up somewhere to ensure her safety, but at what cost?

The thing that had spurred him to visit her tonight in the first place was because the person he'd hired to discretely watch the building had abruptly quit causing Dare to panic. Although Dare would have grasped at any excuse to see Aya again. He supposed he could hire at least three people to take watch tonight until he figured something out.

"Okay."

She scooted away from him. "Okay, what?"

"Go back inside. But please be careful, Aya. I wasn't making it up that someone is watching you."

She rolled her eyes. "Don't start that again. We both know you're the only one who would go to such lengths to have me under your thumb." Aya opened her door and slid out of the car without giving Dare a chance to respond.

He balled his fists in his lap to stop himself from dragging her back to him. There had to be a way to make her believe him. Her very life might depend on it.

Dare watched from the window to make sure she made it back inside safely.

He then dialed in Ronald's coordinates on his holowatch.

Ronald's holographic image popped up. "Good evening, Mr. O'Shaughnessy. What can I help you with?"

"I need you to contact the security firm and have three guards come to the Red District. I need a twenty-four-hour patrol of a certain building."

"Same as last time?"

"Yes. And emphasize to them that they need to be discreet. I want them down here within the hour."

"Of course. I'm on it."

"Okay."

"I'll make sure they're in position by 7:30."

"That will be all for the night. Thank you."

His efficient assistant nodded in acknowledgment before signing off.

Thank you was always a hard word for him to use. He had been taught after all that paying someone was a sufficient enough thank you. But Aya had taught him compassion. She made him a better person. He didn't know what he'd do if he couldn't win her back. But at least in the meantime, he would do his best to keep her safe which is what he fully intended.

And that required waiting in his car in front of her building until he was certain the guards were posted.

Chapter Twelve

Aya was so shaken from Dare's visit that the second she went inside her apartment she collapsed on her couch and closed her eyes, fighting so many old memories. She couldn't believe he'd just shown up at her door as if it was no big deal. It reminded her that she needed to get the codes changed since he'd been able to walk up to her door.

When he'd told her that someone was stalking her, he'd sounded like he actually believed it, but then she remembered all that he'd put her through. If she was truly in some type of danger, he should have told her long before tonight. And to make matters worse, he'd actually tried to kidnap her. As much as she still cared about him, it was time to face the facts; Dare was not a stable man and she'd made the right decision to end things with him. She couldn't spend the rest of her life tiptoeing around him because she was too scared to do the wrong thing. Though he'd never physically hurt her, there was no telling what would happen one day. He could snap.

Aya wished she wasn't burdened by the memories when things were actually good between them. There were moments when they weren't having sex and he'd just hold her and they'd talk about everything and nothing at all.

Aya's eyes felt like they would cross from reading for so long. She couldn't remember the last time she'd had so much leisure time, but the bar was closed for renovations for the grand reopening so it had freed up her day. Dare had several meetings that day, but Aya had decided she wanted to hang out at his house to take advantage of his extensive library. It was definitely more convenient than going to town and to look through hundreds of thousands of digital titles. Besides, Dare had paper books. She loved the weight of them in her hand and turning pages.

She found one book that had caught her interest which happened to be a part of a series. She was on the third book by the time she realized it was getting dark.

"Garrison said you'd be in here." Dare stepped into the library with a slight smile on his face. He walked over to the lounge chair she'd curled herself in and sat next to her. He leaned forward offering his lips, which she eagerly accepted.

"Mmm." Her heart skipped a beat as she stared at this beautiful man. It was so hard to believe he was hers and she was his. "How long have you been home?"

"I just arrived, and when I found out you were here, I needed to see you. Had I known you would be here, I would have come home sooner."

Aya kissed the corner of his mouth. "Well, you're here now."

"What have you been up to all day? Don't tell me you've been sitting here reading?"

She gave him a sheepish grin. "You caught me. I'd only intended to read for a couple hours and then run a couple errands for Uncle Arthur, but I guess I've been here all day."

He eyed the book. "What are you reading that has you so engrossed?"

She showed him the book cover. "Have you read this one before?"

"I haven't, but it's my understanding that it was quite popular in its time. I believe there were movies based on these books, but I'm not certain. What's it about?"

"It's about a boy who finds out that he's a wizard and ends up going to a special school. And something tragic happened to him when he was a baby. It really has a lot going on but I can't put these books down. I think I'm starting to get a headache from reading so long."

"Well, how about you put the book down for tonight. It will still be here tomorrow. And in the meantime, let me make that headache better." He stood up, pulling her with him before sitting back down with her on his lap

Dare then proceeded to give her the most fantastic scalp massage. "How does that feel?"

"Wonderful," she sighed, feeling the tension ease away. "Did anyone ever tell you that you have magic hands?"

"Yes."

Aya felt a little twinge of jealousy. She knew that Dare had an almost insatiable sex drive and he'd probably had several lovers before she'd come into his life, but the thought of him putting his hands on another woman annoyed him. "A former, girlfriend?" she asked with more snark in her voice that she intended.

Dare chuckled. "Do I detect a hint of jealousy in your voice?"

She snorted. "No."

"Of course not, doll." It was clear from his laughter that he didn't believe her. Dare kissed the side of her neck. "If you'll remember, you're the one who told me that I had magic hands last night.

"Oh." Aya's face flamed with embarrassment.

He continued to massage her scalp. "It's okay, love. It's nice to know you care."

"Of course I do. You're mine."

"Always," he replied.

Why did she have to be bombarded with those moments now when the pain was still so raw?

She was brought out of her thoughts when she heard the intercom to her apartment buzz. She jumped to her feet and raced to the door wondering who it could be at this time of night. She never got visitors after dark. She pressed the button by the door and saw a man in a black suit standing outside.

Aya frowned at the stranger. "May I help you?"

"I'm here to pick you up to see Mr. Reichardt."

Aya smacked herself on the forehead. Dare's visit had totally discombobulated her. She'd forgotten that she'd agreed to go to Thor's get-together tonight. She pressed the side of her holowatch and saw that it was eight o'clock sharp. She hadn't showered or dressed and she was certain her hair was a mess.

"Oh, no. I'm so sorry. I completely forgot about the get-together. I'm not ready."

"Take as long as you need Miss. I'll be waiting outside in my car."

"Um, are you sure you're going to be all right waiting out there?"

"The vehicle has a security system that discourages theft if that's what you mean?" the driver responded.

"Oh, okay. Are you sure you'll be fine waiting for me? I need at least a half hour."

"I'll be fine, ma'am."

"Okay. I'll be down shortly."

Maybe tonight wouldn't be such a bad thing. At least she'd have a temporary distraction from her problems.

Aya took a quick shower and found the most acceptable outfit in her closet. She'd left all her fancy gowns at Dare's house. Thor had said the party was casual but what was casual to an Elite and someone like her was night and day. She found a green silk blouse that fell off her shoulder and a pair of form-fitting black slacks. She used a handful of hair cream to refresh her curls and put on just a little gloss and eyeshadow. She didn't look as glamorous as she did when she stepped out with Dare but Aya was pleased with her appearance.

By the time she was finished, she had a few minutes to spare. Just as he said he'd be, the driver was waiting outside for her. Once he opened the back passenger door for her, she slid into the car which was surprisingly a lot like the ones Dare's fleet of drivers used.

She gasped in surprise when she saw she wasn't alone. "Thor. What are you doing here? I didn't know you would personally be escorting me."

Thor's smile was damn near perfect. He by far was one of the most attractive men she'd ever laid eyes on. Even though she was still in love with Dare, if circumstances were different, she could see herself being very attracted to him. "I wanted to be a good host."

"But sending a driver was enough. You didn't have to come out here."

"I wanted to. Can I offer you a drink?" He pressed a button and a panel in the roof opened and a mini bar was lowered.

"No thank you."

"That's right, you told me you're not much of a drinker. But I thought you might want a taste of honeysuckle wine."

"Honeysuckle? I'm not sure if I've ever heard of that."

"It's a tiny flower that produces this really sweet nectar. Since they're so small, it literally takes several thousand to make one bottle."

"That sounds really expensive." Most flowers were genetically engineered because of environmental issues created by the Deregulation Act.

"It is, but I find that cost is inconsequential for the best." He took one of the glasses and poured a small amount of the wine inside before offering it to her.

Not wanting to be rude she accepted the glass and took a small sip. Surprisingly, it was one of the best things she'd ever tasted. It was as smooth going down as it was from the moment it hit her palette. "It's very good." She drank the glass's remaining contents.

Thor poured a more generous amount for her this time.

"You didn't have to."

"I don't mind. I wouldn't be a good host if I didn't. Besides, I see that you enjoyed it. Don't worry, Aya, I have plenty more where that comes from. I have a wine cellar filled with wines and spirits, some as old as the sixteenth century."

"I'm impressed. Sounds like you're a bit of a collector."

"You could say that. I love collecting things. I'd love to show you my museum of items if you're interested."

"As long as you don't have a collection of weapons, I'll take you up on that."

Thor raised a brow, but Aya didn't bother to elaborate. She wasn't even sure why she'd brought that up in the first place, referring the huge collection of weapons Dare used the collect. It seemed like no matter how she tried not to think about him, Dare managed to come up in the conversation.

"Weapons really aren't my thing, but hopefully I have some items that you'd be interested in."

"So what kind of party is this?"

"Just a few friends of mine. We'll have a little dinner and sit around and talk and there will be entertainment of course. I have some live musicians."

"Sounds like a pretty relaxing evening."

"I'm not a huge fan of large get-togethers. I only show up for business reasons."

"Kind of like Dare. He hated those things too, but he said it was a necessary evil." She groaned the minute the words were out of her mouth. She'd done it again. "Sorry. I didn't mean to bring him up." Aya downed her wine hoping it would steady her nerves.

"It's okay. You were with him for what? Almost a year? And you obviously had deep feelings for him. Those kinds of emotions don't go away so easily, but I'm positive you'll eventually be able to move on."

"You sound so sure."

"Sometimes you need to speak things into existence for them to happen."

"You're very wise. I don't know what it is about you Thor, but it just seems like you've led an interesting life beyond what your trappings are."

"Maybe I'll tell you about them some day. But in the meantime, we're here."

Thor's house was just on the outskirts of the Garden District a few miles away from any other houses. His property was surrounded by a thick forest that looked as if it had been man-made. The actual house, however, was just as grand as any of the other houses belonging to a member of the Elite, but it looked as if it had been hidden away from the rest of the world.

"I can tell you're surprised by where I live. I'm a man who values my privacy."

"That's not very surprising. Like I mentioned before, you're not like the other Elites. It's a very nice house."

"You know what I like about you, Aya?"

"What?"

"I like that you're not as impressed with all this as most people are. That's refreshing."

"They're just things, Thor."

"That there are."

When the car pulled to a stop, instead of the driver getting out of the car, Thor got out without waiting for the door to be opened for him, and then he helped her out. She didn't realize he was still holding on to her hand by the time they made inside the opulent mansion and when she did, Aya snatched her hand away in embarrassment. "Sorry," she mumbled.

"There's no need to apologize. Come on, let me show you around."

Soft music played throughout the house from the sound system. "Classical music?" Aya inquired, cocking her head to the side, the dulcet tones filled her ears.

"I find it very calming."

Aya frowned looking around. "I don't mind a tour, but what about your other guests," she asked noticing there wasn't anyone else around.

"They're all amusing themselves downstairs in the party den. Trust me, they're being well entertained. Let me show you around."

Out of nowhere, a woman in a short black dress appeared with a bottle of wine and two glasses. "Welcome home sir."

Thor gave the woman a slight nod. Aya assumed she was a maid.

"Here you go, Miss. This is from one of the finest champagnes from Ma-Mr. Reichardt's collection. It's said to have been a favorite of kings."

To be polite Aya allowed the maid to fill her glass. For just a brief second, she thought she'd seen Thor narrow his gaze, but she must have imagined it because just as quickly his expression was neutral again.

When they were alone again, Aya turned to Thor with a raised brow. "If I didn't know any better, I would think you're trying to get me drunk."

"No, just relax you for when you meet the other party goers. I know these gatherings aren't your thing, but I think you'll fit in nicely. "

"We'll see." Aya took a sip of her champagne. She was no alcohol expert, but it tasted even better than the stuff that was served at the Sapphire Ball and everything there was top shelf. "Mmm. I'm not much of a drinker, but if all alcohol tasted like this, I'd understand why people became alcoholics."

"But you work in a bar."

"True. But most of the stuff we serve is so watered down you'd have to consume a lot of our stuff to get properly drunk, at least that's what I've been told. But it's mainly the hardcore drunks who have said that."

"I imagine they've built a tolerance to it. Let me take you to the first room."

Aya followed behind him taking small sips of her champagne. Thor guided her to a room that was covered in framed disks at least that's what it looked like.

"What is this?"

"Remember when I mentioned the penny to you?"

"Yes. Is this what this room is? Old currency?"

"You're a quick one." He pointed to the closest set. "This one right here are coins that were once used as US currency."

"It seems a little cumbersome to carry those around. What was the value of them?"

"If we put it in today's terms a penny would be worth one percent of one credit. The coin next to it is a nickel, which would be five percent and dime, ten and a quarter, twenty-five. And in the next frame is the paper money which came in increments of one, two, five, ten, twenty, fifty, one hundred and a thousand. A three-dollar bill was introduced just before this type of currency was phased out altogether, but from my understanding, it didn't take off. There it is right there."

Aya was fascinated by so much history in one room. "What are the rest of the coins?"

"Those are monies from other countries, so they no longer exist which makes them even more valuable. Shall we visit the next room?"

She nodded.

The next stop they made was to a room full of framed postage stamps. Thor took his time answering her questions and explaining what each one was worth. Aya was so engrossed that she barely noticed when the maid had entered the room to refill her now empty glass.

Thor then proceeded to guide her to more rooms. It was like a walk through a museum. He had rooms of priceless jewelry, old toys in pristine condition, posters and more things that Aya had never heard of.

By the time he was finished taking her around his home, Aya felt a little dizzy and frowned at her glass. She didn't realize she'd had so much champagne. It was so good, she didn't realize it would have such an effect on her. She swayed on her feet a little.

Thor must have taken note because he was immediately at her side, concerned etched on his face. "Aya. What's the matter?"

"I think I may have had more champagne than I realized. Maybe I should sit down somewhere."

"There are plenty of seats downstairs with the rest of the partiers. Besides, that's also where my most valuable collection is."

"I'm not sure if I'm up to seeing it. I feel..." she clutched her head. "Weird."

"You'll be fine. Here, take my arm."

Aya clung to him so that she wouldn't fall over. She tried to keep up with his long strides, but her short legs failed her and she found herself being dragged along.

"We're almost there," he said in a calm voice. It should have comforted her, but there was something about the way he said it that gave her pause.

"Nooo," she slurred, not having the strength to pull away. By now she was almost certain that it wasn't just alcohol she'd drank. "Thor, something...something was wro-wrong with...champagne."

"Oh, it did what it was supposed to."

The nonchalance of Thor's words put her on alert. "There was no party."

"Of course there is. You're the guest of honor."

Aya's legs were too weak to carry her and she collapsed on the stairs. Thor lifted her in his arms. "Lemme...go."

"So soon? You just arrived."

There were, in fact, people downstairs but they were all women, dressed in the same black uniform. Aya wasn't sure, because of the fog that had fallen over her brain, but she was almost certain she'd seen the same redhead Thor was with before. All the women were lined in front of what looked like glass prisons.

"Welcome home, Master," one of the women stepped forward and bowed her head.

"Help," Aya tried to scream, but it came out as a whisper.

Her last coherent thought as everything went black was that Dare had been telling the truth.

Chapter Thirteen

Dare couldn't shake the feeling that something wasn't right. Last night he'd sat in his car until he was notified that the guards were in place so he couldn't understand this feeling of unease. He'd even checked the tracker on his holo-system to see if it could connect to Aya's VC and just as she'd stated, he could no longer access it.

He should have stayed behind and waited until morning if he had to but seeing that look in her eyes had been more than he could bear. Instead of going straight home after leaving the Red District, he'd headed to his office in the business sector. He couldn't stay in his house without her there. Every room in that house reminded him of Aya from the library where she liked to spend her spare time reading to the living room area where they'd made love on the floor in front of the electronic fireplace. He could picture her sitting across from him at the dining room table.

Being in the bedroom was the hardest. He missed holding her in his arms and inhaling her sweet scent. There was a point in time shortly after he'd realized that he loved her that he let her go because he thought he'd try to do the right thing. It had been excruciating to live apart from her, but they hadn't been in an official relationship and Dare didn't know how good things could be for them then. But having had Aya's love and it being taken away from him was ten times worse.

Every day he woke up with an ache in his chest. He literally felt like he would die. Even though it was probably psychosomatic, the bullet scar on his chest ached. Dare doubted he could go months without her

At his office, he'd thrown himself into his work until he found himself falling asleep at his desk. When he was tired, he showered and slept on his couch and in the morning, he changed into one of his spare suits. But ever since he woke up that morning he was on high alert and he was almost certain it was because something was the matter with Aya.

He noted the time on his holowatch. It was still early, most of his workers were just starting to come in. Dare was certain that Ronald would be in by now so he contacted him.

"Yes Mr. O'Shaughnessy?" asked Ronald's holographic image.

"Could you do me a favor and contact the security agency to check on the guards you sent last night. I need a report right away."

"Certainly. I'll be in touch within the next ten minutes."

Dare paced around his office waiting for his assistant to call back, all while several different scenarios raced through his head. At the very least Ronald would report back to him and assure him that everything was okay and he was just being paranoid.

When ten minutes came and went, Dare grew impatient and contacted Ronald again.

"My apologies Mr. O'Shaughnessy, but there seems to be a problem with the guards. The security company is having problems locating them. They're going to track them through their VCs. I'm just waiting to hear back from them."

Dare's heart felt like it would pound out of his chest as his anxiety rose. This couldn't be happening. Why were these guards not responding? One guard suddenly quitting with no explanation was one thing but three missing guards from the same company was alarming.

"Keep me on the line, we can conference call this."

"Okay. I hear them coming in now. Let me add them."

Another holographic image popped up and a tall, thin man in a black suit with a silver eye patch appeared. "Mr. Briggs, I'm not sure how to break this to you but... according to the vitals on their VC, the three guards are deceased. We're sending a group to the area to find them."

Without waiting to hear more, Dare ended the call and raced out of the office. He had to get to the bar before it was too late. But as he raced through the building, a chilling thought entered his head.

What if it already was?

Aya felt groggy as she came to. Her muscles burned and her throat was raw. Her eyelids were so heavy that it was hard for her to open them. The bed she lay on wasn't as soft as the one in Dare's house or as firm as the one in her apartment and then she remembered.

The memory of last night gave her the strength to sit up. Aya looked at her surroundings. Everything was so bright in this little room which only had enough space for a bed, a small desk with a chair behind it and a chest of some sort. There was a large glass wall that kept her imprisoned. It reminded her of the jail she'd spent a night in when she'd had a run-in with an enforcer, but this was much nicer and cleaner.

A chill made her body shake and she noticed for the first time that the only thing she was wearing was a plain bra and panty set, neither item of which she recognized which meant someone had completely undressed her and put this on her. She wanted to be sick. There was no telling what had happened to her when she was passed out. Now she understood why Thor had kept her champagne glass full. She wouldn't have been surprised that there was also something in the wine that he'd given her in his car. She didn't recall him actually taking a sip from his goblet but then again, her memory was a bit fuzzy.

How could she have been so wrong about a person? Aya believed herself to be a good judge of character. Working in a bar where sometimes she ran into sketchy characters she had to be on alert. But somehow Thor had managed to bypass her creep radar. She wondered if her alarms would have gone off if she wasn't having problems with Dare. Had he noticed and slipped in? She should have questioned how he'd kept appearing wherever she was as if he knew where she'd be. Aya had been so wrapped up in her own problems that what he knew about her were things she was almost certain she hadn't shared.

A previous conversation came to mind when she mentioned that she worked for her uncle. She'd never told him about Uncle Arthur so how he knew about him could only be explained if he'd learned this information before ever meeting her. And in order for that to be possible, he would have to have dug up information on her and had her followed.

Dare had tried to warn her, but she'd refused to listen. She felt like a fool and now she was a prisoner of a madman and she had no clue what he wanted from her. She wasn't even sure why he'd even picked her. They'd never met until that party. It simply didn't make sense.

Aya felt a jolt of pain shoot through her arm and she hissed. When she looked at the source, she gasped in agony. There were stitches on her arm where a long scar was. She gently touched the spot and winced in pain. The area almost looked as if it had been operated on and it occurred to her this would be the spot where her VC was located. Had he removed it? It only made sense that he did and that would make it impossible for anyone to track her. How would she be found and would anyone look for her? She was certain Uncle Arthur would, but what about Dare. She'd said some hurtful things to him and the thought made her want to cry.

She'd completely shut out Foster and Tori because she'd been so angry. She still believed they were wrong to keep something like the fact that she was being stalked away from her, but it didn't matter right now. She was in a predicament she wasn't sure she was able to get out of.

Aya forced herself to get off the bed and walk to the glass wall. She gasped when she saw what was outside of it. There were other glass prisons each one containing a different woman. She could only see so far from where her own cell was located but she counted at least five other cells. There were probably more outside her line of vision. Directly in front of her was the redhead from last night and it suddenly dawned on her where Aya had seen her before. She had been the same woman Thor had been with on the street.

Aya had thought it odd that the other woman had stood in the same spot looking at the curb for such a long time but now it sort of made sense. Thor had obviously had some kind of control over these women and this is where he kept them.

"Hello?" The sound came out as more of a croak than an actual coherent word so she tried again. "Hello?" she yelled.

The redhead looked at her with a startled expression on her face. Aya remembered the woman's name being, Freya. "Freya?"

"Shh, Master is watching. It's quiet time."

Aya licked her lips that felt parched. "What are you talking about? Who is Master?"

"Be quiet before you get us all punished," someone said in a hushed whisper. She wasn't sure which one of the other women had spoken, but they all seemed pretty frightened of some perceived consequence. Even if it was all in their heads, she didn't want to get them in trouble if there was an actual punishment. There was no telling what Thor had in store for them.

Suddenly, a loud siren went off. Aya saw Freya and the other women in her line of vision drop to their knees and place their foreheads and palms to the floor. Aya watched in confusion, but then she understood as Thor appeared. He barely spared the other women a glance before stopping directly in front of her cell.

"Good morning, my beautiful pet. I'm glad to see you're awake. I trust you had a decent night's rest."

Aya glared at him. If there wasn't glass separating them, she would spit in his face. "Let me go you sick fuck!"

She thought she heard one of the women gasp, but she was beyond caring. She'd faced bullies in her lifetime. It was one thing when she believed that he was going to kill her. She wasn't afraid of death, but if he planned on keeping her she wasn't going to put up with this bullshit without a fight."

A smile curved his lips. "Are you thirsty, Aya?" he asked as if she hadn't spoken.

"What's the matter with you?" she demanded. "You can't just kidnap people for your own sick enjoyment." She'd heard about Elites who had their own harems, but most of the women in them were there voluntarily. She certainly never imagined she'd be a part of one.

Thor's expression remained neutral as if her words didn't bother him in the least. "As you've already seen, I like to collect things and this collection is by far my favorite. You see, you probably think I'm just aimlessly taking women for my own sexual gratification. Well, there is that," he paused to chuckle, "but it's so much more than that."

Aya faked a yawn. "I'm sure in your psychosis, you think so, but you're nothing but some weirdo who takes women against their will."

"You think these women are here against their will. He pressed a button on the side of his watch and a holoscreen popped up, he hit several keys and all the glass cell doors opened except for hers."

"Ladies, you may stand."

Each one of them stood up and seemed to wait for his next command.

"Freya. Come." He snapped his finger.

The redhead scurried to his side like a well-trained puppy. "Yes, Master." She bowed her head.

"Aya is your new sister. Greet her properly."

Freya looked in Aya's direction with an eerie smile on her face. "Welcome, Aya. So glad that you can join us."

It was so creepy how monotone the other woman's voice was, as if she was reading from a script.

"Freya, Aya seems to think you're here against your will. Are you?"

She shook her head. "Oh no. It's my pleasure to serve you, Master." Freya turned her watery blue gaze in Aya's direction. "You will love it here, Aya."

Aya was disgusted. It was clear something wasn't right with this scenario. She seemed way too robotic, almost as if she'd been brainwashed.

"And how did you come to be here?" Aya demanded.

Freya furrowed her brows, seeming confused by the question. She looked to him for guidance and he simply nodded. "Master found me and rescued me. He is my savior and I'm happy to be here."

"But you're a prisoner!" Aya screamed in frustration.

"The only prisons that exist are the ones in our minds." All while Freya spoke, she wore that steady smile. That line was clearly something that was rehearsed.

"He must have done something to you," Aya insisted.

Freya's smiled. "Of course he has. He's made me see that my life was nothing before him and you will soon learn that lesson too."

"You must seriously be fucked in the head if you believe I'm ever going to think such a thing.

Thor let out an exaggerated sigh. "That language is very unbecoming for one of my ladies. You're going to have to watch that mouth."

Aya glared at him and slammed her palm against the glass keeping her locked up. "Fuck you. There is absolutely nothing you can do for me except let me go."

His eyes narrowed slightly before the artificial smile returned to his face. "Freya you may return to your quarters. Athena come."

Thor was a tall man, but then again, everyone was tall to Aya who barely made it to five feet but Athena had him by a couple inches.

"Yes, Master." She bowed her head in reverence.

Aya wanted to vomit at the adoration she heard in the other woman's voice.

"Athena, are you here against your will?"

"Of course not, Master. I'm here by your great benevolence."

"Greet your new sister, Aya."

The same scary smile that Freya had worn was tenfold on Athena's face. "Welcome Aya, you're going to love it here. The Master is so generous and kind."

"I think the fuck not." Aya crossed her arms across her chest.

Thor nodded to Athena. "You may return."

Athena gave him a little bow before going back to her spot.

"Shiva, come," he ordered. A brunette appeared this time.

Aya shook her head. "Look, I get it. You have all these women brainwashed and they're all going to say the same thing. But if you think I'm going to become one of your mindless slaves you can forget it, you psychopath."

"It appears you're not in the mood to listen so I'll return when you're more amiable. In the meantime, it's time for your first instruction."

"Instruction? What are you talking about?"

Without replying, he tapped a button on his watch and the screen reappeared. He pressed a button and before she could realize what was happening, she felt the most intense pain she'd ever experienced in her life. She clutched her head to stop the throbbing, but it didn't help.

Dropping to her knees, she cried out unable to bear the ache. "Stop!" she yelled, but that only made her head ache worse. It actually felt as if someone was driving a sharp tool through her skull. But it was a vicious cycle, the louder she screamed the more it hurt and the more it hurt the louder she screamed.

And just as suddenly as it had begun, it stopped. Aya trembled over feeling the residual ache in her brain. Tears burned her eyes, but she refused to let them fall. She refused to let that bastard have that victory over her.

Thor stepped closer to her cell and this time his face had contorted into a sneer, revealing his true self. "Let this be a lesson to you. You don't run shit around her. I do because I'm your Master."

Chapter Fourteen

The second he stepped inside Arthur's Place, Dare knew something was wrong. There were customers, but the mood seemed off. And what was worse, there was no sign of Aya who was usually either walking around the restaurant section seeing to the customers or manning the bar. He saw a woman behind the bar he recognized as the caregiver who he'd once hired for Aya's uncle. They had since become intimate partners. Mera Grise was what he believed her name was. She seemed distracted as he approached.

"Mera."

The older woman looked up at him and gasped. "Mr. O'Shaughnessy! I'm so glad to see you. We can't find Aya."

His heart dropped to hear his worst fears being confirmed. "Do you know how long she's been missing?"

She shook her head. "All we know is that when Arthur and I showed up this morning, the bar wasn't open. There were people standing outside waiting to get in. Aya said she'd open today because she'd taken a few days off and wanted to do it, so Arthur and I didn't come until about an hour or so ago. This isn't like her. Arthur went to her apartment to check on her, but she wasn't there."

"Where is he now?"

"He's upstairs in Aya's apartment looking for clues to where she might be. We thought she might be with you."

"No, she isn't. I'll go upstairs to talk to Arthur."

He saw no point in telling the woman what he knew because she seemed upset enough as it was. Dare took the side door that led to the steps going to Aya's apartment. The door was open so he walked inside. Arthur was there, frantically pacing back and forth when he spotted Dare.

Unlike Mera, Arthur was definitely not happy to see him. Dare understood the older man's animosity toward him, he did, after all, try to ruin Arthur simply because he couldn't get his way. Dare had done all that he could to make it right, but Arthur had never completely warmed to him. But the two men had called somewhat of a truce for Aya's sake. Now that his niece was gone, it appeared that all bets were off for Arthur.

"What the hell are you doing here? I bet you had something to do with this. Where's my niece?" Arthur demanded with his fists balled at his sides. He looked as though he would charge at any second.

The last thing Dare wanted was to fight with Arthur, especially when finding Aya was the top priority. "I don't know where she is." He couldn't bring himself to say this wasn't his fault because it was. If someone didn't have a vendetta against him, Aya would be safe. But it was hard to tell who had taken her because he'd made so many enemies over the years there was no telling who was behind this. As he remembered the threats he shuddered to think what was happening to her. Or if she was even still alive.

No. He refused to believe that Aya was dead. He'd feel it.

"You had something to do with this. I tried to respect Aya's wishes and put aside my differences with you and I did for a while. And as long as she was happy I was willing to do that. But she wasn't happy and you were the cause. Every time I tried to bring it up, it would upset her so I kept quiet. But I'm done biting my tongue. Ever since you came into our lives, you've been nothing but trouble. Just because you threw a lot of money at us to make our situation better doesn't negate what you did. Nothing made me happier when she told me she was done with your ass, but I guess it was too late for her regardless. You introduced my niece into a world of depravity and who knows what else and now she's gone, probably taken to one of those sick auctions, her friend had been a part of."

Dare didn't think there was anything Arthur could say to him that would make him feel worse, but he was wrong. He felt like a huge asshole. The overwhelming shame kept him from refuting the words that Arthur had shouted at him. He hung his head, disappointed in himself.

"Well, boy? Don't you have something to say?"

"What do you want me to say? You're right. Aya is missing because of me. And you're also right that I haven't made her happy in a while. It's why she broke up with me. I've done so much wrong in my life that...I never thought someone like me deserved someone like Aya, so I held on to her as tightly as I could, not realizing I was suffocating her. And then the threats came and I grew even more paranoid of losing her."

Arthur scrunched his forehead. "Threats. What are you talking about O'Shaughnessy?"

"Someone hacked into my system and started sending messages that threatened to take away my most precious possession. And while I have amassed several valuable items over the years, nothing means as much to me as Aya does and the thought of something happening to her was unacceptable to me. So I kept her close and she didn't understand why and I didn't tell her because I didn't want to worry her. I even suggested getting bodyguards for her, but Aya thought I was just trying to run her life, which I wasn't. I backed away, but then the pictures came. The same someone who'd hacked me sent images of her, pictures that could only be taken from micro drones. They were in my house, in her apartment and wherever she went. So I hired a group of stealth guards to keep an eye out for her. Foster wanted me to tell her, but I'd stubbornly believed it was best that she didn't know so she wouldn't live in constant fear. But she found out anyway when she heard me and Foster arguing over it. That's when she broke up with me. But just because she's broken up with me didn't mean that person or people weren't still out there. I saw her last night and told her. She didn't believe me, so I had more guards posted. Whoever it is behind Aya's disappearance must have found out because the guards are now dead and Aya is missing and like you said, it's all my fault. If I didn't fall in love with Aya and selfishly hold on to her, she'd still be here. Look, I know you hate me and deservedly so, but we have to do all we can to find her."

Arthur squinted at him and flared his nostrils. His shoulders were square as if he was ready to swing at any second. Dare braced himself for the hit because it was no more than he deserved, but the punch never came.

Dare wasn't sure what else he could say, but he figured no matter what he did, it wouldn't make things right.

"You know what? I actually believe you."

"I have my faults, but I wouldn't lie to you about something like this."

Arthur's shoulder's slumped and his visible hostility seemed to ease away. "Regardless of how I feel about you, had I known that someone was after Aya, I might have kept it to myself as well because my niece is so headstrong. She'd try to find out who this person was and run right smack into the middle of the danger. Aya has a big heart and is willing to stand up for people who can't stand up for themselves. She's always been a champion of the little dog and she never backed down from a fight. This would have been no different. She'd try to investigate and possibly make things worse. The girl doesn't have a healthy enough sense of fear and that can be dangerous at times."

"That's possible, but maybe I should have told her and she would have at least agreed to come with me last night."

"Well, tell me what else you know. You said something about micro drones? I've heard of drones before, but not the other thing."

"They're microscopic cameras that can be used to spy on people without them being aware, unless there's some kind of security system in place to detect and disable them. When I arrived last night, I placed a small device on the wall of the building that would deactivate any that are in this building. I'll need to have a team sent to sweep through the building to find them. It occurred to me on my way over here that if we can find the drones, we can trace them back to the original user."

Arthur scratched his head. "Why haven't I noticed these things? Wouldn't someone have seen them?"

"No, because they're the size of the tip of your finger and they have the ability to camouflage themselves to fit into their surroundings so it would be hard to detect from the naked eye."

"Even still, maybe we should do a quick sweep of the apartment, just in case. I'll take the front, you check the back rooms."

Dare looked through the bathroom and then came to a small room that made his heart ache. This was Aya's bedroom. He'd been in it before when they were still together. Her scent still clung to the walls. Everywhere he looked he saw bits and pieces of Aya. The outfit she'd worn the last time he'd seen her which was a pair of jeans and a white top with a heart on it was still on her bed which told him that she must have changed before she disappeared. He took a seat on her bed and looked at the glass frame that lay on its side as if it had been knocked over. He pressed the on button and holo images appeared, a lot of the pictures were of people who frequented the bar. Some were of her uncle. There were a few of Macy and then finally there were a lot of her. Aya's picture frame told the story of the people in her life she cared about and seeing that she'd collected so many pictures of him, some he wasn't aware she'd taken made it obvious that she'd cared a great deal about him. Some of the pictures had captions on them.

One of the final images that rotated on the frame was one of him where he was sitting in the bar, looking at his holowatch. He was probably waiting for the bar to close so he could have Aya all to himself. The caption read: *He doesn't know how much I love him.* Seeing that made him realize what a huge fool he'd been. If, no when, he found her, he'd do whatever it took to win her back.

As he stood up, something on the floor caught his eyes. He bent down to see a gold chain peeking out from under the chair. He picked it up and saw that it was the locket he'd given her. Aya had made no secret of the fact that this was one of the favorite things he'd gifted her and since he had, Dare had never seen her without it. The fact that she'd thrown it on the ground, with a broken clasp suggested that whether he found her or not, it might be too late for him.

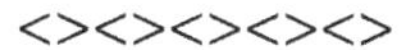

The darkness and the lack of sound was beginning to drive Aya crazy. After leaving her writhing on the floor in agony, a metal shield-like door came down in front of the glass one and the lights were cut off. Then suddenly everything went quiet. Behind the glass wall, she'd been able to hear everything, but now there was absolutely nothing. She couldn't even hear the other women shuffling around. As the time stretched, Aya realized that Thor had turned her cell into a sensory deprivation cell. It was so dark, she had to feel her way around the room to get back to her bed. She pulled her knees against her chest and waited. And waited. Nothing happened.

Time continued to stretch until she began to hum to herself just to hear another sound. She wasn't sure what was worse, that pain in her head she'd felt earlier or this. Aya felt like banging her head against the wall as she cursed herself for being such an idiot where Thor was concerned. Now that she knew he was the one behind the messages that Dare received she tried to think of his motive. Aya knew she wasn't a bad looking woman, but she also understood that people were drawn to her because there weren't many women who looked like her. Her mother had beautiful golden brown skin, but she'd inherited her father's darker skin. She couldn't keep track of the number of people who pointed out how rare and unique she was or how many times she'd been propositioned because of it. Somehow Thor didn't seem to strike her as the type to be caught up in something as trivial. Most of the women she'd seen in Thor's containment cell had pale skin. There were a couple of ethnic looking girls, but she couldn't make out an exact pattern.

There was something that Freya has said about him rescuing her that made Aya think there was way more to Thor's method of crazy than just him collecting women. And then the names of the women. Just as she'd recognized that Thor's name was tied to mythology so was Freya's and Athena's. She wasn't sure about Shiva, but it wouldn't have surprised her if that also didn't belong to an ancient goddess. She wondered if Thor was even his real name. Now that she thought about it, he'd said that he'd known Dare for a long time. But the time she was talking to him at the party and Dare was being his normal overbearing self, the look in Dare's eyes hadn't been one of recognition.

Did he take her as some personal vendetta against Dare? And if that were the case, how did that explain the other women, and what had he done to them to make them think he was some kind of savior.

Unable to take any more of the darkness, she swung her legs off the bed and felt her way to the glass wall. "Let me out!" she screamed and banged on the barrier if for nothing else than to break the deafening silence. "I don't want to be here! Thor, let me out."

Aya screamed until her throat went raw and hit the glass until her fists were sore. Finally, exhausted, she slipped to the floor.

"Please," she croaked out even though she knew no one could hear. "Let me out."

Chapter Fifteen

Aya wasn't sure if she'd fallen asleep or not because the darkness had stretched until she was certain she was hearing voices. She was cold, hungry, her throat was sore and she'd emptied her bladder when it became too excruciating to hold. The scent was starting to get to her and she had to talk to herself so that she wouldn't go crazy.

"You're going to make it through this, Aya. You're a survivor. You've been through so much worse. You're not going to let this psycho break you down."

She thought of Dare, but immediately pushed thoughts of him from her mind. She wasn't sure how to feel about him right now. On the one hand, had he been honest with her about why he'd been having her watched things wouldn't have turned out this way, but then again, in his own overbearing way he was just trying to protect her. His heart had been in the right place, but his execution of it left a lot to be desired. At the end of the day, it all boiled down to trust.

But as hard as she tried to stop thinking about him, the memories began to assail her. The good ones were the ones she held dear to her heart.

One of the advantages of living with Dare at his huge estate was the gorgeous landscape. There was so much grass and manicured vegetation, unlike the Red District where the roads were barely paved and the dirt stretched for as long as the eye could see. There were tufts of grass here and there, but nothing like this, which is probably why this area that the Elite occupied was called the Garden District. Aya liked to go out in the back of the garden at night and sit on one of the stone benches where she could get a clear look at the stars unlike in her home area where the smog obscured them.

Dare had hosted a few business associates that night and Aya had played hostess. It wasn't as bad as usual since the group wasn't as large, but by the time the dinner was over she wanted to get outside for some fresh air. She'd dragged Dare out to look at the stars with her from her favorite stone bench in his garden.

"I'm not sure what it is about looking at the sky that fascinates you so much," Dare said once they'd taken a seat.

Aya raised her hand to emphasize the majesty above them. "Don't you see the beauty? There are millions of stars out and on a night like this they seem so close, but so far away. Look at how they twinkle." She stared at the celestial majesty as she spoke.

"I do see beauty and it's quite breathtaking," he'd said softly.

Aya tore her gaze away from the stars and realized that Dare wasn't looking at the sky at all, but instead, his steady gaze was trained on her. Goosebumps raced up her spine and her heart fluttered. There was so much love in his eyes when she looked at him. Dare had a reputation for being a hard and sometimes cold man. But there was nothing cold about him now.

Aya couldn't keep the smile off her face. "I'm not talking about me."

"But I was."

"Be serious," she gently prodded, taking his hand and scooting closer to him. Dare placed his arm around her shoulder and she rested her head against his chest. "Look up. Do you see it now? How wondrous it is. Just think, the sun is a star. So can you imagine all the inhabitants of other planets

in the universe looking at the sky and seeing our sun as just another star? It kind of makes you think of how insignificant we all are in the grand scheme of things."

Dare didn't answer right away, but when he did, he dropped a kiss on top of her head before replying. "Honestly, I never thought of it that way. To me, it wasn't that profound, but thank you."

"For what?"

"For helping me to see the world through your eyes. You make me glad to be alive." He held her tight as they stared at the stars and talked until close to dawn.

But there were no stars now to light her way and the longer she sat in the dark the more listless she became. Suddenly the lights flashed on. Aya cringed at the brightness. The metal wall rose and standing on the other side of the glass was Thor holding a plate of food. Aya eyed it hungrily wanting to claw her way through to get to it. Her stomach growled in response.

"Well, Aya, I hope you enjoyed your reflection and meditation time."

Aya licked her parched lips, not taking her eyes off the plate in his hands. "Ho-how long were the lights out?"

"Oh, I felt you needed some time to calm down. Not long. Just forty-eight hours."

He made it sound like sitting in the dark with no sound or any sensory stimulation wasn't its own form of torture. If he let her out she vowed to herself that she would scratch his eyes out. Uncle Arthur was probably sick with worry if she had been gone for two full days. There was no telling what Dare's reaction would be.

It was clear Thor saw himself as some type of savior so maybe she could appeal to that side of him. "Thor, you said—"

"You will address me as Master."

The irony wasn't lost on her that she'd accused Dare of trying to control her life, but Thor was the one who had the one control issues. She refused to call him by anything other than his name. "You said, that all the other women were here of their own free will. But I'm not. I don't want to be here. Please, if you actually care about my feelings, you'd let me go."

"You just don't know what you want and apparently right now you don't want to eat. I gave you an instruction. I am the Master and you will obey."

Before she had a chance to respond the metal wall went down again and the room went dark again. "Nooooooo!"

Dare had never felt so helpless in his life. Aya had been missing for three days and no one seemed to know where she'd gone. It was as if she had disappeared without a trace. He'd exhausted every avenue he could think of. Arthur had asked people who usually hung around the bar if they'd seen anything. No one seemed to know.

Not being able to concentrate on anything work related, Dare had postponed all of his business meetings until further notice and left everything in the hands of Ronald while he was on his hiatus. Until Aya was found, he didn't intend to do anything else other than look for her.

The signal on his holowatch dinged to alert him of an incoming call. Pressing the side button, he answered to see the image of Travis Dawson, the head of his cyber security team. "We've been trying to trace the micro drones that were found at Miss Smith's residence and they were all untraceable. But, we have been able to narrow down who in this area would have access to purchase this many and the company who produced them. We're working on that list right now and we should be able to have a list compiled shortly."

"Have it done before sundown."

"We're on it."

Dare clicked off without waiting for a response. He then tapped in Foster's coordinates. Foster popped up.

"I'm just pulling up to your place now. We'll be there in a couple minutes."

Dare was thankful to have Foster on his side. Even though the two of them had had their share of differences through the years, when either one of them was going through a crisis, they could count on each other. And thus far Foster hadn't let him down. When he'd found out about Aya's disappearance, Foster immediately reached out to his underworld and black market contacts to see if there were any new groups or prostitution rings that women were being kidnapped for.

Dare paced the room impatiently waiting for his friend to come inside. To his surprise Foster wasn't alone. Tori was with him and she looked as if she'd been crying. "I'd planned on calling before I came over, but I figured since you were expecting to hear from me anyway I thought I'd drop by. How are you holding up?"

"How do you think? The longer Aya is out there, the less likely it is that we'll find her." Dare felt like punching the wall and destroying shit, but the last time he'd done that, the staff had worked overtime to replace everything. It wouldn't have been fair to them and plus it was counterproductive. Destroying things wouldn't bring Aya back. He wondered where she was, and how she was holding up. Was she scared? Was whoever had her hurting her? The thought that she was being harmed infuriated him. He shoved his hand into his pocket and grasped her locket. Since Dare had found it on her bedroom floor, he'd kept it with him. She'd worn this close to her heart and him having it somehow gave him comfort. He felt that as long as he had the locket, she'd have to be found so he could eventually give it to her again.

"I hope you don't mind that I tagged along," Tori said stepping up to Dare.

He hadn't seen her since the ball when he'd blown up at her. He regretted doing that because it had pissed Foster off as it rightfully should have. If anyone had talked to Aya the way he'd talked to Tori, he'd rip their fucking heads off. But he mainly hated that he'd done it because she didn't deserve it. He knew that the other woman cared about Aya. He did his best to put on a smile even though his lips wouldn't quite curve into one. "It's fine. I'm glad you're here."

"I wanted to apologize for telling Aya something I had no business saying to her. I didn't mean to and—"

Dare held up his hand to stop her. "No need for apologies. I hope you haven't been carrying around this guilt the entire time. My problems with Aya started long before you said anything and I should have been the one to tell her myself. Had I done that then she wouldn't be in the predicament she's in. So if we're placing blame, I'll take it. I'm the one who needs to apologize. I'm sorry for the way I spoke to you at the ball."

Tori placed her hand on his arm. "It's no big deal. I understand that you were upset. I didn't take it personally. I just want to do whatever I can to help."

Dare let out a heavy sigh. He wasn't exactly sure what she could do, he appreciated any help he could get at this point. He turned to Foster, who had been silently looking on. "So, any update?"

"I've been in touch with some of my contacts who I thought I'd never have to deal with again, but this is for Aya and I'd do anything to get her back safe."

Though Foster was a respected member of the Elite class whose family had made their money through the banking industry, few people knew that his grandfather had garnered most of that wealth through illegal means and had groomed Foster to continue those illicit activities. Since talking helm of his family's business, however, Foster had steered everything toward more legal avenues even though Foster still had contact with the world he had vowed to leave behind. That he was willing to even reach out to people on his behalf, humbled Dare.

"And I appreciate it. But did anyone give you any information that could be helpful."

"Unfortunately, when you're dealing with these type of people, they don't always answer at your beck and call. These things take time, but they are aware that I've put my feelers out and they'll be in touch. I think I may have a lead regarding missing women, but it's an overseas operation."

"Could it have reached over here?"

"It may have considering some of the women inside the organization hailed from the states. It sounds like it's something like the auction, but different. I don't want to say too much on it right now only because I don't want to give you any misleading information."

"Just tell me. And if it's not right then we'll figure out what is later," Dare insisted.

"Fine," Foster sighed. "It has something to do with a reprogramming game. Instead of selling women as is like at the auction, the purpose was to take women and program them to be compliant to the point where they would never want to escape, in fact, if you tried to rescue them, they'd actually fight you. It's my understanding that the will would have to be weak in order for the program to work. So the key is to break the women down until they are able to accept reprogramming."

Dare felt sick to his stomach at the thought of something like that happening to Aya. Though he was scared to ask, he had to anyway. "And do you know how they break these women down?"

"I wasn't told much, but have dabbled in breaking people down myself. I imagine it would include torture, starvation, and exploiting the victim's darkest fears. But before you panic, for all we know, Aya may not have anything to do with this."

Dare hoped not. Aya was full of spirit, he doubted she could be easily broken down, so it frightened him the lengths someone would go to get her to that point. He took a deep, calming breath to keep himself from panicking. "You said this operation took place overseas. What country is the headquarters for this place located?

"Nuldanria."

"Fuck!" That country was a hotbed for tons of illegal shit. There were very few regulations in the United States, but in some countries, it was basically anything goes. The wealthy went there to get away with any and every indulgence they wanted. Things that were frowned upon by people with even a modicum of decency here didn't even register in a country like Nuldanria. If people had the desire for sleeping with children, tasting human flesh or any kind of depravity imaginable that would be the place for it. It wasn't surprising that a reprogramming racket would be based there. "I think I should fly there."

"But we don't know for certain that it has anything to do with Aya yet. It could be a wasted trip."

"It's a lead we need to follow up on. I can have my jet fueled and ready in an hour."

"And if we go and she's not there and we find that there's another lead here. Then what? You need to be here. If you need someone to go so badly then I'll go."

"And I'll go too," Tori chimed in.

"Absolutely not," Foster objected forcefully.

"But Aya is my friend. I need to feel like I'm doing something useful."

Foster took Tori in his arms and kissed her on top of the head. "You are. You're a huge support to me in this."

Dare felt a small surge of jealousy within watching Foster and Tori interact when he himself didn't have that luxury because Aya was missing. He wished he could turn back time and he do things differently. He'd be more open, he'd do whatever it took to keep her by his side. He wondered who had her and what they were doing to her. Was she injured, was she in pain? The thought made him shudder.

Foster closed the distance between him and Dare and placed his hand on his friend's shoulder. "I promise we'll find her."

"But in what condition," Dare whispered the words of dread and he felt as if his entire world was caving on him.

Chapter Sixteen

The next time the lights when on, Aya was almost certain she was hearing voices. Sometime during her solitary confinement, she'd found the strength to get off her bed and crawled to what she believed to be the sliding wall to bang on it and demand that it be opened. When no one came, she found her body wouldn't cooperate with her when she told it to move.

Aya had been lying in the same spot yet she didn't know how long. She felt disgusting lying in her own waste, being sickened and disgusted by the smell. The stench was enough to make her throw up, but there was nothing in her stomach, so she dry heaved until she passed out.

Each time she'd come to and find herself in the darkness, she wanted to cry, but her body wouldn't produce tears. Aya was so hungry she was ready to eat her own hand.

"I will survive," she mumbled to herself. The more she said it, however, the less she believed it. It was clear that Thor would starve her to death.

But when the metal wall came up along with the glass one, Aya was startled. She barely had the energy to raise her head, let alone to get up and make a run for it as she desired. All she saw were a pair of expensive shoes as she continued to lay on the floor.

She felt herself being lifted in a pair of strong arms and carried. Her vision was blurry as it took some time to adjust to the light. The only thing she could determine was that she was being carried to a different part of the house. The next thing she knew she was being submerged in a tub of water so hot she screamed in agony, but with her head under the water, she swallowed water and felt herself drowning. Somehow she found the strength to struggle, but the hand holding her head under was too strong.

She was going to die and she saw flashes of her life flash before her eyes.

Dare's face seemed to be hovering over the water and just as suddenly as the vision appeared it disappeared.

Just when she hovered at the line between life and death, the hand grasped her by the hair and pulled her to the surface. Aya coughed and sputtered while trying to gasp for air.

"All clean. We couldn't leave you in those filthy quarters. You've been a naughty girl, Aya, wetting yourself like a bad little girl."

Thor.

Aya almost wished he would have let her die. Her throat was raw and she was still too weak from lack of food and drink that all she could muster in a fit of defiance was a glare.

He smiled. "Still have that spark I see. No matter."

Aya was pulled out of the tub and practically dragged to another part of the room. She felt several pairs of hands on her body, some were drying her off while others rubbed oil into her skin. Others were combing and putting some kind of product in her hair. One of them pressed something against her lips.

"Eat," a woman's voice urged.

Aya wanted to weep for joy. She didn't know what it was, but at this point, anything would have been welcome. She nibbled greedily on what tasted like some kind of protein bar. It could have been dirt at this point.

Finally able to focus on what was going on, Aya noted that several of the women had surrounded her and were aiding in her toiletry while Thor watched from the corner with his arms crossed.

When she was finished eating the bar that was offered, a bottle was placed against her lips. Water. She never thought she'd be so glad to have it. She was only allowed small sips at a time, but it was enough to soothe her parched throat.

The women worked on her for countless minutes while Aya passively lay there and let them. All the while her gaze was trained on Thor and she thought of what she'd do to him if she got free. She wanted to rip his balls off and feed them to him. The sick fuck.

By the time she was thoroughly fed and groomed, the women helped her into a fresh set of bra and panties. Only then did Thor approach her. Aya had regained a little bit of her strength so when he lifted her up this time. She raked her nails down the side of his face.

He hissed in pain and dropped her to the hard concrete ground with a loud thud followed by a swift kick to her stomach. She grunted in pain and started to cough as the air whooshed from her lungs.

"That was a warning. If it happens again, your punishment will be more severe." Thor grabbed her by the hair and dragged her. Aya grabbed his hand to stop the burning in her scalp.

"Lemme go!" She struggled against him.

Ignoring her, he continued to pull her into yet another section of the basement. He yanked her up and threw her in the chair. Thor then strapped her wrists to the arms of the chair and did the same with her ankles to the chair legs. He moved until he was standing directly in front of Aya. "Are you comfortable, my pet?"

She glared at him.

Thor leaned down until their noses touched. "I beg your pardon? What did you say? I require a response when I speak to you."

Aya mustered all the moisture she could manage in her mouth and spit in his face.

Thor pulled away and backhanded her. Her head snapped to the side.

"The extra thirty-six eyes in confinement didn't seem to teach you did it? But I know something that will." He touched the button on the side of his watch again.

The raging pain she'd felt in her head came back twice as strong as the first time. "You son of a bitch!" she screamed in agony

There was a point in pain where it was too much to bear, the body would shut down and a person would pass out, but it seemed Thor only took her to the edge where she couldn't completely black out, so Aya continued to endure the excruciating torture.

By the time it stopped, Aya whimpered from the residual ache.

"For one so small, you sure have a lot of fight in you. I knew you were special, but nonetheless, you'll break. They all eventually do. I just have to figure out where your limit is."

"Why?" she managed to ask. "Why me?"

He shrugged as if her question should have been obvious. "Because I wanted you. At first, it was because you belonged to *him*. I was going to take you to a different location, have you trained, and give you to one of the program's rejects. I wanted you to disappear and never be found again so that he would suffer as I have."

What was he talking about? "I don't understand."

"You don't need to. All you need to know is that the more I observed you, you intrigued me. And when we finally met, that sealed your fate. I decided that you would be the ultimate treasure amongst my collection of beauties. You really are a rare find." He caressed the side of her face with the back of his hand, but she flinched away. Thor gripped her chin and squeezed hard. "Don't pull away from me again," he said through gritted teeth.

"Or what?" Aya challenged defiantly.

Without warning, he hit the switch again. When the pain hit her this time it felt as if her brain was melting. Thor didn't make it last as long this time. "This is what happens when you speak out of turn, Aya. You know, for the past few days, I've been wondering what goddess name I should gift you with, but your name suits you. When I looked it up, it had many meanings, all of which suited you, 'beautiful, art, miracle.'" He caressed her cheek again. "Because you are indeed a miracle. You made the beast feel. And you're the key to destroying him."

Not caring if he turned his pain device on again, she needed to know. "You just wanted me to get back at Dare?"

"Like I said, that was my intention at first, and it still is because I'm sure if I were to lose someone as valuable as you, I'd be driven crazy as well. He'll know how it feels to lose someone. Really, he only has himself to blame. He had the opportunity to save you, but he wanted to do things his way, making it very easy for me to step in."

"What do you have against him?"

"You know Aya, I'm giving you a lot of latitude by answering your questions. But I'll tell you this one final thing."

"Dare O'Shaughnessy was responsible for something being taken from me. Something that meant the world to me. And now I'm returning the favor. I've been waiting for this moment for a very long time and revenge tastes so sweet."

"He'll find me and he'll destroy you."

Thor grinned gripping her bra strap and releasing it so that it snapped painfully on her shoulder. "Oh? You think so? Don't you think I've done my research? Infiltrated his company with my own people. I have people on the inside my dear, reporting his every move to me. He may have figured it out about the drones, but if even if does manage to trace them, I've seen to it that they'll lead to someone else. My mole will keep me informed and I'll stay one step ahead. It is, after all, how I was about to take you."

"You were able to take me because you exploited the problems Dare and I were having. I wouldn't be surprised if you helped exacerbate them."

His smiled widened. "I'll never tell," he taunted in a sing-song voice. He ran his fingertip down her arm and if Aya could have flinched away, she would have. "Such beautiful skin. When I watched you making love to O'Shaughnessy, I wondered what it would feel like when you're finally riding my cock like you rode his. And how those big dick sucking lips would feel around me. You certainly looked like you enjoyed doing it."

"Finally? It's never going to happen unless you rape me. And trust me, I won't make it easy for you." She was disgusted that he would think that she would voluntarily allow him to touch her. If she weren't anchored to this chair, she would have been fighting in earnest.

He cocked his head to the side as he stared at her. Finally, he smiled again. "You know what? You're absolutely right. I could allow the electronic head screw to do the job for me, but if I were to use it too much, it would eventually liquefy your brain. Honestly, I've never had to use it on my women as often or as much as I've had to use it on you and you haven't been here that long. But there are other ways.

Thor gripped the front of her bra and with one hard tug, he ripped it off, leaving her breasts exposed. Aya fought against her restraints, but it was no use. "Don't do this." She was reminded of a time when she was younger when she'd defied her Uncle Arthur to go out at dark to see some friends. On her way to her destination, Aya was cornered by three boys who had had every intention of raping her. Though she'd fought with all her might and had even gotten off a few good licks, there were too many of them and they were too strong. She remembered being pinned down and her clothing ripped. But by some miracle, Uncle Arthur had found them and he had a rock in hand and had bashed one of her attackers in the head, knocking him out. Her other two assailants, not wanting any trouble had run off. But that incident had left a lasting impression on her. It was the reason her uncle had insisted she keep her head shaved and her clothes baggy until it had just become a habit for her.

Aya supposed protecting herself and others from the lascivious nature of people who would take advantage of those they perceived as weaker had been so ingrained in her that it had shaped most of her existence. The fact that she was able to open herself up to Dare had been a miracle in itself because she'd never intended to fall in love with anyone for self-preservation reasons. But when she'd let love in her heart, she'd fought against it. Dare had made lots of mistakes, sure, but some of the fault lay with her as well. She'd been so focused on being independent and fighting against his overprotectiveness that she'd blatantly ignored the real danger.

Now here she was in the middle of her biggest nightmare, the prisoner of some madman who truly saw her as nothing more than a toy.

"You've got a beautiful body, Aya. So compact. So perfect." Thor tweaked one of her nipples and she instantly felt sick to her stomach.

"Don't fucking touch me!" she growled uncaring about what kind of pain he inflicted on her."

Instead of releasing the tip, he squeezed and twisted it so hard, she thought he might actually pull it off.

She cried out in agony.

"Who the fuck do you think you're talking to?"

"You."

He grabbed her other nipple and gave it the same treatment, turning and yanking on both of them roughly until she wanted to beg for mercy. By the time he released them, they had gone numb.

Thor bent over and ripped her panties off. Aya didn't understand why he'd bothered to put any kind of undergarments on her if he'd just intended to tear them off anyway, but then again, the mind of a psychopath was something she didn't want to figure out. Aya squirmed in the chair, terrified what he had in store for her next now that she was completely exposed to him.

"So pretty," he murmured more to himself than to her. Thor slid a finger along her slit and Aya could only glare at him. He seemed to be taking pleasure in her discomfort.

"What kind of man are you to take a woman against her will? You are a sick freak."

He pushed a finger inside of her and gasped in despair because she didn't feel the least bit turned on. "Hmm, you're not wet. But I can fix that." He stared at her with what she now considered scary purple eyes and a smile so sinister curving his lips that a shudder ran up her spine. She couldn't believe that she'd once thought him to be handsome. Of course, he was aesthetically pleasing to the eye, but now all she saw was an ugly monster.

Thor reached into his pocket and pulled out something that made Aya widen her eyes in horror. She began to shake her head vehemently. "No! Not that," she screamed eyeing the small black sphere that fit in the palm of his hand.

"Oh? So you're familiar with this are you?"

"Please don't." This was the closest to begging she was going to give. She recognized the tiny device because it had been used on her before and it wasn't an experience she wanted to repeat. The Pleasuretron Ultra was meant to be used as a sex toy that could be inserted inside of a woman's vagina or anyone's anal cavity. It would give off a set of vibrations that would make a person orgasm as much or as little as they liked. It could be programmed to go off at a specific time. On the flip side, it could also be used as a torture device that could cause multiple orgasms which created a significant amount of stress on the body.

The last time that thing had been used on her, Aya had felt the effect for a week after it had been removed from her. She'd twitch and spasm at the sight of anything spherical.

Ignoring her pleas, Thor parted her pussy lips with one hand before roughly shoving the device into her without the benefit of lubrication. Thor slowly backed away from her then and watched with a gleam of anticipation in his eyes.

It didn't take long for the vibrations to begin and Aya fought hard to not respond to the sensation coursing through her. A warmth spread throughout her body and she tried to clear her mind completely to stave off any sensations that came remotely close to pleasure. But this thing inside of her was designed specifically to generate the desired effect and Aya was powerless against it.

To her dismay, moisture began to drip from her and puddle in her chair all while Thor looked on with a smile on his face. "That's it. You're almost there."

"No, no, no, no," Aya chanted to herself, doing the best that she could to fight off her oncoming climax.

"You can fight it all you'd like, but it's going to happen, over and over again. You see, you might have had the pleasure of experiencing this little toy before, but the one that's inside of you is slightly different. You see, the old versions created the vibrations you're feeling now in intervals, this one…it doesn't stop."

"Noooooooooooooo!" Aya screamed just when she was pushed to her peak.

And it continued to go on just as Thor told her it would until her body couldn't take anymore and she welcomed the darkness as she passed out.

Chapter Seventeen

Time seemed to become a meaningless thing because Aya hadn't seen direct sunlight for a while. The only difference that allowed her to distinguish when a new day began was the routine. At nights, she was locked back into her cell, although she noticed that the other women were sometimes allowed to roam the area as they pleased. They even talked with each other as if they were in the middle of a huge society party. Some nights, Thor, would select one and take them with him and the individual he selected, would act as if it were some huge honor.

During the day there would be some new torture for Aya. She'd be removed from her cell and taken to a room where Thor would attempt to get her to refer to him as Master and every day she refused.

The Pleasuretron Ultra had been one of the worst punishments. It had taken her days for the effects of that thing to wear off and she was still sore between her legs. Some days she'd get sensory deprivation time with no food. Other times, she'd be submerged in cold water until her body nearly went into shock. Thor would hit her at times, but never enough to cause lasting bruises. It was as if he was trying to preserve her in some way, like a collector.

Most of his torture, however, was psychological. Yesterday's torture had been particular nightmare inducing.

Aya nibbled on her protein bar trying to make it last as long as she could because she had no idea when her next meal would be. It wasn't as if they were consistent. She noticed the other women were delivered real meals on silver trays by servants. She'd eye them enjoying their food making her wistful for one of Uncle Arthur's specialties, or something prepared by Dare's chef, but she figured she was being fed what amounted to scraps as a form of punishment.

Still, she would rather eat these tasteless bars than have real food if it meant she had to bow and defer to Thor. She was surprised she hadn't seen him today. Maybe she would get a reprieve.

Almost as if she'd conjured him up, Thor appeared in front of her cell. When it opened, she didn't bother to move, knowing that if she did, whatever he had in store for her would be so much worse. Two of his women were with him, Freya, who seemed to be a favorite of his and Diana, a brunette who was nearly as tall as Athena.

"Good afternoon, Aya. I hope you didn't think I've forgotten you. I unfortunately had business to take care of that I couldn't allow anyone else to handle. But I have something very special for you today."

"I'm sure you do," she muttered under her breath.

He raised a brow. "What was that?"

"Nothing." Aya may have still hated his guts, but she wasn't a fool. Why make things harder on herself than they already were?

"Come, or do I need one of the ladies to assist you?"

Aya wobbled to her feet. She hadn't been at full strength since she'd been in this forsaken place, but she wanted to cling to a little of her dignity. "I can walk."

"Still holding on to that pride I see. But as the old saying goes, pride cometh before the fall. Keep that in mind when I introduce you to some friends of mine.

Diana and Freya stood on each side of her as the three of them followed Thor to what Aya dubbed his torture chamber. This is where all the punishments occurred. In the middle of the room was a large black box that appeared big enough to fit a body inside and upon seeing it, Aya was almost certain that it was meant for her.

Thor nodded toward his two minions. "Ladies, you may return to your quarters."

"Yes, Master," they spoke simultaneously before hurrying out of the room.

"I'd like to show you another one of my collections. Do you by any chance know what entomology is?"

She shook her head not bothering to answer.

"I used to collect these when I was a boy. It didn't cost any credits, only the time to find them, especially the rare ones. Aya, I want you to get to know this collection as well as I have."

He then opened the box and gestured her forward. She walked to the box and squealed in horror. "Oh no!" She shook her head back and forth. "No. I can't.

Living in the Red District she'd seen lots of creepy crawlies, but never so many at once in one place. There were insects of the six to hundred-legged variety, roaches, ants, beetles and some she didn't recognize.

"Get in."

She backed away, her hand over her mouth. "I can't."

"We have this argument nearly every day and I always win. When will you learn that you will not get your way? Now get in the mother fucking box!" Thor gripped her by the hand and pulled her toward the box.

Knowing the longer she fought him the longer her time would be in the box, she trembled as she stepped inside, feeling something squish between her feet. Bugs crawled over her bare feet and legs since she wasn't allowed to wear anything besides the uniform of bra and panties.

"Sit down."

Reluctantly Aya did as she was told. Though she was short, she still had to pull her knees against her chest to fit inside. When he closed the lid on top of her, she wanted to scream but was frightened that one of those things would crawl into her mouth.

"Don't worry, Aya, none of them are poisonous...at least none that should leave any lasting effects." She could hear him chuckle outside of the box.

Aya whimpered and screamed on the inside as the bugs crawled all over her. There was no room inside this miniature prison to swat them away. She twisted and turned her head as best as she could to keep them from going into her ear and nose. The feel of them moving along her skin had placed her in a special kind of hell. She pressed her hands over her mouth and released a muffled scream after scream.

The really humiliating part about that punishment was when Thor finally decided to take her out of the box. He had one of the women examine all of her orifices to extract any stray bugs that may have crawled into them. They'd found two in one and one in the other.

Aya could still feel them on her skin and every now and then she would flinch and itch. She didn't know how much longer she could keep up the fight. With each new torture, Thor broke her down a little more. She should have been grateful that he hadn't actually raped her. He claimed that when they had sex, she would be a willing participant. He was clearly delusional if he thought that would happen.

Just as she finished eating her glass door opened and Thor was nowhere to be seen. She wasn't sure if this was her chance to go, but something told her it may be a trap.

Athena appeared in front of her cell. "It's social time, come on Aya."

"Social time? What do you mean?"

This was something new.

"Master generously allows us to congregate for a certain amount of time a day and to stretch our legs. Don't you want to get out of your quarters?"

Aya nodded as she scratched her arm, certain there was a bug crawling on it. She stood up and followed the blonde to another part of the room where chairs were formed in a circle. There were eight women in all, including herself. They wore matching undergarments like herself.

Aya took the empty chair between Athena and the one she'd heard referred to as Brigid, a beautiful woman who looked to be a mixture of several ethnicities.

"Aya, welcome to social time." Freya smiled at her. It was clear that she was the leader of this group because the other women seemed to take direction from her, and she also seemed to be the one Thor would choose for his special events most often.

Aya scratched her leg, unable to shake the feeling that she wasn't alone in her skin. "What do you guys have to be social about? You barely get out."

Freya frowned. "About Master's generosity, of course. It is by his grace that we are all safe from the dangers of the world. He is our savior and for that we are grateful. You should be too, Aya."

"Grateful? For what? It's been one round of torture after another for me and you all helped him. Don't you see? He's brainwashed everyone here," Aya tried to reason with them, hoping she could find an ally amongst all the crazy surrounding her.

Each woman looked at each other and then to Freya for guidance. "Aya, Master has been very patient with you and has shown a remarkable amount of restraint. You shouldn't test him. He wants to take care of you and protect you."

Aya had heard that before and it didn't sit well with her the first time, but now she realized just how different those statements were in context. "But what about your friends and family? Don't you think they would worry about you? Have any of you seen them since your so called Master has kept you locked away?"

"I…I saw my mother once when Master took us on an outing. She wanted to take me away from Master. She said some horrible things about Master. Master knows what's best for us."

If Aya didn't know any better, she thought she'd seen the suspicious sheen of tears in Shiva's eyes. Was it possible she could get through to the other woman somehow?"

"Shiva? You don't miss your mother even a little bit? I'm sure this is probably the same woman who took care of you and kept you safe until you came to be with Master. My mother is dead. She died when I was young and if I had a chance to see her again, I'd do anything to make that happen. Don't you miss her? Even a little?"

Freya narrowed her eyes seeming frustrated with Aya's line of questions. "Master would be very displeased to hear your upsetting line of questions."

Aya placed her hand against her chest. "I'm upsetting? Maybe the fact that you guys are being held as prisoners should be the real cause for upset here. Look at Shiva? There are tears in her eyes. She's missing her family and I'm willing to bet some of you are as well."

"Why are you so stubborn?" Brigid asked with anger tinting her tone. "Master provides all. We want for nothing under his care."

Aya ignored Brigid and focused on Shiva who hastily wiped a tear from her cheek. "Is that how you feel? Does Master provide you a mother's love?"

"He…" her voice trailed off and she burst into tears.

While a few of the women went to comfort the crying woman, a couple others shot dagger-like glares in Aya's direction. Had she found a weakness? Maybe if she could exploit it, she could get more people on her side. But before the thought had a chance to fully take hold, a shadow fell over her and a pair of arms clamped down on her shoulders.

"Is there a problem ladies?"

Aya's heart began to pound. She felt like a fool. Why did she think this so called social time wouldn't be monitored? This was just another means of control for Thor. It was clear he gathered these women together so they could keep each other in line.

Seeing that he had joined them, all the women with the exception of Aya knelt down with foreheads to the floor. If this garnered her another punishment, then so be it. Fuck him. But even as the thought crossed her mind, she started to twitch feeling as if a bug was crawling on her skin.

Thor released her shoulders and walked over to Shiva. He got down on his haunches and stroked the back of the woman's light brown hair. "Shiva, look at me."

Shiva raised her head. "Yes, Master?"

"Do I make you unhappy?"

"Of course not Master. The only thing that makes me happy is serving you." Shiva's voice wobbled a little as she spoke and it was clear the woman was terrified of Thor, the way she trembled.

"Hmm, then why are you crying, my pet?"

"I…I uh…these are tears of joy because I'm happy to be here…to serve you."

"Is that so? And it has nothing to do with missing your mother?"

Shiva's eyes widened. "Master, you are the only one I care about."

"I want you to prove it to me."

Shiva nodded eagerly. "Anything."

He caressed the woman's face. "I'm glad to hear you're so willing to please me. And that you'll obey my command. I want you to know what's about to happen next is only because I'm looking out for you. You have to know that when someone tries to come between me and you it can cause doubt and doubt leads to pain. Grab your left pinky and bend it back until it snaps."

Aya was out of her chair. "No!"

Without a second's hesitation Shiva quickly did as Thor commanded, creating a sickening snap. The woman screamed in agony and tears gushed from her eyes.

"How could you do that to her?" Aya looked around the room at the rest of the women who remained in the positions of worship. She charged at Thor only to be met with the back of his hand. He was so quick she didn't see him move. Aya fell back on her ass.

"Athena, sit up."

The blonde did as she was told.

"Break your left pinky."

Athena did exactly that and Thor called on Diana.

"No! Please, Thor! Don't!" Aya cried. He was making them hurt themselves on her behalf and though she would take his abuse, her conscience wouldn't allow others to take her punishment."

Thor whirled on her with narrowed eyes. "What did you call me?"

"I…" she opened her mouth, but the words wouldn't come out.

Though he kept his gaze trained on Aya he pointed to Diana. "Do it!"

There was a snap followed by Diana screaming and crying in agony as the two before her had done.

"Now what the fuck did you call me?"

"Ma-master." As soon as the words left her lips, Aya burst into tears.

Chapter Eighteen

Four weeks.

Aya had been gone for nearly four whole weeks and they weren't getting any closer to finding her than they were before. Foster's trip to Nuldanria had been a huge bust. Dare had believed they were on to something when he'd learned about the reprogramming operation, but it had been a huge dead end. Even Foster's underground contacts had come up with nothing.

Tracing the purchaser of the micro drones had led them to a whole bunch of nothing as well. Dare was starting to lose hope and the longer Aya was gone, the further into depression he spiraled. The only thing that kept him semi-sane was his work, but even that wasn't enough. He needed Aya. Nothing was the same without her. When she'd broken up with him it hurt beyond any pain he had ever suffered, until now. Not knowing if she was safe or not was driving him crazy.

He thought about all the things he could have done differently to keep her safe. Maybe if he would have stayed outside of the bar the night when she was taken things would have been different.

He was slowly losing his mind. Everywhere he went, he thought he saw her. Dare was even beginning to have conversations with her. "Aya, where are you?" he whispered to the air. He sat in his home office without any lights or electronics on, just taking in the silence. It was the only way the visions of her didn't constantly haunt him.

"Dare, why do you work so hard? You should take some time off." Aya moved behind him and gave him a shoulder rub as she kissed the side of his neck.

"Are you trying to distract me?" he asked, losing his will to focus on the holo documents before him.

"Absolutely. Uncle Arthur says I should take some time off from the bar. I think we should take some time off together?"

"And what do you propose we do?" He leaned into her touch, feeling the tension drain from his body as she worked his muscles with her dexterous hands.

"I'd like to go somewhere? The beach maybe?"

Before he'd met Aya, he'd done an extensive amount of traveling. There were times when he hadn't seen the inside of his house for weeks at a time because of business, but since Aya, he'd delegated a lot of his work that required travel to his executives. Dare had only gone on a few trips since they'd been together, but none of them lasted for more than a couple days. The thought of a beach trip with Aya seemed appealing, especially if it meant seeing Aya in a tiny bikini. Most of the beaches in the US were so polluted that the only habitable ones were privately owned. Dared owned a small private island in the Mediterranean that might be the perfect getaway for them.

"The beach sounds like a good idea. As soon as this latest merger goes through, I promise I'll take you to my island and we can relax on the beach all day and make love at night

"Oh yeah, I like the sound of that. In the meantime, we can get a head start on the making love part. I'm wearing a skirt." She then bent over and whispered in his ear. "With no panties."

Dare's cock immediately jumped to attention. Aya knew it drove him crazy when she wore skirts, especially little ones that showed off her sexy legs. Thankfully, she only wore them around the house because he was jealous enough as it was without having to fight off every man that checked her out.

"Let me see." He pushed his chair away from his desk to give her enough space to stand in front of him. Aya turned her back to him and spread her legs before raising the skirt to reveal her bare ass and pussy. Her lips were already damp with juice. Dare inhaled sharply. It was one of the most beautiful sites he'd ever seen.

He inserted two fingers deep inside her moist channel. "Is all this for me doll?"

"Oh yeah." She slowly began to wiggle on his fingers as he drove them in and out of her, soaking his hand. "When I was at the bar today, I was thinking about you and it made me horny. I got off early so I could be here before you got home, but I saw that you beat me here, I thought I'd change into something a little more…oh" she groaned, "accessible."

"And I like it a lot. But you know what I'd really like right now?"

"Mmm, what?"

"For you to sit on my dick."

"I thought you'd never ask."

Dare took his fingers out of her dripping pussy, long enough to unfasten his pants and free his cock. Aya reached behind her and wrapped her fingers around his girth before aligning it with her entrance. Dare grasped her by the waist and pulled her down until he was so deep inside of her they had become one unit. Aya raised herself and then sat down. Though Dare kept his grip on her, Aya was in control and he loved this aggressive side of her as she bounced up and down on his cock.

He loved this position because he could go very deep. Dare brought his hands up to fondle her tits which jiggled as she moved. Her cunt felt so good and tight around his length that he didn't think he'd be able to hold on for very long.

"I love you!" he yelled as he shot his seed into her. Aya continued to move up and down until she reached her own completion. When she was finished, she curled in his lap and wrapped her arm around him. "I love you too, Dare."

Ever since that day, whenever he was in his office, he thought about her, but then again, there weren't many rooms they hadn't had sex in. They never got around to taking that trip because the threats had started to become more frequent and he'd become paranoid where Aya's safety was concerned. If only...

The lights in the dark room suddenly came on and Garrison's holographic image appeared in the center of the room. "Sir, I apologize for interrupting, but a Mr. Lane is here to see you. Should I allow him inside?"

Dare frowned. "Of course. Let him in. Mr. Lane is Miss Smith's uncle. He's never to be turned away. Take him to the living room and offer him refreshments."

Garrison turned red. "I'm sorry, sir. I had no idea. I'll let him enter right away." The lights went off again when the estate manager's image disappeared.

"Lights on," Dare commanded. He walked to the bathroom to take care of his disheveled appearance.

When he stepped into the living room the older man who appeared to be pacing around halted when he saw Dare. Dare hadn't seen the other man in weeks since they'd first learned of Aya's disappearance. Arthur Lane wasn't exactly a fan of his and considering what Dare had done to him, it was understandable. The fact that Aya's uncle had even shown up at his house meant that things were serious. Arthur looked as if he'd aged over these past weeks, his face had thinned which made his weight loss evident and his hair, which had already been liberally sprinkled with gray hairs seemed even grayer. There were shadows under his eyes.

"Lane. I'm assuming you're here concerning, Aya."

Arthur balled his fists at his sides as if it was difficult to get the words to come, but finally, he spoke. "I wanted to know if you've heard anything about my niece?"

Dare raised a brow in confusion. He knew Arthur had his coordinates because Dare had given them to him the last time they'd seen each other in person. "I'm surprised you didn't call me to ask."

"Look, this isn't easy for me, O'Shaughnessy? Do you think I would have come over here if I didn't think it absolutely necessary?"

"Probably not. But as far as finding a lead as to where Aya may be, no. There hasn't been any word on that."

"I need you to do something for me, boy."

"Yes?"

"I need you to look me in the eyes and tell me you didn't have anything to do with her disappearance. I need to know in no uncertain terms that you don't have her locked away somewhere and this isn't some elaborate ruse. I couldn't do that over no damn hologram. So man to man, I want the truth."

Dare understood why Arthur would have such a low opinion of him, but to think Dare would stage a kidnapping just to have Aya to himself was something that even he wouldn't stoop to. "The truth? The truth is I've spent four weeks of sleepless nights doing nothing, but think of Aya. And when I'm not doing that, I am using all my resources to find her. I have men in other countries looking for her. I know Aya and I didn't start in a good place, but I love that woman with all my heart, so uncle or not, you don't get to come into my home and make these ludicrous accusations. I did not kidnap Aya." Dare bore his gaze into Arthur's never wavering stare.

The two men didn't break eye contact with each other for what seemed like several minutes, but it was probably only a matter of seconds. Finally, the old man sighed, backing away. "I guess I have to believe you."

"I would never intentionally hurt Aya." Dare held up his hand when Arthur looked as if he wanted to object as he continued. "I know that I've made a lot of mistakes where she was concerned, but it's because she's the best thing that ever happened to me. I love her more than I love myself. Hell, I didn't know how to love before I met her. I've been so frightened that one day she'd wake up and realize she's made a mistake being with me and she'd leave me. I thought she'd see right through me and leave me for someone who was worthy of her. So I acted like a jealous fool. And then I started getting threats, taunting me by saying that they would take away my most precious possession. I value Aya above everything, so I panicked and made a lot of bad decisions, but I thought what I was doing for Aya's own good."

Arthur gave Dare a long assessing stare before collapsing into the closest chair. "Who am I kidding? I'm just as much at fault as you are. Ever since my sister died, I vowed to take care of her. I love Aya and raised her like my own. As far as I'm concerned, she is mine, and I guess at times I've been overprotective of her, always making sure I knew of her comings and goings and having her downplay her looks so the boys wouldn't notice even though they did. I raised her to be street smart, but she's naïve in a lot of ways as well, like when it comes to men and relationships. I didn't talk to her about those things because I wanted to keep her young forever. But then somewhere along the way, Aya became a woman and I wasn't sure what to do with her anymore except love her and protect her the best way I could."

"I was scared for her because despite being tough at times, Aya has a big heart and while she may be cynical when it comes to Elites, she really just wants to see the good in everyone. And then you came along. Do you think you're the first man or person for that matter to proposition her? She'd been able to handle them just fine. But I could tell you were different. You wouldn't be deterred no matter what. I recognized that look you gave her whenever you looked at her. It was the look of a man in love even though you didn't recognize it at first. You were trouble even before you did all those things to disrupt our lives. If I'm being completely honest, I used what you did as an excuse to hate you. I mean what you did was pretty bad, but in the end Aya forgave you and I should have respected that. I think I would have hated any man who came along and turned my baby's head. Aya means the world to me and I'm finally looking at you as one man who loves her to another. You really do care about my niece don't you?"

"With all my heart. Her disappearance has been killing me. I just wish we had some kind of clue about that night. It just doesn't make sense that no one saw her go off with anyone and no one is willing to talk."

Arthur wrung his hands in his lap. "That's been bothering me too. Most of the locals, well the ones who aren't troublemakers, look out for one another. Aya is loved in our community because of what she does for everyone. But not one person knows where she is. The thing is, there's usually a gang of people who usually hang out across the street and when I looked at the camera footage that night, they weren't there. In fact, they haven't been hanging out there since. But the strangest thing happened, I saw one of them the other day, when Mera and I was closing up the bar. He was just walking down the street, looking all dressed up like he had somewhere important to go."

Dare frowned at this bit of information. "Do you happen to know his name?"

"I don't know him personally, but I think he goes by the name Slim, at least that's what I've heard people call him. They don't come to the bar because none of them ever have any credits. Aya may have known their names because I'd occasionally see one or two of them in line when she was handing out leftover food to the hungry."

"And you say he was all dressed up? How? Like what was he wearing?"

"I'm not talking about dressed up in a suit or anything like that, but his clothes seemed much nicer than what I was used to seeing him in. "

That seemed odd. "Do you know where he works?"

Arthur shook his head. "I barely remembered his name. But I could ask around. Do you think he knows something?"

"Possibly. Do you think you could transfer the footage of the night Aya went missing directly to me? Specifically, from around 7:30 on."

"Okay, I can do it right now. This fancy holowatch can do just about anything. Don't know how I managed before I was able to afford one of these babies."

Dare knew he could never truly repay the older man for what he'd done to him, but he was glad that the large sum of credits he'd transferred to him had offered Arthur some measure of comfort and from the looks of things, he was able to live a little more comfortably. He waited patiently for the man to figure out the watch's settings, but it appeared he was having trouble figuring out how to get to what he was looking for.

"Hmm, you know I thought I had the hang of it. Mac showed me how to use it. The young people always seem to know how to work these gadgets."

"Perhaps I can assist you," Dare offered.

"Sure, you have a try at it."

After a few minutes, Dare was able to pull up what he needed and then transferred the information to his system. "Hopefully we can figure this out soon enough."

Arthur nodded. "I hope so."

At least one good thing had come out of Aya being missing, Arthur and he had seemed to form a tentative truce which was good because Dare needed all the help he could get.

Time was running out.

Chapter Nineteen

The sound of the alarm went off signaling that *Master* was coming. Aya hopped off the bed and took the position. Every time she knelt on the floor for him, she felt a part of her dying on the inside. But he'd found her weakness. It wasn't the torture to herself. It was the hurting of the others. She didn't know these women and they certainly didn't give her a chance to get to know them because they were basically mindless robots. The only thing they seemed to talk about was how benevolent Master was.

But Thor had realized that the best way to hurt Aya was by exploiting her compassion. Whenever Aya stepped out of line, he would have one of the other women tortured while she watched. The last lesson she'd learned had been one that she would never forget.

Social time was becoming unbearable. It was difficult sitting in a circle with a bunch of women who didn't know they were in prison, but she played along for their sake. Because every time she made a misstep, Thor would give one of the other women the punishment that he thought Aya deserved. For not bowing when he came to their area, he'd taken Oshun, one of the more quiet ones of the group and had tossed her into the box of insects. It had made Aya itch just watching. What was worse, the woman's agonizing screams were more than she could take. For several nights, Oshun would wake up screaming from her nightmares.

Another time Aya had spoken out of turn and he'd triggered the electronic head device on Freya. He left it on for so long that Freya's nose had started to bleed and the blood vessels in her eyes had burst. Aya was very careful to follow the routine after that.

The thing that made the entire situation worse was that the women didn't seem to blame her. In fact, they thanked her for allowing Master to use them as a form of instruction. Today's social time seemed to be a particularly chatty one.

"Master says that he'll be choosing one of us to go out with him tonight," Diana spoke, her voice full of enthusiasm.

"I hope he picks me. I haven't gone on an outing in ages," Brigid piped in, but then as if rethinking her statement she said, "but I will be happy for whoever he chooses because just being able to serve him is an honor in itself."

"I'm very glad to hear, that Brigid."

Thor had a way of sneaking up on them without being noticed. Instantly they all went into a kneeling position, Aya included.

"Very good my, pets. You have all pleased me. You may reclaim your seats."

Aya was happy to sit in her chair again. She was careful to avoid looking directly at him because this was another rule that someone else had been punished for on her behalf. Never look Master in the eye unless he specifically requests it. *This was a rule that Aya didn't mind following because she'd grown to hate his face.*

"Which one of you lovelies should I take with me tonight?"

Aya hoped that she wouldn't be the one selected.

"I think I shall take Shiva with me tonight. Shiva, it is your honor to be my chosen."

"Thank you, Master."

"And how do you properly thank your Master?"

Shiva walked over to Thor and knelt before him, unbuckled his pants and wrapped her lips around his dick.

And that was the exact reason Aya was relieved he didn't select her. He still hadn't demanded sex from her, but she felt it was just a matter of time before he coerced her into fucking him. Though she would loath to do it, she felt that he was playing a game with her. Making sure she was completely on edge before he made his move.

Aya hoped that the disgust she felt for him didn't show on her face as Shiva pulled away. Thor ejaculated in the woman's face. "Thank you, Master. It was a pleasure to serve you."

"Aya, is there a problem?" he asked softly, but she could hear the menace in his voice.

She shook her head. "No…Master."

"Shiva, fix my pants." The other woman tucked his cock back into his pants as if it were the rarest of artifacts and redid his pants.

Thor then moved to stand in front of Aya. "Look at me, Aya." He grasped her by the chin giving her no choice, but to obey his command.

"Did you see a problem with the way Shiva showed her appreciation for her Master?"

"Of course not, Master," Aya quickly answer. She hated that the words so easily rolled off her tongue.

"That's good to hear because in the future, I trust you'll show me the same appreciation."

Unable to help herself Aya snorted in disagreement.

Thor shook his head. "Still so much to learn. "Athena, come. Aya needs another lesson."

Aya wanted to protest, but she knew that if she spoke up, Athena would get it worse.

"Aya, follow us, please."

Tears burned her eyes as she followed him. Thor directed Athena to go inside her cell. Thor hit the side of his watch and the glass door closed and the metal wall followed.

"Perhaps when Athena gets out, you will have had time to think about how lucky you are, Aya."

He left Athena in her cell for four days straight. By the time she was released, the blonde was so dehydrated, Thor had to take her to an undisclosed location for medical attention.

Aya's guilt kept her in line, but something told her that Thor was growing impatient with her. She could hear his footsteps as he approached and they sounded as if they had stopped directly in front of her cell. When she heard her door open, Aya fought the urge to look up and see what was going on. This wasn't a part of the normal schedule.

"Aya, you may rise."

Aya slowly wobbled to her feet but kept her head bowed. When he caressed her face, she just managed not to flinch away. He took her chin. "Look at me."

Reluctantly, she obeyed.

"You've come around quite nicely my pet. You're almost there, but not quite yet. Are you ready for the next stage of your training?"

She moistened her suddenly dry lips with the tip of her tongue. "Yes, Master."

"That's what I wanted to hear."

To her surprise, he leaned forward and pressed his lips against hers. Aya wanted to pull away but knew if she did, something would happen to one of the women. With a growl, he pulled her against him, cupped her bottom and grinded his erection against her. When he pushed his tongue past her lips, Aya didn't think she had it in her to keep going, but the last thing she wanted was someone to get punished because of something she'd done.

Finally, to her relief, he pulled away, seeming satisfied with himself. He stared at her with a raised brow as if he was expecting her to say something.

"Thank you, Master."

He smiled. "Yes, you're definitely ready for the next phase of your training. I need you to take this." Thor reached into his pocket and pulled out a green pill. "Open your mouth."

Aya hesitated briefly, but when she saw Thor's eyes narrow, she opened her mouth. He placed the pill on her tongue. It sizzled as it melted when she closed her lips.

Almost instantly, she felt slightly dizzy. She stumbled backward, but Thor caught her and lifted her in his arms. The next thing she knew, he was carrying her out of the prison and then everything went black.

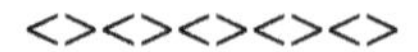

"What the fuck? You can't be serious." Dare shook his head in disbelief.

Arthur shook his head. "I know I can't believe this either. I called you as soon as I found out."

"Fuck!" Dare screamed, drawing attention to himself from the people in Arthur's place.

"Perhaps we should take this to somewhere more private?" Mera suggested coming over to them."

"Yes, that would be a good idea," Foster agreed.

Dare was thankful his friend had come along with him or else he would have been tearing things apart in frustration.

"Maybe we can go upstairs to Aya's apartment. We won't be disturbed there," Arthur suggested.

"You boys go ahead, me and Mac will keep things running." Mera jerked her thumb toward the boy behind the bar.

Dare's gaze fell on Mac's barren wrists and couldn't figure out why that bothered him so much so he pushed the thought out of his head momentarily. He had more pressing matters to deal with at the moment.

Once the three men were in the apartment Dare was the first to speak. "How did it happen? Where was the body found?"

Slim was dead, which seemed awful convenient for whoever it was they were trying to track down. It didn't seem like a coincidence that just when they'd had a lead he wound up dead.

"He was in an alley. I had one of the local kids ask around for him. I said I'd pay for the information. This morning I heard some people in the bar talking about the body of a kid not too far away from the bar. His head was bashed in. I don't think it was a coincidence."

"Who knew you were looking for Slim?" Foster asked.

"I told Mera, but I know she wouldn't have hurt the kid if that's what you're implying."

"No one is implying anything, but we're going to have to face facts," Dare spoke. "There has to be someone working on the inside who's preventing us from getting answers. We keep getting fed false leads and then when we think we're getting close to finding answers something like this happens. Someone is tipping off whoever took Aya."

Foster nodded his head. "I've been thinking this for a while now, but couldn't be certain. This confirms it. I don't believe in coincidences and there have been too damn many in this case."

"But who could it be?" Dare asked more to himself than to anyone else in the room. "It would have to be someone who's aware that she's missing and we've kept it on the hush because we don't want the news outlets to get a hold of this.

"Well, we could make a list of all the people who know about this," Arthur suggested.

"Well, on my end, the only people who know are Tori and Macy," Foster mused, rubbing his chin.

"What about your underworld contacts?" Dare asked.

"I've been discreet when making my inquiries. None of them know that Aya is missing specifically because trust me, if they knew, they would extort a whole lot of money out of me for any information because she's connected to you.

Dare looked in Arthur's direction. "How about you? I'm sure there are plenty of people at the bar who have realized that Aya's been gone for a while."

"The regulars have asked about her, but I told them that she's taking a long vacation. Even the staff thinks that's the case. The only people who know are Mera, like I said and Mac and neither one of them would be involved with this. Mac is a good kid, he's been running errands for the bar for a long time now. Because of the money I got from you, O'Shaughnessy, I was able to hire him full time so he practically runs the bar for Aya and me when we're not around. And Mera is always with me so not only would she not have the opportunity to be involved in any wrong doings, she's a good woman." Arthur seemed so certain that Dare had no choice, but to believe him.

"As for me, who you named are the only ones who know and Ronald of course."

Just then a loud beeping sound emanated from Arthur's holowatch. "Damn, this thing is always going off. Hmm, I'm going to have to get Mac to help me with it again. I was fiddling with the alarm on it, but I guess I programmed it wrong."

Dare walked over to the old man and took his wrist, he hit the button on the side of the watch to make the screen come up. He noticed a red dot in the corner of the screen and did a double take to make sure he wasn't imagining things. Without giving any warning, he ripped the watch off Arthur's wrist, threw it on the ground and stomped on it, crushing it until he was sure it was completely disabled.

"What the hell?" Foster demanded.

"Boy, do you know how much that thing cost me?" Arthur glared at him. "Are you crazy?"

Dare didn't bother to respond because if his suspicions were correct, he couldn't waste a single second. He raced out of the apartment and headed to the bar area. Mera stood behind the bar. The other employees were taking care of customers.

"What happened to Mac?" Dare demanded.

Mera frowned. "He had to check something in the back, but—"

Not waiting for her to finish, Dare raced around the bar and into the back, he navigated his way around the boxed just in time to see Mac slipping out the back door. He raced to catch the boy and just managed to grab a handful of his shirt. As he held on, he delivered a blow to the back of Mac's head.

The kid crumpled to the ground.

As he stood over Mac's body, Foster appeared. "Are you fucking insane?" his friend demanded.

"No," Dare answered feeling exactly the opposite. "I think this is the first time I've seen things clearly in a while."

"O'Shaughnessy. What the hell is the matter with you? Why would you do this?" Arthur asked as he finally caught up to him.

Mac rolled over with a groan and clutched his head.

Dare kicked him in the side. "Why don't you ask Mac, why he's been recording your conversations?"

Chapter Twenty

Whenever Aya found herself dozing off, an electric jolt when through her body. Her back was stiff and her bottom was sore from being strapped in this uncomfortable metal chair. Her last coherent memory before waking in this pitch black room where dots of light flashed and soft music played. A voice had whispered suggestively in her ear and it spoke of the Master's benevolence.

Each time her mind fought against it, she'd be fed a pill, until her resistance was weak and then everything had faded. Now she was in this room watching holo images of herself, sad, crying and upset, and then images of Master. The same images played over and over again until she'd memorized them all and knew in which order they would appear.

Aya bent her head to rest her eyes for just a minute, but then she was shocked again, waking her. The reel started from the beginning again. This time she made it to the end without closing her eyes. Once it was at the last image, she thought it would start over again, but instead, the screen disappeared.

The lights came on and she heard the soft footfalls get closer and closer until they stopped. A hand caressed the side of her face and she leaned into the caress.

"Aww, I trust you've had a productive night, my beauty?"

"Yes, Master," she answered without thought."

"I'm glad to hear that." Master moved around the chair until he was standing directly in front of her. He gripped her chin so that she was looking at him.

"Do you understand why I had to do this, Aya?"

"Yes, of course, Master. Before you came along, I was unhappy and alone. But then you rescued me. Thank you, Master."

"I'm glad you finally understand that. I only did what I did because only I know what's best for you."

"Of course Master, only you know what's best for me."

"Very good, my pet." He bent over and pressed a soft kiss to her lips.

The second his lips touched hers something didn't feel right, but she didn't understand what it was, after all, this was her Master. She pushed the feeling away and returned his kiss with all the enthusiasm she could muster.

He pulled away with a smile on his face.

Aya sighed with relief. Good. She'd pleased him.

Master then unfastened her restraints. "You've pleased me. I want you to get cleaned up and dressed. Someone will help you pick out an outfit for my approval. Tonight, you will show me how much you appreciate me."

"Anything for you, Master."

Foster had to hold him back several times because Dare wanted to fuck this kid up. His first clue the errand boy that worked at the bar may have known more than he'd let on was when Arthur had casually mentioned

Mac helping him program his holowatch. They were expensive gadgets that most people in the Red District wouldn't be able to afford. While he was certain that Arthur paid the kid a reasonable salary for working at the bar, was it enough to purchase a holowatch? But he'd dismissed it thinking it could have been gifted to him, Dare had after all transferred enough credits to Aya and her uncle so that they didn't have to work if they didn't want to.

Knowing Aya the way that he did, and a little about her uncle, they were generous people. But then he'd seen Mac behind the bar and he wasn't wearing a holowatch. How would he know how to program one if he didn't own it? But what finally gave it away was when Arthur's alarm had gone off and he saw the red dot in the corner, he knew exactly what was going on. If he was recording Arthur's conversations, the watch that was receiving the recordings would have a green light on the side indicating that they were receiving a transmission. Mac must have been tipped off when the connection had ended abruptly.

So once Dare had explained what he'd figured out, they dragged Mac to Arthur's office and closed the door. They'd found Mac's watch in his pocket and sure enough, when Dare had pulled up Mac's system he could see a dozen conversations in the voice log.

"You'd better start speaking, Mac before I let him loose and it's not going to be pretty," Foster warned him.

"How could you do this son? We treated you like family. Aya was your friend." Arthur shook his head, looking more hurt than angry.

Mac hung his head. "You don't understand."

Dare managed to tear out of Foster's grip and raced across the room. He grabbed Mac by the collar and began to shake him. "What's to understand you little shit? You helped the person who took Aya. For all we know, someone could be hurting her. I swear, for everything she's suffered, I'm going to make you feel tenfold, so you better tell me what the fuck is going on."

"I was promised she wouldn't be hurt."

Dare released Mac only to slam his fist into the kid's face, causing a sickening crunch.

Mac held his face as blood gushed from between his fingers. "Aww, fuck. I think you broke my nose."

"I'm about to break something else if you don't tell me more," Dare threatened.

Tears streamed down the sides of Mac's face, mingling with the blood. "I'm sorry. I swear I didn't know she'd be taken. I helped after the fact."

"Did you kill, Slim?" Arthur asked.

"No. I didn't kill anyone. I just called my contact and transmitted the conversation Arthur had with Dare. After Aya was kidnapped, I was just as upset as everyone else. I mean, she's been a good friend to me. You guys gave me a chance when no one else did. But I was approached by a man who only goes by the name, Jones. He offered me a lot of credits to doctor the video from the night Aya was taken. I just erased the part where a car came to pick her up and the footage of the witnesses who saw her get into the car. They were paid off to disappear from my understanding, but I guess Slim didn't take the hint."

"But you're transmitting the conversation to this Jones person was what got Slim murdered and because of that, you're indirectly responsible for his death. The blood is on your hands." Foster's words were ironic because, at the moment, Mac's hands were literally covered in blood. "So you did all this for credits?"

Mac looked as if he was ready to break but then raised his chin defiantly. "And why the hell shouldn't I get paid? You fucking snobs don't want to give folks like me a chance. Won't give us decent paying jobs so we can earn a decent living and look down on us when we do what we have to do to survive. You call us Dregs for living in the conditions that you people made possible. And then Aya goes and falls for one of you. All that talk of injustice she spouted and there she goes sleeping with the enemy. And even after what you did to her, she still stayed with you. She didn't want me, but she chose you." Mac glared at Dare with so much hatred, if looks could kill, he'd be dead on the spot.

"Is this because you had a thing for Aya?" Dare asked incredulously. He'd suspected the kid had a crush on Aya, but seeing as how Aya had never treated Mac as anything other than a friend, Dare hadn't been overly concerned plus he thought he was dating Macy for a while."

"Did you have feelings for Aya while you were with Macy?" Foster asked.

Mac shrugged. "Macy seemed like a sweet girl and I thought she'd help me move on. But she was no better. Dumped me for Dare's driver. His fucking driver! She probably saw how much he made in that job of his and dropped me without a backward glance. Women are all the same." Mac didn't bother to hide the bitterness in his voice.

"Mac…" Arthur looked at the young man as if he couldn't believe what he was hearing.

Mac rolled his eyes. "Don't look at me like that. You landed on your feet, Arthur. Through all this, you talked about what an asshole Dare is and how much you hate the Elite, but you weren't above taking that Elite money were you? So when I was offered a lot of credits, I took it. Bought me all those fancy gadgets you've been showing off. I got to see how the other half lives for a change instead of being left behind. Do I feel bad for betraying her? Sure I do, but she paid the price for involving herself with you bastards." Mac looked between Dare and Foster.

Dare believed if he stayed in this room for another second, he would murder this kid before they got all the information. He looked to his friend.

Foster raised a blond brow. "Do you want me to handle this?"

Not trusting himself to speak, Dare merely nodded before storming out of the room. As soon as he was out of the office, he threw a punch against the wall and instantly regretted it. He grasped his fist in pain. "Shit."

He hit the side of his watch and pulled up the reading on his VC. The chip stated that his hand wasn't broken, but he'd bruised his muscles. It would smart for a couple days, but it wasn't anything he couldn't manage with a couple pain pills.

"Are you going to be okay?"

Dare didn't realize Arthur had joined him. Dare turned to the old man. "You didn't stay in the office?"

"No. Foster thought it would be best that there be no witnesses. Do I even want to know what's about to happen in that office?" Arthur looked behind him. And a loud scream came from the inside.

"Does that answer your question?"

"You Elites sure are strange ones. And here I thought Foster was the nice one. He's not going to kill him, is he? I mean I know what he did was wrong, but…I don't want a dead body on my conscience."

"Arthur, there are some things that are far worse than death. I suspect however that by the time Foster is finished with Mac, he may wish he were dead, but at least we'll have the information that will hopefully get Aya back soon."

Another scream came from the office and Arthur sent a worried look toward the door. "Maybe I should go out front to make sure no one else hears that. When we had the renovations done, we soundproofed the area pretty good, but I need to make sure.

"You do that. I'll wait for Foster to finish up."

Arthur took one last look at the office before going to the front. Dare leaned against the wall and waited as he silently cursed himself for his foolishness. How hadn't he seen the clues up until now? Aya had been gone for a month and only now they'd gotten their first real clue.

He'd give anything to have her back safe and as much as it pained him, if she didn't want to be with him he'd have to accept that. Just knowing that she was okay, would have to be good enough for him.

Periodically he would hear Mac's screams which alternated between pleas for mercy. Despite knowing about Foster's underworld connections it still surprised him at times that his usually easy-going friend had such a dark side. It felt like hours that the door remained closed when in actuality it couldn't have been more than ten minutes before Foster emerged. There were splotches of blood on his otherwise pristine white shirt.

Dare raised a brow. "Is he…?"

Foster shook his head. "He's still breathing. He's going to need some medical attention. I don't think he'll be recognizable for a very long time, but he'll live. I called some men to come clean up the mess and take him away. And when he's all patched up, he's going on a nice trip and won't be bothering anyone again."

Dare thought it best that he didn't ask any more questions in that regard. "So what did you get out of him?"

Foster hesitated for a moment. "How well do you trust your staff, Dare?"

He froze. "What are you getting at?"

"This mysterious Jones person he's been in contact with...I pulled up the coordinate numbers in Mac's watch and I dialed it see who would pop up. Don't worry, I placed the call so that my image wouldn't pop up, only his."

"And?"

"And I think we need to find Ronald Briggs before he has a chance to get away."

Chapter Twenty-One

"Are you sure you want to go in there alone?" Foster placed his hand on Dare's shoulder before he could go to what was waiting for him behind the door.

"I need to do this on my own. If I need you, I'll holler."

Foster nodded backing away. "Okay. I'll be out here waiting."

Dare took a deep breath before walking into the dark room. "Lights on," he commanded. A flood of lights suddenly bathed the room which was located in the middle of an abandoned warehouse. It was one of Foster's properties that he hadn't gotten around to developing. It was far enough outside of the city that it was the perfect location for hiding bodies…if the situation called for it.

Gagged and bound to a chair in the center of the concrete room was Ronald Briggs. Thankfully Foster had had the foresight to call in some men to round him up before he could make his escape. They both agreed that when Ronald figured out that he was no longer able to communicate with Mac then he would figure they were on to him.

Dare looked at the man who had been his executive assistant for the past eight years, the man who had basically run his corporation for him while he was on his hiatus. He'd trusted this man with all his business secrets and Ronald had been efficient in his job never giving Dare reason for complaint.

But knowing that he was one of the people behind Aya's disappearance, propelled Dare across the room with his fist raised. He punched Ronald with enough force to make the other man's head snap back. Other than a grunt, Ronald barely reacted, so Dare punched him again and again, pummeling him as he alternated between fists.

If it weren't for Ronald's grunts and the bruises starting to form on his face, Dare would have thought he was he hitting a dead body. "You motherfucker! You knew all this time. You let someone take Aya and you knew how fucking frantic I was. You knew I would give anything to get her back. And you fucking did this to me?"

It infuriated Dare that he didn't get the reaction he wanted. Dare kept going until his rage burned out. "Fuck!"

By the time he was finished with Ronald, both of the other man's eyes were swollen shut, he had a busted lip, a large knot on his forehead and Dare was pretty sure his nose was broken.

The pain had been reactivated in Dare's hand, despite the pain pill he'd popped a few hours earlier, but he didn't care. Now seeing his handy work, his only regret was that the man might be dead before he could get answers.

Dare moved closer to see if Ronald was still breathing. Even though his body slumped over, the shallow rise and fall of the other man's back told Dare that he was still alive.

"Have nothing to say for yourself?" Dare demanded when Ronald didn't so much as beg for mercy. "What the hell is wrong with you?"

"Besides the fact that I'm choking on my own blood?" he wheezed.

"You have yourself to blame. How could you have done this Ronald? I trusted you and yet this is what you do to me? To Aya? She was actually very kind to you. What did she do to deserve this?"

"Nothing."

"So why?" Dare demanded.

"Does it really matter? It's done and there's nothing we can do about it now. I'm guessing soon enough he'll figure something is wrong when I don't check in soon. And then it will be all for nothing."

"What the hell are you going on about?"

"Thor Reichardt. He had a real vendetta against you. That's why he took her."

Dare frowned. Thor Reichardt? He barely knew the man and had never done business with him. He'd seen Thor at a few functions and up until recently, the man did most of his business overseas. But now that Dare thought about it, he recalled Aya talking to him at a party.

At the time, he'd had an uneasy feeling about the other man, but then again, he felt that way about most of the men Aya talked to. He'd just put it down as jealousy. And then there was the time Thor had randomly been at the same restaurant as Aya. Because of their problems, he didn't put two and two together. But he didn't understand why out of all the women Thor had set his sights on, it had to be Aya. Those notes he'd received seemed like the person behind them had some kind of personal vendetta against him and as far as Dare knew, he had no dealings with Thor, business or otherwise.

"If you're going to kill me, go ahead," Ronald whispered. "It's no more than I deserve. I failed her." It almost sounded as if Ronald was talking to himself instead of Dare.

"What are you talking about Ronald? Aya? Yes, you failed her."

The bloodied man shook his head. "No. Not her. Kelly."

Dare frowned. Had he beaten Ronald into delirium? "I don't know who you're talking about. Who's Kelly?"

Ronald made a sound that seemed like an attempt at a laugh, but instead, he ended up coughing out blood. "You don't know a thing about me. I've devoted eight years of my life to you and your company and you don't know me. You've never asked about how I was doing and up until Miss Smith came into your life, you barely said thank you. But I did my job because it was what I was paid to do, and I was compensated very generously for it. I was able to take care of my mother and sister. A boy from the Red District. I worked from the time I was a kid, hustling and doing whatever I could to get a paid education and earn a good living and…" he broke off in a fit of bloody coughs.

Dare wasn't sure where Ronald was going with this, but the more the other man talked he felt slightly guilty. "Ronald, why are you telling me this? You were of course investigated before you were offered such a high ranking position in my company. I already know about your background."

"Yeah, but I'm sure after you were satisfied I wasn't likely to sabotage your company you forgot about everything else, like how my father was already married and my mother was his favorite whore in the brothel. When she got pregnant with me, he gave her enough to retire, but by the time my sister Kelly came along, he found a new flavor of the month and kicked us all to the side leaving my mother without means to support herself so back to the brothel she went. But she'd aged out of her old brothel and had to work in one of the low-end ones. I did errands around the brothel for a few credits and it was my job to keep Kelly out of trouble and away from customers who had a taste for young girls."

"Ronald..."

"You want information and I'll give it to you. You don't even have to torture me for it, because regardless, no matter what happens, I'm dead, whether he kills me or you do. But at least for the first time, you'll *see* me. I mean really see me for the first time. As a person and not just your efficient machine."

Dare wanted to crack Ronald's skull open, but if this was how he was going to find out where Aya was then so be it. "Fine, but make it quick."

Ronald chuckled. "Even when in this situation, you have to be in control don't you?"

"Are you going to tell me or do you plan to keep rambling?"

Ronald raised his head, but Dare couldn't read his expression because most of his face was swollen. "My mother, never really had too much use for me, because I reminded her too much of my father. But she adored Kelly. It was always about her, but I didn't mind because I loved her too. She was one of the few good things in this shitty world. I did protect her and kept her out of harm's way. She was such a sweet kid, very loving so for her, and to get us out of the Red District, I worked my ass off to save up enough credits to get a decent education.

And eventually I lucked into getting a position at one of O Corp's companies, and soon I began working for you. I made a decent living, was able to get Kelly and my mother out of the Red District, and saw to it that Kelly also got an education so she wouldn't have to make a living off her back. And about six months ago when you were busy being worried over Miss Smith's comings and goings she went missing."

"What?"

"My sister was taken. You might even recall how I had requested some vacation time, but you yelled at me for taking time off during an important transition in the company. It didn't matter to you that something might have been wrong or that I hadn't taken a vacation for years because I've been at your beck and call 24/7. But when I pointed that last fact out, you relented begrudgingly and gave me half the time I requested. I wanted to tell you to shove this job up your ass, but I doubted I would get the kind of credits at another job that I got from you. So those three days I drove myself crazy trying to find her, and that's when Thor contacted me. Said he had Kelly and if I wanted her back, safely, I'd do everything he told me to. I just had to wait for his instructions. So I waited for weeks in agony wondering if Kelly was all right. And not once did you ask me if I was okay, even though my mother's mental state was deteriorating because Kelly was missing. You were too wrapped up in yourself."

"So I started receiving images of Kelly, in these horrible torture contraptions. And that's when I started to receive instructions. I was the one who sent those messages, that's why you couldn't trace them. Since you had put me in charge of tracing them, I made sure you couldn't. I hired that company with the guards, but they weren't watching Miss Smith for you. They were watching her for Reichardt."

"And those three guards that were killed?"

"Not guards, just some random guys I paid to stand in position to make you think they were out there to watch her."

"And you had them killed?"

"I was told they'd be paid so they could disappear. It's unfortunate what happened to them, but I was willing to do what I had to do to get Kelly back."

"All those dead ends were because of you. We could have found her weeks ago, but..."

"I actually liked Miss Smith, but I won't apologize for what I did. I wanted to get Kelly back. Ironically, I did have a moment of contrition, but then the bastard sent a message to me saying that Kelly would meet my mother to ensure that she was still alive. Do you know what happened? My mother begged Kelly to come away with her, but Kelly didn't want to go with her. According to my mother, she was clinging to that bastard like he was some kind of savior. She was even going by a different name. Sheila or something like that. After that, my mother had a complete breakdown and that's when I knew I had to continue the plan. He must have brainwashed her or something because I can't think of any reason why Kelly wouldn't go with our mother. So there you have it. I did it, and I'd do it again."

Dare wanted to be angry with the beaten man, but then he thought about the lengths he'd gone to get Aya back and that he'd literally kill for her. He would figure out what to do with Ronald later, but for now he had to find Aya. "Ronald, one of the reasons I hired you was because you're a sharp man. I bet you've traced his location haven't you?"

"He told me if I traced his locations he'd hurt Kelly, but I saved all of our calls and I've been able to figure out where his home base is. Now, I'm not sure if this is where he has Kelly or Aya, but I'm pretty sure this is where Reichardt lives." Ronald then rattled off an address that Dare committed to memory. "I also learned that he owns a private jet that takes regular trips overseas to Nuldanria."

"Nuldanria? But Foster personally went there himself."

"And I knew about it. It was easy to cover everything up once I warned them ahead of time."

"Does Reichardt run the reprogramming operation?"

"From what I could dig up on him, he's heavily involved, but the ringleader is some guy named, Larys Morton."

Dare froze. He'd heard that name before. It was etched in his brain forever. "Are you certain?"

"Positive. But if I were you, I would hurry. I have a certain amount of time to check in with him every day at specific times so if I don't make my check in, it's a signal to him that something is wrong. My guess is that he'll disappear."

"And when are you to check in?"

"I've lost track of time. I've probably missed my check in at this point."

"Then I need to get going. Someone will be by to get you."

"I suppose you're going to kill me then?"

"I haven't made up my mind yet." And with that Dare walked out of the room.

Foster was waiting for him outside the door.

"Well?"

"Thor Reichardt."

Foster furrowed his brow. "Reichardt. We've never had any dealings with him. Most of his business is done overseas…in Nuldanria. Shit, so the reprogramming operation was actually a thing. I swear when I went there I couldn't find anything on it."

"That's because Ronald had called ahead to warn them. But apparently, Reichardt has a partner and I don't know how it's possible."

"Why isn't it possible? People have silent partners all the time."

"Not dead ones."

Chapter Twenty-Two

"It's time to go Aya." Master had appeared without warning.

Aya who had been in the middle of putting on the dress Master had gifted her, dropped to her knees. But Master gently touched her back to halt her. "No, you don't have to get into position now. Allow me to help you get dressed. We have to leave now."

Aya knew better than to question him even though something in the back of her mind told her to question him. He'd told her that she would get a day of pampering and indeed she'd been taken to his private bath by one of the servants who brought the women their meals and cleaned their quarters. She had taken a scented bath with bubbles. Afterward, she'd been given a full body massage and her hair was styled. Once her grooming had been completed, Aya had been led to a bedroom where a beautiful green dress was laid out for her.

Master seemed to think of everything. Part of her mind told her that she should be grateful for his benevolence, but in the back of her mind, she couldn't shake the feeling that something was off. The color green reminded her of something…of someone. Briefly, a pair of jade colored eyes appeared in her mind and the very thought of it gave her a brief flash of burning pain in her head. As soon as she was able to push the thought away, the pain was gone.

Aya had hesitated for only a moment before getting dressed. She was being silly, of course. She was happy Master had chosen her tonight to be taken somewhere special. So when he entered the room, she didn't understand why she felt apprehension. She remained still as he finished zipping her up.

When her dress was properly fastened, he wrapped his hands around her waist and pulled her against him. She could feel the press of his erection against her rear. He dropped a kiss on the side of her neck before he captured her earlobe between his teeth. "I wish I could enjoy you properly tonight. But our plans have changed. I had intended to take you somewhere special and then when we returned home, you could then show me how much you appreciate me. But instead, we're going to a new home."

He cupped her breasts and continued to nibble her ears. "Hot damn, you get me so fucking horny. I don't see why I can't get a little sample of what I plan on getting later on?"

With one hand still on her breast. He used his free hand to lift her dress. "Spread your legs a little for me, Aya."

Something told her to resist, but then that brief flash of pain hit her making her gasp. She immediately obeyed. Master moved his hands between her thighs and roughly caressed her folds before finding her clit.

This is wrong, her brain screamed.

But the more he stimulated her pussy the more aroused she became.

"That's it my pet. Get wet for me." He inserted two thick digits into her sex and began to pump furiously.

"I've dreamed of doing this to you for a long time. You're a greedy little slut who can't get enough of it can you? I watched you ride his dick and love him in ways he didn't deserve. And you're going to do everything to me that you did for him. And you're going to love every second of it."

Aya wasn't sure what he was talking about. All she knew was that every time she tried to think about the past, her head would hurt. Right now, her body seemed to have a mind of its own. It was less painful to focus on the sensations working through her body.

Master sucked on her neck as if he was trying to leave his mark on her as his movements became more savage. He squeezed her breast tight, fingered her harder and bucked his erection against her ass until she was very close to her peak.

"Master, may I cum?" she asked, the words sounding foreign on her tongue.

"Yes. Cum for me, Aya."

As she came, he bit down on her neck. Hard.

She screamed her release.

Master held on to her as she slowly came down from her high. He continued to kiss her neck until her breathing calmed down. Finally, he released her. "Get yourself together. It's time that we head to our new home."

As he pulled her along with him, she adjusted her dress. Thankfully, he didn't look back at her as a single tear slid down the side of her face.

As Dare and his fleet of security approached the property Ronald had given him the address to, he saw that it was gated. He was certain this was the place because he'd confirmed with one of his contacts that this house deed was in the name of Thor Reichardt, so this had to be the place.

His holo device began to beep. "How should we proceed with the gate?" We have a device that will disable any lock in under thirty seconds." Clark's voice spoke. He was the head of the security team Foster had organized.

It wasn't like this was a pleasant visit and he doubted Reichardt would let him in. "Do it." Dare ordered.

"Before we enter the property, my team is going to have to do a thorough sweep to make sure there aren't any other security measures implemented to keep people out. Some of these systems can be quite deadly."

"And how long will that take?" Dare demanded, getting impatient. He had to get to Aya and every second that they took was another second apart from her.

"Should take about ten minutes. We have to scan the area because most of these traps wouldn't be detected by the human eye."

"Do what you have to do. And don't contact me until we're ready to proceed."

"Yes, sir."

Dare tapped his thigh, feeling restless. All the way over here, he'd tried to rake his brain how Thor Reichardt was connected to his father's old groundskeeper. Larys was the one who had informed on his fellow servants for being overly friendly with Dare as he remembered. Dare had been a lonely child who lived in terror while his father was around. The servants, however, were kind. He'd congregated with them when Aeden O'Shaughnessy wasn't around. There was even a kind-hearted couple who'd taught him how to dance. He would gather with the servants and laugh and have fun as children should. But Larys ended it all because he'd gotten scared that Dare's presence would get them in trouble. He might have even thought Aeden would give him some kind of reward.

Little did Larys know, Aeden had already known and was setting a trap for Dare, but as Larys was the one to speak of it first, he'd been taught an extremely harsh lesson. Aeden had beaten the man within an inch of his life with a warning to never be seen in the area again.

Dare didn't think he would see the man again, but he did under unfortunate circumstances.

Dare trembled as he walked to his father's office. The only time he was ever summoned there was to be disciplined or taught some life lesson that was equally traumatic. Before he knocked on the office door, he took several calming breaths, to slow down his rapidly beating heart. His father had a way of sensing weakness and if Dare showed the slightest sign of being nervous his punishment would be swift and severe.

He knocked on the door with a confidence he didn't feel.

The door slid open. "Well, it took you long enough, Alasdair. Come in."

When he stepped into the office, he noticed, Larys, the old groundskeeper. He hadn't seen the man in over a year when his father had beaten the man bloody."

Next to Larys was a woman. The two of them looked extremely nervous.

"Do you remember when Larys was here last?"

"Yes, Father," Dare answered without hesitation knowing his father hated when he prevaricated.

"And do you remember what I said?"

"Yes."

"What did I tell him?"

"You told him to not show his face around town again or you'd kill him."

"I did indeed say that. I'm pleased that you at least listened. But apparently Larys didn't. Not only didn't he leave town, he found employment with one of my business associates. I found his charming wife was also an employee there as well, so this will be a two for the price of one deal."

The woman next to Larys burst into tears.

Larys dropped to his knees. "Please, Mr. O'Shaughnessy. We don't have the means to start over. We couldn't afford to move because I didn't receive the pay that I was owed plus we have a child. He's not quite finished his schooling and..."

Aeden abruptly stood and strode over to the trembling couple, stopping in front of Larys. He yanked the man to his feet. "Have some damn dignity. You're a grown man begging for a life that's already been forfeited."

"You can't do this to us. There are laws," Larys' wife spoke.

Aeden narrowed his gaze at the woman. Without warning, he reached back and picked up a diamond ball that had served as a decoration on his desk and smashed it against the woman's head. Aeden brought the object down with such force that it caved the side of her skull in. The look of shock was still on her face as she dropped lifelessly to the floor.

"Della!" Larys screamed kneeling next to his wife's dead body.

As Larys mourned his wife, Aeden brought the ball down on the back of his head and kept hitting him until blood splattered against the wall.

While his father bashed the poor man's brains in Dare stood stiff as a board, his gaze never wavering because he knew if he looked away, there was no telling what his father would do to him. When Aeden seemed satisfied with his handiwork, he looked at his son.

"Do you know why I did this?"

Dare shook his head. "The lesson is to always be a man of your word."

Dare had always known that his father was a little off balance, but he'd never actually witnessed him murder anyone. Aeden O'Shaughnessy was the reason why Dare had shut down his emotions because he was afraid of becoming like his father. But in ways, by refusing to feel, he'd become exactly like him. That day his father had not only murdered Larys Morton, he'd killed the last ounce of Dare's innocence.

But what that had to do with Thor still remained a mystery.

He was so deep in thought he was startled when he received a signal from the men. "Are we ready to go?

"Yes sir. We're moving on."

The motorcade of vehicles proceeded through the gates, then through a thicket of trees that surrounded the area. Dare hadn't realized this land had been developed. It provided the perfect hideaway for someone who valued their privacy or for anyone who had something to hide

The security team burst through the front door first, with Dare on their heels. He was armed with a demobilizer that he was ready to use if necessary. As they went through the rooms he had the scene of being in a museum. Reichardt seemed to have an eye for things that were rare or obsolete, but with each room they searched, his frustration grew. There was no sign of any women. When they made it upstairs. There was no sign of life at all, and it seemed odd that there were no servants around for a house this size.

"I found something," one of the men yelled from another room."

Dare rushed the source of the voice. A couple men standing in the middle of the hallway. "What is it?"

"Listen," the head guard instructed. He stomped his heel against the floor.

Dare shrugged in confusion. "So what?"

"It's hollow." Clark hit another spot with his foot and then tapped on the previous spot. There was definitely a different sound. "We think this is a hidden entrance. It might take a while to figure out how to open it. The scanner detects that its's made from some incredibly thick metal. We can laser our way through it or we can set off a mini bomb to coerce it open."

"Do whatever works the quickest. She could be down there."

Clark nodded. "Explosion it is. We're going to need to move at least twenty feet away."

Dare's frustration level was reaching a breaking point, but he felt that they were so close to finding her. Whatever was down there, he'd at least have some more clues to where Aya was.

He jumped when the mini bomb went off making the room shake causing paintings to fall off the wall and ornaments to crash to the floor. When the debris cleared, there was a large hole in the floor that revealed a set of stairs and confirmed what Clark had suspected.

"We'll go down first, you stay behind us, Mr. O'Shaughnessy."

Dare shook his head. "No. I have to see what's down there. I can handle it myself." He took the lead as he carefully went to the stairs, careful to avoid the chunk of door and wall that had fallen. When made it downstairs, it was like stepping into a completely different house. There was a long concrete corridor with four different doors. Thankfully the doors weren't locked, and with each one opened pieces of the puzzle fell together. One room looked like a torture chamber of some sort with tools he didn't recognize. In another room, there was one large chair that reminded him of an old electric chair that he'd seen in history books. It was an archaic looking death trap. There was another room with eight chairs formed in a circle. In the final room was a large metal door with a keypad next to it.

"I'll put the decoder on to figure out the sequence to get in." Clark put his device over the keypad.

After a minute, the door opened. As Dare stepped inside, his mouth fell open. Before him were cells with glass walls and each one of them contained a woman bowing on the ground. This had to be it. Dare frantically searched each cell until he came to the one at the end. It was empty. His heart sank because, in his heart of hearts, he knew Aya had been in there.

"Get them out of there," Dare ordered. "One of them has to know where Aya is."

Clark's men went to work using the decoder on the women's cells, but as the doors opened, none of them moved. They remained in their position. Dare walked over to a redhead who was only clad in bra and panties as were the rest of the women. Dare tapped her shoulder. "You can get up. You're free."

She didn't move. Something was definitely wrong here. He was certain she wasn't dead because of the steady rise and fall of her back. Dare shook her this time. "Why are you still kneeling? That bastard who held you prisoner is gone. You don't have to do this."

Still, she remained in the same spot. Dare looked around in confusion and saw that the other men were having the same problem getting the women up. With the last bit of his patience gone, he yanked the woman to her feet. Her eyes widened in fear and she shook her head. "No! I need to get back into position. I have to stay here until Master returns!" She fought against him and managed to pull out of his hold and immediately went back to her knees.

This must have been the reprogramming part. What the hell had Reichardt done to these women that had gotten them so spooked that they were scared to disobey him?

Dare tried again, pulling her to her feet and anchoring her against him tightly enough so that he made it difficult to break the hold he had on her. "Please! Master will be displeased."

"What is wrong with you? He's gone and you're free to get out of here. You don't have to listen to him."

She continued to fight in earnest. "Let me go. Don't want to make Master unhappy." Suddenly she burst into tears and it chilled Dare to the core of his soul. Is this what that bastard had done to Aya? Was she brainwashed to the point where this man had become the center of her world? And knowing how strong-willed Aya was, what did he do to get her to that point. From what he saw in those rooms, the thought was sickening.

"If you tell me where Aya is, I'll let you. I promise I won't tell him that you got out of position," Dare tried to inject as much calm as he could in his voice to soothe her.

The redhead sniffed. "She was chosen. Master has decided to take her somewhere special."

"And this somewhere special is out of the house?"

"Yes."

"Do you know how long ago they left? The last time you saw your Master?"

"Twenty-seven minutes ago."

"How can you be certain if you have nothing to indicate the time?"

"I count the seconds when Master is away from us. Now please, let me go."

Dare released her and she immediately scrambled to the floor resuming her previous position. This woman was so far gone, Dare wasn't sure if there was any coming back from what her mind had been warped into. This woman didn't seem to have the details of Reichardt and Aya's whereabouts, but at least he now knew that they'd basically just missed them, which meant they couldn't be that far away.

He hit the side of his watch and pulled up Foster's information.

Foster's image popped up. "What did you find?"

"She's been here. He was keeping her along with several other women in holding cells. But he and Aya are gone. They must have just left prior to us arriving. Are you on your way to the second location?"

Foster nodded. "And if he just left I'm suspecting he's on his way to the airfield. I believe I can get there in time to intercept him. But in the meantime, I'm going to call in a few favors to get the flights for the night grounded for a few hours. That should buy us some time if he has nowhere to go."

"Good. I'm on my way." Dare signed off.

Clark approached him and made a sweeping gesture around the room with his hand. "What should we do with these women?

Dare suspected that the women would fight them tooth and nail, but they deserved to be out of this prison and reunited with their families. He could have his men take them to one of Tori's safe houses and perhaps they could be eventually reunited with anyone who was looking for them. Maybe one of these women was

Ronald's sister, but he'd worry about his former assistant and his predicament later.

For now, he had to find his woman.

Chapter Twenty-Three

"We're on our way to our new life, my pet. Far away from here. I'll take very good care of you." Master took her hand in his and kissed her on the knuckles. "What do you think of that, Aya?"

"I think that sounds very lovely, Master." Aya continued to look out the window. Her mind screamed obey, but that niggling voice in the back of her head told her to get away. With every thought of rebellion, her head ached, and it dulled her thoughts. She wasn't sure why she was fighting so hard and why the color of her dress was bringing back these images in her head, of another man…of another time. She didn't understand why this was happening. There was no other man than Master. He'd rescued her from an unhappy situation. Her heart didn't know real joy until he'd come into her life.

She should have been happy that he had chosen her and was taking her somewhere special, but something was causing her anxiety and she wasn't sure what it was. Aya continued to stare out the window, trying to figure out why she couldn't seem to get her brain to work properly. Every time she tried to remember something either her head started to hurt or she found blank spaces.

"Aya, look at me."

She looked over at Master, who sat close to her. He really was quite handsome. A smile formed on her lips. "Yes, Master."

"Have you ever been outside of the country?"

"I..." She wanted to answer the question, but she wasn't sure what the answer to that was. Why couldn't she recall? "I'm sorry, Master. I don't have an answer to that question."

He patted her hand indulgently. "That's okay. If you don't remember this will be a brand new experience for you. I want to take you to my home on the beach. You can see blue ocean for days. Nothing, but sun and relaxation."

"The beach...." That sounded so familiar but why?

"Would you like that?"

"I would love that Master."

He raised a brow as he examined her face as if not quite liking what he saw. She stiffened. "Is there anything the matter, Master? Have I displeased you?"

His purple gaze narrowed. "Your beautiful lips say one thing, but your eyes say another."

"I don't understand Master...don't I please you?"

"Very much, but I fear that..." He released her hand with a curse. "Shit. Needed more time on her." Though he muttered those last words under his breath, Aya still heard them.

She was going to ask him what he meant by it, but was interrupted when the partition in the vehicle went down. "Mr. Reichardt, my apologies for interrupting, but there seems to be some kind of disturbance at the airstrip. The planes have been grounded for the next hour or so."

Master's face turned almost as deep a shade of red as his hair. "Disturbance? What kind of disturbance? Whatever is happening shouldn't affect my flights."

"Sir, I don't know what the exact problem is either. It could be a possible terrorist threat like the one from a few months ago, when a group of activists got inside the airstrip and blew up a few planes, I'm trying to get as much information as I can."

"Well, at the very least we can get on the airfield and board. I own the damn jet!"

"Sir, I'll call in and see what I can do."

"I don't want you to see what you can do, I want you to fucking do it!" Master raged, making Aya flinch with each word.

As if of their own volition, she placed her hand on the door handle. All she had to do was push it open and run, but the pain started again and this time it was so intense she bent over in agony. "Ahh."

Master stroked the back of her head. "Aya were you just having naughty thoughts?"

She was in too much pain to answer.

"Just relax your mind, my pet and it will be all right. In the meantime, I have something that will make you feel better. Sit up."

Aya shook as she struggled into a sitting position.

"Open your mouth."

As soon as she did, he placed a pill on her tongue and then handed her a glass of wine he poured from his mobile bar.

Just as he said it would, the medication relaxed her.

"Do you feel better?"

"Yes, Master."

He caught her by the chin and pressed his lips against hers. Just as Aya leaned into him there was a loud crash and they were both jolted forward.

The partition when down and Master screamed, "What the fuck was that?"

The drivers' face must have hit the control panel because his nose was gushing blood. "We've been hit."

And then there was another crash. Each time Aya was tossed across the car. She hit her head and everything got fuzzy. And then they were hit subsequent times, from the sides, the rear and the front. Aya clung to her seat for dear life.

"Get us the fuck out of here!" Master yelled.

"Sir, I can't. We're surrounded."

"Fuck! I'm not going to let that motherfucker win. He's taken away too much and I'm going to make sure he loses." He pulled out a vial of black liquid. "It's really a shame. I was hoping you and I could start a life together. I was ready to start fresh. With you. But even now, Alasdair O'Shaughnessy comes out on top. I'm not going to survive this night, but I'm going to make damn sure he knows the meaning of the word loss by the time everything is said and done. He handed it to Aya. "Drink this. It will make you feel better."

Aya looked at the small glass container and felt a sense of dread in the pit of her stomach. His speech didn't feel right even though he was supposed to have her best interests in mind. The mention of the name that sounded so familiar made her hesitate as he continued to hold the bottle out to her.

"What the hell are you waiting for? Take the bottle!" He raised his voice, making her flinch.

"Who…who is Alasdair O'Shaughnessy?"

Master gripped her face. "Forget you ever heard that name and take the fucking bottle. You're making me very unhappy. Obey!"

This definitely wasn't right. She didn't like the looks of that stuff. Her hands began to shake as she twisted off the cap and slowly raised it to her lips.

"We were about to track his vehicle based on my intel. He was just about to pull into the airport, but we sent that message to the air traffic control team. We have his car surrounded. How far away are you?" Foster asked through holo communication.

Dare's heart sped up at the news. Could his nightmare be coming to an end soon? "We're just up the road. I should be there in under a minute. Are you certain it's him?"

"We were able to use a satellite feed to trace the vehicle that had left his property around the time you said and we traced it here. The fact that he'd headed to the private jet entrance, tells me he had planned to make his escape tonight. And I'm almost certain that Aya is in the car with him."

Dare knew he was close when he saw a circle of vehicles with one in the middle. "I see you. We'll pull up and get out of the car."

"He may have a weapon in there. We have to be cautious for Aya's sake," Foster cautioned.

"Gotcha." Dare signed off without waiting for a reply.

As soon as the vehicle stopped, he was out of the car. Foster met up with him. The blond nodded toward him. "Let's do this."

Clark and two members of his team went ahead and smashed the passenger side window with a sonic blaster, which was an effective weapon against the shatterproof glass that was made for luxury vehicles. With the window broken, they were able to yank the door off its hinges.

One of the men yanked Reichardt out of the vehicle who was laughing maniacally. "It's too late, O'Shaughnessy. She's going to die and you'll have to suffer just like I had to when your psychotic father murdered my parents."

Dare didn't know what the hell Reichardt was talking about, but he had to get to Aya." He dove into the car in time to see her hold a black vial against her lips, tilt her head back and start to drink.

Dare slapped the little jar out of her hand, but he could see that she'd already ingested a little. He yanked her out of the car and pulled her against him. "Someone help? She's drank some kind of poison."

One of the security team approached. "Do you know what it was?"

"If I fucking knew what it was I would have told you," Dare yelled in frustration. "There's a little vial that I knocked out of her. It looks like she only had a few drops of the stuff."

Aya crumpled in his arms.

"Aya!" Dare screamed.

Her eyelids fluttered open and it appeared as if she was struggling to keep them open. "Dare?"

"Yes, it's me. Just hold on. We'll help you. Just try to keep your eyes open."

"I…I rem...remembered you." And then she went limp.

"Aya!" he screamed. "Aya!" He shook her, but there was no response. And all while he was trying to get a response from her, Reichardt's maniacal laughter rang in his ears.

Chapter Twenty-Four

"Dare, you're going to have to sleep sometime. How about you go home and rest and I'll stay with Aya until you get back?" Foster suggested.

Dare clutched Aya's nearly lifeless hand and squeezed. He refused to leave until she opened her eyes. She'd been like this for three straight days with no sign of change. The doctors had said that they had been able to get the little poison that she drank out of her system, but it was a type so deadly that it could instantly shut down the organs once it went to work. Even for the few drops that had passed her lips, enough damage had been done.

One of the members of the security team had a medical kit at his disposal and was able to administer a P-pen that stopped poisons from spreading in the body long enough for proper medical attention to be received.

His men had taken Reichardt away and he didn't ask for details. Dare figured he'd deal with the other man later. Right now, Aya was his priority. He just wanted her to wake up.

She seemed so fragile lying in the stark white hospital bed. She'd already been a petite woman, but she'd lost a lot of weight. She looked as if a small wind would blow her over. The doctors weren't sure when she'd wake. And if she did, they weren't sure what her mental state would be. From what Dare had learned about the reprogramming operation, the women went through an extensive amount of brainwashing that often took a few months to complete. The fact that Aya was only with Reichardt for a month might work in her favor, but that didn't mean she still wouldn't face challenges.

"No. I'm going to stay here until she wakes."

"You can't go on like this. Don't you think Aya would want you to get some rest? You haven't even showered in the last couple days. The only time you've gotten out of this seat was to relieve yourself. You probably wouldn't eat if I hadn't forced that meal on you."

Dare looked up at his friend. He understood Foster was coming from a place of concern, but he didn't want to hear any of this. Aya was fighting for her life and he needed to be here to give her his strength when she couldn't hold on. "I know you mean well, but what if this was Tori? I bet I'd have a pretty hard time dragging you away from her side."

"True, but—"

"Then you should understand why I can't leave her side. I've made so many fucking mistakes in my life and I never thought that they would eventually cost me the love of my life. If I lose her it will be because she no longer wants to be with me. But I refuse to lose her because she died paying for my sins. That psychotic bastard has been holding on to a damn grudge since we were kids. And you know the funny thing is, I barely remember him."

What angered Dare most about Thor Reichardt, or Larys Morton Jr. as they'd discovered was his actual name before he'd changed it and left the country, was that he'd made Dare pay for a crime that his father had committed. When he was a child, Dare used to play with the servant's children until his father had put an end to that. Thor had been one of those children. Dare remembered seeing the boy when he'd sneak away and join the servant's celebrations. But after Larys was unceremoniously beaten and fired, that was the last time Dare had seen the kid. He hadn't even thought about him until very recently. The fact that he'd held a grudge all this time blew Dare's mind. Dare supposed since Reichardt couldn't take his revenge on Aeden because of his passing, he'd transferred his anger toward Dare. In his warped mind, he saw Dare as the reason his parents had been banned because Dare was the one who had fraternized with the help against his father's wishes, thereby incurring Aeden's wrath. It made no sense, but then again, in the mind of a mad man, not a lot did.

"Fine, but at least eat this meal I've brought for you. You're not doing Aya any good if you starve yourself to death."

"I'm not really hungry."

"Eat, or I won't go away. Here, I got you a boxed meal from the restaurant you enjoy so much. Just a sandwich and a side salad. Think you can handle it?"

Dare took the box. "I got it. Now you can go away."

Foster looked like he was on the verge of saying something, but changed his mind. He sighed placing his hand on his shoulder. "Alright Dare. Just call me if you need anything. I have to check on the package and I need to put in an appearance at the office for a meeting I can't avoid, but I'll be back, later on, tonight. Victoria and Macy will be coming by later for a visit."

Dare nodded in acknowledgment before turning his focus on the comatose woman lying so peacefully in bed. When they'd gotten her to the hospital the doctors had worked on her for hours. They'd done a full scan of her body and found that there were thin pins inserted into the base of her skull that when activated by a remote device could generate pain in any part of her body. Dare figured that was probably how Reichardt had exerted some type of control over the women so that after breaking them down they were probably more susceptible to mental manipulation. Thankfully the doctors were able to remove the tiny torture devices. But as it was explained to Dare, the trauma of the surgery coupled with the general stress her body had taken over the past month and the malnutrition that Aya was fortunate to be alive. The poison certainly hadn't helped either.

Reichardt must have skipped steps in the brainwashing process to force Aya under his control in under a month. The scary part was, no one knew what Aya's mental state would be when she finally woke up. Dare refused to consider the possibility that she wouldn't wake up. The one good thing from this at least was that Ronald had been reunited with his sister who was one of the girls in those cells. Unfortunately, the poor girl was so far under Reichardt's thumb that she kept asking about the whereabouts of her Master and had only wanted to be referred to as Shiva, the name Reichardt had given her.

Dare felt a sense of betrayal from Ronald that he couldn't explain. Sure, Dare hadn't always been the best of employers and he could be a hard taskmaster at times but had Ronald just come to him, he would have helped to get his sister back. Instead, he'd severed a trust that couldn't be repaired and Dare had lost the best executive assistant he'd ever had. He saw no point in making the man pay more than he already had, but he and Ronald had both agreed that it was best that Ronald take his family and leave town. Perhaps wherever he went, he could get help for his sister. But none of that mattered now, Ronald was no longer his problem. His sole focus at the moment was Aya's recovery.

Dare bowed his head and closed his eyes momentarily, but jerked his head up when he felt himself dozing off. He reached into his pocket and pulled out a bottle of pills which helped him to stay awake. He was about to pop one when the door opened.

Arthur strode into the room. "What are you doing? What are those?" The old man looked at the bottle in Dare's hand.

"Just some concentrated caffeine tablets."

"Why are you taking those?"

"Obviously to stay awake. I need to be alert for when Aya wakes."

Arthur sighed, taking a seat next to him. "Son," Arthur began which surprised Dare because the other man had never referred to him as anything other than a boy or O'Shaughnessy. "You can't keep doing this. You haven't left her side since she's been here. It won't hurt if you caught a few hours of sleep. Aya wouldn't want you to suffer."

"I have to be here for her. She may be able to hear my voice. I want her to see me when she wakes up."

"I know you love her, but you're doing more harm than good. You need sleep and if you keep popping those pills you'll bring more problems on yourself than you already have. Give me the bottle."

"I can't."

"Why not?"

Dare's chest grew tight as panic set in. "She needs me."

"Who are you trying to prove it to? Her or yourself?"

"I love her so much. I can't live without her." Dare finally admitted out loud. Deep down he knew that when she woke up there was the possibility that she still wouldn't want to be with him, but maybe if she saw the lengths he'd go to for her she'd come back to him.

"I know you do, son." Arthur patted his shoulder. "I know. It took me a long time to finally admit it, but I know that you do. I can tell by the way you look at her, the way she makes you smile when you don't think anyone is watching you. To be frank, one of the reasons I didn't like you was not because of what you did to us even though that in itself was reason enough, but somewhere along the line, she fell for you too. And that's when I knew I'd lost her. Like I've said before, Aya is more than a niece to me. She's like my daughter and it was me and her for a long time, but I've held her back because I was scared to let her go. The bar had become her life. She'd work at the bar and go home and then the cycle began again, but I was okay with that because at least she was with me and I could pretend that she was still my little girl. I never really gave her a chance to grow and be the woman she wanted to be. Don't get me wrong, Aya is an amazing person, so full of life with a huge heart and always standing up for the underdog. But I've done her a disservice by raising her to just work at a bar. I could have used my settlement money for any number of things, like investing in her education or even taking her around the world. But I chose this option."

"There's nothing wrong with your choice. It provided you with a stable living so that you could take care of her."

"True, but I've received offers over the years to sell the property, and I would have gotten enough credits to retire and give some to Aya to do whatever she wanted to do, but I didn't because I couldn't let her go. Maybe I was trying to hold on to my sister's memory. Aya looks just like her mother did at that age. And then you came along and I saw the writing on the wall. I fought against it and you gave me reasons to not like you, but eventually I should have backed off when I realized that you were who she wanted."

"Why are you telling me this now?"

"I'm going to sell the bar. I think it's time for Aya to spread her wings and go at it on her own. It's time for her to discover what she wants to do with her life and not what I want. I'm an old man and I won't be around forever. Mera showed me that it's okay to let Aya go because she's strong and she'll be okay. The bar has become too much of an anchor for her and honestly, I think she sometimes uses it as an excuse to not follow her heart's desire because she thinks she'll be letting me down. Thanks to you she has enough credits to do whatever she wants. And you're going to have to be prepared to let her go. I mean truly let her go if that's what she wants. Even those few months you released her that first time, you never truly did."

"I don't know how I can."

"You're going to have to Dare. If by some chance the two of you end up together, then it was meant to be. Don't try to hold her by guilting her into being with you. It has to be her decision. Aya is a free spirit and the reason the two of you were having problems was because you held on to her too tight."

Though Arthur's words were killing him, Dare knew he was right.

As if he sensed the heaviness in the room, Arthur redirected the conversation. "Any changes?" He nodded his head at Aya's prone figure.

"No. Not even a little."

"Aya's a fighter. Have faith. She'll pull through. I'll leave you alone with her, but don't take those pills okay?"

Dare nodded, not trusting himself to speak. Arthur patted him on the shoulder before standing up and leaving. Once he was alone again in the room, Dare felt wetness on his cheek and hastily wiped it away before realizing that he was crying. It had been drilled into his head that crying was a weakness, but now he couldn't stop. He grabbed her hand again and squeezed it. "I love you so much, Aya. I don't want to lose you, but I want you to be happy. Just wake up okay and I'll give you anything you want, even leave you alone. Just give me a sign that you hear me. Any sign."

When she remained motionless he lowered his head and released all his misery in an outburst of tears. Dare cried until his chest hurt and throat was raw.

Abruptly he raised his head when he felt a twitch in his hand. He thought he imagined it at first, but it happened again.

Aya squeezed his hand.

Chapter Twenty-Five

Dare didn't think he'd step back into this hell hole again, but this was where Foster had left the son of a bitch which was somewhat fitting. When they'd uncovered the mysteries of Thor Reichardt/Larys Morton Jr. they'd found a world of debauchery, crime, and blackmail. Apparently, after his parents were killed, Larys Jr. had been in and out of trouble with the law. His crimes had varied from petty theft to assault and eventually, he graduated to running illegal sex trafficking operations. After his last stint in prison, he disappeared.

That must have been around the time when he'd left the country and settled in Nuldanria where he changed his name to Thor Reichardt and built his illegal empire of sex trafficking and importing stolen artifacts. Because so many people went to Nuldanria to participate in illicit activities, Thor was able to gather information that people didn't want to get out. It gained him access to even more wealth and entrance into the Elite circles. The biggest feather in his cap was the reprogramming operation that was mostly used by wealthy men and women who wanted docile sex slaves. Some of these women went for as much as several million credits.

Dare had found it curious that Reichardt would pop up at social functions. He didn't know much about the other man's business except that he had several interests overseas. Now he knew how Reichardt had wiggled into his social circles. And now it was time for Dare to face him for the final time.

The house was just as he'd last left it. The hole was still in the floor and all the paintings that had fallen were in the same position. Dare walked down the stairs to the cell area.

In one of the cells, Reichardt lay in bed staring aimlessly at the wall. He must have sensed Dare's presence because he sat up. A smile split his lips. "Well, well, well. I suppose you came to gloat."

Dare watched the other man dispassionately. In the past several days, he'd felt many emotions regarding this man most of them angry, but now when he stared at the other man he felt nothing. "No. I just wanted to come here to let you know that when I walk out of here, I'm never going to think about you again. I just want you to see my face and know that I'm still standing. And Aya is alive and eventually she'll forget about you too."

"Oh? She's going to forget about how I made that sweet little pussy weep?"

Dare clenched his fists at his side. No. He shook his head. He wasn't going to let this asshole get to him. He could only imagine what he'd done to Aya, but he vowed to help her get through the trauma she'd experienced if she wanted him. But as for this fucker, after all the damage he'd done, Dare refused to let him win in any way.

"Like I said, she'll eventually forget about you. And really does it count if you had to brainwash her to get a response from her? What kind of monster are you? Mind control? What's the matter? Can't get it up without having to reprogram a woman?"

"You know what it's about. It's control and after what your father did, what you did, my world was in chaos. So I took it back and did what I had to do to rise to the top. You can look down your nose at me all you want, but the two of us aren't so different. You did after all have the Run. Think of all the women you took advantage of, tricking them into participating in a game they couldn't win. That's right, I was at one of those Runs. It's there I found the first girl for my program so I have you to thank for that." Reichardt smirked.

Dare would forever regret the role he played in keeping the Run going. To him, it was just a lucrative operation that his father had started. He'd since learned the error of his ways, but he did what he could to pay for his past transgressions. "No, I'm not better than you, but we're not the same. I've learned from my mistakes while you're still blaming others. I didn't kill your parents, but for a long time, I blamed myself. But I'm no longer going to take responsibility for something I had no control over."

"You did! You should have left well enough alone, but you had to go slumming with the Dregs. My parents would be alive today if it weren't for you!" Reichardt slammed his fist against the glass wall.

"My father was out of his mind. He could have snapped at any time, so no one was safe, but if it makes you feel better to blame me, there's nothing I can do about it. I just hope your thoughts keep you comforted for as long as you live, which by the way…will last as long as it takes for the dehydration to set in. But before I go, I want you to know that I intend to dismantle everything you built, including your collections. You and your name will be wiped off the face of the Earth and no one will care."

Reichardt turned bright red. "You can't do this to me, you fucker!"

Dare's cyber team had rerouted the controls to the cells to his personal system so he touched the button on his watch to bring up the holo screen before pressing the button to bring down the metal wall of Reichardt's cell. The bastard would never see the light of day again and within a week's time, Dare would implode this house with Reichardt's withering body inside of it.

Once his task was complete, Dare walked out of the room without a backward glance.

Aya stared out the window of her apartment. She couldn't believe that Uncle Arthur was closing the bar. This place had been her life for as long as she could remember and now it was like a chapter of her life was closing. She should have been sad, but for some reason, she wasn't. She felt slightly relieved even.

Her uncle hadn't made the formal announcement to the locals yet, but it probably wouldn't go over well. The only thing that worried her were the few people they had been able to employ. It would be hard for them to find decent jobs, but Aya had promised that she would help them find placement elsewhere.

It had been nearly three weeks since she'd been released from the hospital and it was only now that her mind didn't feel like it was in a haze. Each morning she would wake up with a headache as she tried to remember things that should have come easily to her. The doctors had said it was likely a side effect of the brainwashing and the mind altering drugs she'd been fed.

She still shuddered when she thought about those horrific experiences. Some nights she'd wake up screaming from nightmares. She still couldn't sleep without a light on. Uncle Arthur had wanted her to stay with him and Mera so that she wouldn't be in the apartment alone and be scared, but Aya insisted that she stay here otherwise she would never conquer her fear. Besides, if she allowed the fear to rule her life, Thor had won. She compromised with her uncle instead and had someone stay with her. Macy had volunteered. It was nice to have her friend around.

Aya was glad she'd never have to see that monster Thor again. However, what he'd done to her was bad enough, but what he'd done to the other women was horrific. She hated that she'd given in to him. She told herself that she could have fought harder even though she realized it had been because of his mind control techniques.

One of the things that hurt the most out of this entire experience was learning of her friend's betrayal. She'd known Mac since they were children and that he would turn on her so easily was hard for Aya to wrap her head around. Had it just been a money issue, then she would have gladly given him all of her credits if it made him happy. But it had been deeper. He'd had feelings for her that she just couldn't return. It didn't help matters that things didn't work out with Macy. But Mac had a lot of issues that he had to work out for himself.

She didn't know what his fate had been because all she was told was that he had been taken care of. Aya didn't want to ask any more questions after that. As long as she didn't know what happened to him, she could still pretend he'd gone off in the world somewhere and was happy with whatever he was doing. Despite the wrong he'd done her, she forgave him, but he was someone she had to put firmly in her past as she moved forward to the next stage of her life.

Aya just wasn't sure what that was. She knew she wanted to do something to help people, but she wasn't sure what specifically. And then there was Dare.

Throughout her captivity, it was thoughts of him that got her through those particularly tortuous early days. Even when Thor had scrambled her memory, the thoughts of Dare had never truly gone away. But she hadn't seen him since he'd rescued her from the limo. Uncle Arthur had said that he'd stayed by her side the entire time she was in a coma, but when she opened her eyes he wasn't there. It was as if he'd dropped off the face of the Earth because even Foster didn't know where he'd gone. He'd only left his friend a message saying that he would be back. Aya wanted to see Dare if for nothing else than to have some form of closure. She'd made a mistake in not believing him when he'd told her about someone stalking her, but they still had their problems. She wondered if there was a possibility that they could start over again or did her time with Thor made her look at Dare more favorably. There was no denying she still had feelings for him and everyone had ensured her that he still loved her, even her Uncle Arthur. But if that was the case, then where was he?

"Aya, I'm home!" Macy called.

Even though Aya didn't mind living on her own she liked having her friend around. Since Macy had moved to a house with her younger siblings and had decided to resume her education, Aya hadn't seen her as much.

"Hey Mace, I'm in here."

Macy walked into Aya's bedroom. "Why are you sitting in the dark? Lights on."

Aya winced as the room flooded with light. "My eyes are still adjusting. I'm still getting used to bright lights again."

"Have you been sitting in your room all day?"

"No. I went downstairs for a while to help Uncle Arthur at the bar. It won't be much longer before it's closed."

"Yes, I heard. And I think it's a good idea. It's time for you to get out of this district and pursue something different. Maybe you can go back to school."

Aya shrugged. "I don't know. I'm not really sure what to do with myself. This is really all I've known. And you make it sound like moving is the answer to everything. I like it here. I grew up around these parts."

"And you know just as well as I do, that it's not always safe. I get the feeling that you're clinging so hard to this bar and this area because you're scared of change. You think that if you move away from here, you'll be judged and the people you grew up with will resent you. Maybe some of them will, but you can't let other people determine what's best for you."

"It's not just that, what if I become like them?"

Macy scrunched her forehead and crinkled her nose. "Become like who?""

"What if I became another Elite snob? What if I forgot where I came from and start looking down on people the way the Elite look down on people who aren't wealthy."

Macy threw her head back and laughed. "Is that what you're worried about? Aya you're not that kind of person. And quite honestly not every single person who has wealth is a total asshole. Sure a lot of them are, but for the most part, people are just people. Where you live and how many credits you have doesn't determine who you are, it only amplifies it."

"You might actually be on to something. When I was with Dare, I'd sometimes get angry with him for how nonchalant he was about spending money because it made me feel guilty that I was living a privileged life while others were suffering."

Macy took a seat next to Aya and threw her arms around Aya's shoulders. "You're going to have to let that guilt go. Some people are lucky enough to move up in life and others aren't. That's life and it isn't always fair. But it's how you live yours that counts, not what you have. Do I feel a little guilty when I come back to the Red District after enjoying my life on the other side of town? Sure. But it doesn't stop me from enjoying life. My siblings have a better life now. They can go to school and they have opportunities that weren't open to them before. I wouldn't exchange that for anything and I damn sure not going to let guilt get in my way. Look at how well Tori has settled into her life? Do you think being with Foster and sharing in his wealth has made her the terrible Elite you think you'll become?"

"No. In fact, she's doing something great by running those shelters and I…You know what? I think I know what I want to do."

"What?"

"I think I want to buy this property from Uncle Arthur."

Macy raised both brows. "Really? Do you think he'll sell this place to you? Wasn't the goal to close the bar to get you out of the neighborhood?"

"Actually, the bar will stay closed, but I can do something different with this building. Something to help the people around here. But I'm going to need some help. Some business advice and I know just who to ask, but..."

"But what?"

"I don't know where he is."

It was a novel experience for Dare to visit Foster at his office. It was usually the other way around. He told Foster's assistant that he didn't want to be announced so when he knocked on Foster's door and stepped inside, Foster jumped to his feet in obvious surprise. "Where the hell have you been?" Foster demanded. "I've tried calling you, but you haven't responded. I even went by your house, but Garrison said you hadn't been there for some weeks. I was ready to send out a search team for you."

"I left the country. I made a promise that I intended to keep."

"What the hell is that supposed to mean?"

"I took some men with me to wipe out the reprogramming operation in Nuldanria. Then I spent some time negotiating some business deals that will allow me to liquidate some of my assets, sell off some of my companies and then I took a little time to myself to reflect and think about what I wanted to do with myself when I got back home."

"And on top of all that, it seems you had time to grow a beard," Foster pointed out.

Dare caressed the scruff on his face and chuckled. "Yeah, one day, I just didn't shave and then I kind of liked how I looked with the hair."

"You know you could have contacted me. I was worried about you."

"I just needed to handle these things before I could face Aya again. I didn't do these things for her specifically, but hopefully, it's a start of me being the man that she deserves."

"What do you mean?"

"My last confrontation with Reichardt opened my eyes to a few home truths about myself. I'm not that much different from him. When I owned the Run, how many women came through desperate because they needed the credits to provide for their families or even just to survive. My game took advantage of them. I justified it by telling myself that those women had volunteered and they were paid for their participation, but the game was rigged. And for what? Bigger profits? Not only was I no better than Reichardt, I was no better than my father. I want to right some of the wrongs I've done. Most of my life I was so scared of becoming my father that in a way I became him anyway. That's why I clung so tightly to Aya. It was because I was scared that one day she'd see right through me and leave. I wasn't secure in our love so I foolishly caused more harm than good in our relationship. If I get another chance with her, I want to be a man worthy of her love."

Foster didn't say anything at first.

"Foster?"

The blond raked his fingers through his hair. "Wow. Who are you and what have you done to my friend Dare? Are you a clone?"

Dare smirked. "I know. I deserve that. And I just came to say, thank you."

"For what?"

"Just for being a friend. I haven't been the easiest person to get along with, but you've been there for me through it all and I appreciate it."

"Okay, man. Don't get all sentimental on me." Foster's smile belied his words. "So, since you liquidated some of your companies, what are you going to do now?"

"I didn't get rid of all of them, just the ones that require the most of my time. Even though Ronald turned on me, I still have to learn to trust my employees and give them more responsibilities. I'm going to take a step back and only handle what is necessary. I'll eventually get another assistant, maybe even promote Ronald's secretary to that position as she's always been quite capable. And then I was thinking of trying my hand at philanthropy."

Foster raised a brow. "Are you doing this to impress Aya?"

"No, I'm doing it for me. I've done a lot of wrongs, and it's time for me to start righting them. There's no telling whether or not I'll get her back, but at least at the end of the day, I'll finally be able to look at myself in the mirror again and be proud of who's staring back at me."

Chapter Twenty-Six

The regulars in the bar were somber today because Uncle Arthur had posted his closing sign on the building. This was more than just an establishment where people came to get a few drinks or a bite to eat. People had congregated here, laughed, cried, and some had met the loves of their lives here. This was a staple of the community and it would all be gone soon. Aya knew how they felt and the uncertainty of times to come for the people who took advantage of day old food Aya handed out to the needy. For some that was their only meal of the day.

"Are you okay dear? You've been moping around the bar all day," Mera observed.

Aya could forgive Mera for not understanding why she was a bit down. She didn't have the connection that Aya did to Arthur's Place. To Mera, this was just another bar, but to Aya, it had been her life. "I feel bad for the regulars. There aren't a lot of places like this in the community. Some of the other bars are pretty rough going."

"I guess that's understandable. Arthur feels bad about closing up shop, but he felt it was for the best and I think it is too. He sees this as an opportunity for you to go out and be your own person."

Aya shrugged. "Yes, I understand. I've heard that speech."

"And I think he deserves to enjoy the rest of his years relaxing. I'm not saying raising you was a burden because he would never think of you in that way. But he's made a lot of sacrifices and it's time for him to reap the rewards of all his hard work. I hope I'm wording that right. I don't want to cause any offense."

"You're not. I get what you're saying and you're right Mera. I want Uncle Arthur to enjoy the rest of his life and I'm glad he has you to spend it with."

"Thank you for saying that. I know I haven't been in your life very long, but if I had any children, I would want them to be like you. You're a beautiful, kind, smart and resilient young woman. I feel you will succeed in any endeavor you set your mind on."

"I appreciate the vote of confidence. But now I have to go do a run through of the inventory, probably for the last time."

Mera smiled. "I'll do it. Besides, I think you're going to want to personally see to the next customer yourself." She nodded toward the door.

Aya turned around with a frown and gasped when she saw a bearded Dare walk into the bar. She froze, unsure how to act after not seeing him for all this time. It had been a few weeks without a word from him. She tried to shove away the resentment she felt that he hadn't at least checked up on her to see if she was okay even if they were technically broken up.

He approached seeming uncertain in his steps which surprised her because when Dare entered a room it was always as if he owned all that he saw. The arrogant tilt of his head was gone and there was something in his eyes, she'd never noticed in them before. Humility.

"Aya, hello," he greeted as he halted in front of her.

"Dare, what are you doing here?"

"I thought it was obvious. I came to see you. I was wondering if maybe we could talk."

She hesitated. Aya had waited for this moment for weeks, but now that he was here, she was tongue-tied. "I, uh…I mean. I'm working right now."

Uncle Arthur, who Aya swore was in deep conversation with one of the regular patrons raised his head and waved his hand to shoo her off. "It's okay. Go ahead. The place won't fall apart without you girl."

She sighed. "I guess there's your answer. We can go up to my apartment."

"I was thinking we could go for a drive. That is if you don't mind."

"I guess. Let's go."

She followed him out to his vehicle and was surprised to see a sporty two-seater instead of the chauffeured sedan that he usually rode in.

"Why the look of surprise?" Dare asked after helping her inside.

"I just never saw you drive yourself before."

"I am capable of driving. These vehicles can basically drive themselves to be perfectly honest, but every now and then, I like to take it off autopilot, put it on manual and do the work myself. It relaxes me. I've been doing a lot of driving lately. I go out to the countryside and see some of the land the industry hasn't completely destroyed. You wouldn't believe all the old abandoned homes out there and land that people have forgotten about."

"That sounds nice, Dare, but I'm sure that's not what you wanted to talk to me about. But what I would like to know is where have you been? I was told that you stayed by my bedside when I was in the hospital. It was strange because when I was unconscious, I thought I heard your voice. You'd talk to me and it made me fight when I wanted to give up. I dreamt that I was in the dark and I kept hearing your voice and I'd walk toward it. But then I woke up and you weren't there."

"I know, and I'm sorry. I felt you squeeze my hand and I alerted the doctors and I waited to hear word. They told me you'd opened your eyes and I contacted your uncle to come to the hospital right away."

"But you left. Why?"

Dare didn't answer.

"Dare?" she prodded.

"I need answers. Why did you leave?"

"Because I was scared. I was afraid that when you woke up and looked at me, you'd hate me because you'd remember all the things I'd done to you and blame me for what Reichardt did. It was no more than I deserved of course, but I don't think I could have handled seeing that hatred in your eyes."

It was a rare occasion when Dare allowed her to see his vulnerable side. It was one of the things she loved about him. It made him more human. "Dare, I don't blame you for what happened. The person I hold solely responsible for what happened was Thor. He was a sick individual with control issues. Some of the things that he made me do...and made the other women do. It was... I still have nightmares about it and probably will for a long time coming. It's going to take a very long time before I walk down the street without looking over my shoulder again. That was all his doing, not yours."

"But if I had been honest with you about what was going on in the first place, maybe he never would have gotten ahold of you in the first place."

"You can't beat yourself up over this. But if you came looking for forgiveness, I'm not the one you need it from.

You're going to need to learn how to forgive yourself." She reached over and placed her hand on top of his.

"Does this mean you're willing to maybe give us another chance…I mean. Could you really love me again?" he asked hesitantly.

"Dare, I never stopped loving you. I just hated how it felt like you only saw me as a possession. That you didn't value my feelings.

"It wasn't about me viewing you as a possession, it was the fact that I never thought I was worthy of you. I'm not that much different from Reichardt—"

"Don't say that," she interrupted with a shake of her head. "That man was a maniac. You are nothing like him."

He grasped her hand and gave it a light firm squeeze. "Let me finish, please. I've told you about my father and how he raised me. I lived in fear of him before I grew old enough to fight back against him. But even when he was gone, the damage was done. I'd tried so hard not to become a monster like him that I became a different kind. I was cold and unfeeling and took my pleasure wherever and whenever I wanted. I wanted so badly to be better than my father that I focused on building my wealth to something even he couldn't imagine. That was my focus. Making money, and disregarding the people I thought was lower than me which was basically everyone. And then along comes a fireball from the Red District who pierced my heart without me even realizing it. In my mind, she was just going to provide me with a means to get my dick wet and then I'd be able to discard her like the others. But she wasn't like the others. And I went to extreme lengths to get her. But somewhere along the way, I realized that I loved her. You, Aya. I loved you so much I didn't know how to handle it." Dare fell silent before abruptly pulling over to the curb on an empty stretch of road.

He turned off the vehicle and turned to her. Dare cupped her face in his palms. "You quickly became my everything, but I feared that one day you'd realize that I'm a shit human being. So I grew jealous, paranoid, and acted out. And all that did was drive you away. It felt like my worst nightmare was coming true when I received those messages. I didn't want to lose you so I did what I thought I had to in order to protect you. But I made the wrong choice in not telling you what was going on. You asked me what I was up to these past three weeks, well, I was making sure that Reichardt and his associates will never be able to do to any other woman what he did to you and all those other women. I sold off a large chunk of my businesses. I have more money than I'll ever know how to spend in several lifetimes and I no longer have anything to prove. I'm tired of living under my father's ghost. I want to use my wealth for something other than status. But I want you by my side while I'm doing it. If you'll just give me another chance, I swear I'll spend every day doing my best to be the man you deserve. I'm not a perfect man and I'll make a lot of mistakes, but I can promise that I'll love you for as long as I draw breath."

By the time Dare was finished speaking, tears streamed down Aya's face. "Dare, I know you're not a perfect man, but you're perfect for me." She leaned forward and pressed her lips against his.

Dare pulled her against him and gave her a hungry kiss. Aya could barely breathe, but she loved every second of it. Finally, she pulled away with a laugh as she tried to catch her breath. "Slow down Dare."

He kept his arms around her. "I don't want to let you go because I fear that this is a dream I'll wake up from."

"It's real. We're real. And like you, I'm not perfect either. I admit that I've made plenty of mistakes myself and I allowed my fear of becoming something I'm not to keep me closed off from you. I should have shared those fears with you and been less judgmental of the lifestyle. So when it's all said and done, you're not perfect and I'm not perfect. Let's be imperfect together." Aya finished as she connected her lips to his.

"Are you sure you want to do this?" Dare asked as they entered his house, holding hands.

"Yes. I can't think of anything I want more than to be with you again. Like this." Aya wrapped her arms around his neck and stood on the tips of her toes to meet Dare's lips. He lifted Aya off her feet and she immediately wrapped her legs around his waist. After their talked, they had been able to get many things off their chests. They shared their fears with each other as well as their dreams for the future. Aya had never felt so close to anyone than she did with Dare in that moment. And she couldn't think of anything better than getting to know him again, intimately. Instead of taking her back to her apartment, Aya suggested that they go back to his place for more privacy since Macy was still rooming with her. She wanted to wipe the slate clean between the two of them and she could see no better way than this.

Just as their kiss was getting more intense they were interrupted.

"Welcome back, Miss Smith."

Garrison appeared in the corridor.

Aya tried to untangle herself from Dare's hold, but his grasp remained firm. "As you can see, Garrison, we're in the middle of something."

For a second she thought she saw a faint smile on the otherwise stoic man's face. "Of course sir. I'll leave you two alone. I'll be around if I'm needed."

"We won't be needing you anytime soon." There was agitation in Dare's voice.

"Very good." Garrison nodded before leaving them alone.

"I think we should take this upstairs," he growled, burying his face against her neck.

Dare gripped her bottom and she held on to him as he carried Aya to their destination. He gently put Aya back on her feet and looked deep into her eyes. As he stroked the side of her face, he whispered, "You're so beautiful. I love you so much, Aya."

"I love you too, Dare." Her heart felt so full right now she thought it would burst.

"Are you sure you're ready for this? After what happened—"

She placed her finger against his lip to silence him. "I refuse to allow him to dictate how I live my life from here on out. I'm the one in control of me and I want to be with, you, Dare. Make love to me."

"With pleasure." He slowly undid Aya's top and kissed her exposed shoulders and neck. Aya trembled partially from fear and arousal. She'd been a bit scared that when she made love again, she'd remember her trauma, but right now, all she could think about was Dare and how magnificent his hands and lips felt on her body.

By the time he'd removed the rest of her clothing, Dare had kissed every inch of her exposed skin on her.

Aya trembled in delight, reveling in the sensation of his touch.

"My turn," she stated firmly when he went to unbutton his shirt. Aya smacked his hands away.

Dare chuckled. "Well aren't you just the aggressive one tonight.

"I missed this." Once his bare chest was exposed, she ran her tongue along biceps, loving the salty maleness of him. She circled his nipples and gently sucked on them each in turn. Dare held her head against his chest as she went to work, caressing his body with her mouth.

As Aya continued to lick his chest, she unfastened his pants and pushed them down his lean hips. She slowly worked her way down the length of his body, moving her lips along his hard planes. Finally dropping to her knees, she circled his cock in her hand and wrapped her lips around his engorged length.

"Oh, yeah, doll. Your mouth feels so damn good, love you so much." She licked and sucked him, taking as much of his cock in her mouth that she could.

Without warning. Dare hooked his hands beneath her arms and pulled Aya to her feet.

Confused, she asked, "What's wrong? Didn't you like it?"

"That's the problem. I liked it way too much. When I cum, it's going to be deep inside of your walls." Dare carried Aya the short distance toward his bed and climbed on top of her.

He nudged her thighs apart and guided his cock to her entrance before locking his gaze with hers. "I love you," he whispered again before entering her.

Aya sighed at the delicious sensation of her walls being stretched to their limit. Every part of her could feel him. They were one as she wrapped her legs around his waist, pulling him deeper into her core. They moved together as one. Aya loved this man with all her heart and she silently pledged her body and soul to him forever.

Her climax was swift and powerful as it took her to heights she'd never thought she'd experience again.

Dare shouted his release as he shot his seed deep inside her womb before rolling to his side and pulling Aya along with him. He kissed the top of her forehead. She couldn't remember a time when she'd felt so content and safe. The world was changing around her with Uncle Arthur moving on to the next phase of his life with Mera and the bar closing. But no matter what happened, she knew things would work out because she was a survivor, most importantly, however, was that Dare would be by her side.

A comfortable silence fell across the room as they held each other. Dare stroked her back and was the first to speak. "What are you thinking?"

Aya placed a kiss on his chest. "I'm just wondering what's in store for us."

"Well, Aya, whatever happens, we're in this together."

Epilogue

"I'd like to welcome everyone to the official opening of *Aya's Kitchen,*" Aya announced to the crowd who broke into thunderous applause. She was on the verge of tears seeing her dream come to life. When she'd had the epiphany about what she knew she wanted to do with her life, Aya realized that it would involve a lot of hard work.

Aya had a passion for helping people. Nothing gave a more fulfilling feeling than when she was volunteering at one of Tori's shelters. She wanted to do something similar, but she wanted to help the people in her neighborhood, which meant seeing to the revitalization of the block she grew up on. After some doing, she'd managed to convince Uncle Arthur to sell the building to her. It was her intention to reopen as a soup kitchen, but run it like a restaurant so that people could maintain their dignity while receiving a meal. Payment was donation based meaning they paid what they could and if they had no credit, they pledged to volunteer their time around the district to help keep the area safe and clean.

Because there were so many abandoned buildings, Aya saw it as an opportunity for people to start their own businesses which would create jobs within the community. When she'd explained her idea to Dare, he was more than willing to lend a hand. In fact, he'd started a program that would provide grants to people who wanted to start their own business in impoverished neighborhoods on the condition that they could only hire local people. So far, a handful of entrepreneurs had taken advantage of this deal and the area was changing. What Aya and Dare were doing had even garnered media interest. Aya suspected that it was only because Dare's name was connected to it. And because he still wielded a considerable amount of influence among the Elites, Aya had received several donations.

She wasn't fooled into thinking that most of the money came from the heart. People wanted to curry favor with Dare which was fine with Aya because it didn't matter what their motives were. Their credits spent the same way and would go a long way to keeping her dream alive.

"So what is everyone waiting for?" Aya asked. "Let's go inside!"

The crowd funneled inside of her restaurant. Aya wiped away a hasty tear as she started to follow them in, but she was held back. She turned to see Dare smiling down at her. "I'm so proud of you." He gave her a gentle kiss on the lips.

"I couldn't have done it without you. This dream has been two years in the making and I can't believe that it's actually happening." Aya had lived and breathed this project for so long and every step of the way, Dare had been right there with her.

"No," he disagreed. "You would have found a way."

"Well, let's just say things went a lot smoother with your help." She got as close to him as her body would allow as she pressed herself against him. She was about to give him another kiss when she felt a hand fall on her shoulder.

"Hey you guys, are you going to come inside or do you plan on standing out her to make out?" Foster asked with a chuckled. Tori stood at his side holding their one-year-old son who looked like a miniature version of Foster.

"We were having a moment." Dare glared at his friend even though there was no real animus behind his words.

"We see that, but you have people waiting for you." Foster pointed out.

"Come on, let these two have their moment," Tori tugged on her husband's sleeve with her free hand. "Congratulations by the way. The place looks fantastic."

Aya grinned. "Thanks, Tori."

Once the two walked into the restaurant, they were about to kiss again when Aya noticed Macy and Ben walking toward them.

Dare groaned. "I'm never going to get a moment alone with my woman."

Aya patted him on the chest indulgently. "Take it easy, baby. We'll have lots of moments tonight when we're alone."

"Aya," Macy and Ben joined them. "Sorry we're late, but we had to go downtown to file the final paperwork. We've been approved!"

"That's' wonderful news you guys. I'm so excited you two will be opening up a business together in this district. This area could really use you guys."

"Thanks, Aya." Macy grinned. "And thank you Dare for the grant. Ben and I wouldn't be about to open the tech shop without it."

"My pleasure." Dare nodded in acknowledgment. "Why don't you two go inside and join the festivities."

"Are you two coming in?" Ben asked.

"We'll be there shortly," Aya assured them.

Macy and Ben walked inside holding hands. Aya suspected that it wouldn't be long before those two made it official. It made her happy to see her friends doing so well, including Uncle Arthur, who was still going strong with Mera.

"Now," Dare put his arms around her. "How about that kiss?" He lowered his head and captured her lips in a deep, wet kiss.

"Mmm. Tonight can't come soon enough."

"I know. But remember to take it easy, okay? And if you need to take a break, do it. And let other people help you. I know how you are."

"I know. I know." Aya sighed in exasperation. She knew he was doing it out of concern for her well-being, but it wasn't like she was the first woman to ever be in her condition.

"You say that dismissively, but I mean it. Take care of yourself. You don't have just yourself to think about." He placed his hand on her swollen stomach. In two months they were having a little bundle of joy of their own. Aya hadn't planned on getting pregnant, but her schedule had been so hectic in the past several months that she'd forgotten to take her birth control shot. The second VC she'd had implanted after the first one was removed, hadn't been programmed with the reminder so as a result she and Dare would soon be parents. Aya was a little worried at first, but Dare, who had been excited about the news, had assured her that everything would be okay. And she knew it would be.

These past couple of years with Dare had been a dream come true. They still argued from time to time, but they always made up. And the making up was the best part. Dare had wanted to get married right away and Aya wanted to wait until her restaurant was open, but when she became pregnant, Dare got his way. But she didn't mind because it felt right. Other than seeing her dream come to fruition, her happiest day was becoming Mrs. Aya O'Shaughnessy.

"Okay. I'll take care. I promise."

"Good. Now let's go inside and live out your dream."

Aya took Dare by the hand and looked him in the eyes. "My dreams came true a long time ago."

About the Author

NYT and USA Today Bestselling Author Eve has always enjoyed creating characters and stories from an early age. As a child she was always getting into mischief, so when she lost her television privileges (which was often), writing was her outlet. Her stories have gotten quite a bit spicier since then! When she's not writing or spending time with her family, Eve is reading, baking, traveling or kicking butt in 80's trivia. She loves hearing from her readers. She can be contacted through her website at: www.evevaughn.com.

More Books From Eve Vaughn:

Run

The Auction

Whatever He Wants

Relentless

Mistress to the Beast

Laid Bear

Made in United States
Orlando, FL
23 March 2022

16029106R00147